Beast of the East

Kenneth Wolfson

BEAST OF THE EAST   **1**

Act I: Winter

Chapter One

The rider tracked mud onto the tavern's dry floorboards. The half-dozen day travelers strained in their seats and looked at the newcomer. She wore a tan duster with fleece lining and was caked in mud to the thighs of her oily trousers. Her skin was black and, contrary to fashion of men and women of the region, her hair was short, curly, and uncovered. She hunched under the weight of a massive railgun. The slit muzzle was caked in black yet shined as if freshly polished. She sat down at the bar, and placed a rectangular copper two-chip on the table.

"Barkeep, I'd like one whiskey. Black Malt," she said. She ignored everyone's stares, from the blushing young cowgirls huddled around a booth, to the grizzled white beards playing cards. The preacher in black, sitting on the floor in a corner opened a verse in her bible.

The bartender was a boy too young to have his own beard. "Here you go, ma'am." He poured, then stooped behind the bar. "We've raised our prices. That's four creds now."

"Raising prices on the verge of winter," she said acidly, and produced another copper.

"Apparently war's on the horizon in eastern parts. A couple big cities about to have a go of it. All our stocks tightened, everywhere 'round town."

"Fair, that," she said with a nod, and sipped her drink. She pursed her lips at the molten black tar as it sent prickles of feeling into her numb face. With renewed feeling she said, "War never profits. Hell do they want to kill each other for?"

"I'm sure someone in the velvet lounges is making money, miss," the boy said.

"Of course they be." She finished her drink. As she put it down, the two whitebeards leaned in in conference. There were frantic looks at her. She only looked at the boy behind the bar. "You have breakfast?"

"Biggest eggs you'd ever see."

"Two, please, fried." She dropped a silver ten-chip. The boy turned.

"Mary, two fryers fresh!" as he spoke, the preacher took two steps forward. The rider didn't hear, but she saw the flicker of movement. She tilted her head, to catch the black form in the reflection of her own glasses.

"Does they want a third for free? We've got one left from last week," a young woman's high voice yelled back.

"Miss, do you want a slightly old egg for free?" the boy said.

She smiled slowly, grin curling across her small-pox scarred face. The disease had been fought off before it did long-term damage, but even its defeat had left a few marks. "Can't pass up free food."

"She does!" the boy said and hurried off. A second set of footsteps matched his. The preacher leaned on a beam of dark wood and rusting hat hooks and read a passage from her sacred scroll. She'd closed the distance by half. Her face was hidden beneath a veil of black. It was caked in dried mud, only moving with the words she spoke aloud. Yet, the rider noticed how clean the hems of her robes were. And how perfectly they fit her body. The rider had grown up in an orphanage, she knew how shapeless and anonymous a preacher's robes were meant to be.

The whitebeards stood and approached. One sat down on either side. The rider slipped a hand into her jacket. She had a revolver and a knife there. Distance was too close for gunplay, so she closed her hand around the knife. "Pardon ma'am. Have we met? Your name's Samantha, right?" the white beard on her left said, and tipped his hat.

The rider slouched. She studied his beaked nose and heavy whiskers. "We did. The Calross gang hunt. You shot their preacher off his horse," she said.

"I knew it. And you made the killing shot on Calross from half a kilometer. Best I'd ever seen," he said and replaced his hat.

"It was a day's work," she said, and hid her satisfaction at his crestfallen expression as she cut down his ideas. She wasn't much for telling spectacular stories. "That was five years ago. What you on? I've forgotten your name."

"Holden. I'm traveling to visit my daughter. I want to spend Winter's eve around their fire, telling my stories to the mob of grandkids. I like kids, they're easy to impress and difficult to control," he said with a grin.

She smiled, removing her hands from her jacket. "I have a son, he's somewhere in this region. I'm supposed to meet him—if he can find a signpost in a town square." That was a bad way to joke about it. She could have tracked him down wherever he'd ever wanted to go and no matter who he'd paid to hide him. That wasn't how parenting should work. So, she'd sent a letter to the address he'd left, with a meeting place, and would hope he cared enough for her to turn up.

"Well, good luck to you. Perhaps your next meal will be cooked on a hot under the stars?" he said.

"The best there is," she said. When she stopped, silence fell. The preacher had shut up. Where was that woman? Sam swept the room, pretending to exchange words with the other fellow. No sign of that black clad form. Where were the exits? The door to the kitchen was shut. The front doors would have rattled as they swung open. A stairway went upstairs but that was still in her vision. "What's your friend for?"

"We was just playing cards now. Salman's a local and a fine host to an old fart like me," Holden said and punched the fatter man's shoulder. She noticed Salman sat back on his haunches, fat billowing up under his shirt. This was not a hardcore traveler. He didn't even have a weapon and had no room to hide one in his taut red shirt.

"Do you own this establishment?" Sam said.

The fat man laughed and his belly strained at his buttons. "Good guess, ma'am. I own about half the buildings on this street. Means I get an employee discount," he said and winked.

Sam grinned back. "My son was going to go to university for accounting. He's good at math." And damn smarter than her and his father combined.

The eggs arrived. Three of them filled the plate with white goodness surrounding three yellow suns, still sizzling with the hot bacon grease off the well-used frying pan. Sam smiled, imagining she was delighted and letting that hide the paranoia as she searched the corners of her vision. There was only one place the preacher could have gone. And only one way to draw her out.

The shadows flickered, as Sam reached for her fork. As she grabbed it, she planted her boots on the bar and shoved, throwing herself back.

A curved sliver of steel filled the air where her throat had been, and continued on with its passage. The rider exhaled and tensed her chest just in time to slam into the ground with a clatter of wooden chair and skull on old boards.

The bartender shoved the belling double muzzle of his shotgun over the edge and fired. The air shattered with the cannonade, old boards groaning and nails splintering on the floor. Splinters flew in the air over her head as the whitebeards threw themselves to the ground, howling in shock that convinced Sam, unharmed beneath it all, they hadn't been involved.

She rolled and her hands found the trigger grip of the railgun and wrenched it free of its leather wrapping, softened to cracking by decades of use. The boy had stopped, looking for her in the mess he'd made overhead. Sam swung the railgun up and saw his eyes go wide.

The bar split down the middle. Glass behind it shattered as liquor mixed with blood. A chunk of vinyl bartop flew into the air and landed amongst the shelves of liquor behind it, scattering broken glass

She yanked the lever action of the railgun down, then back up, jamming a fresh round into the chamber. She rolled back over and leapt to her feet, sweeping the room with her railgun. There wasn't much left of the boy above the waist. His shotgun lay amongst his twitching remains. It was a fresh weapon of silver, utterly unlike the rusted old thing still strapped under the bar. The door burst open in the back and a young woman emerged, blonde hair flying out with her revolver. Sam swung the railgun around, the lengthy barrel heaving slowly.

Holden leapt up, a revolver in each hand and firing through the floating splinters. He scored a hit, and the girl stopped in her tracks. The next blast of magnetically-propelled projectile removed her pretty young face from her head.

The rider swung about. Saloon doors swung, and wet footsteps splashed down the street towards the garage.

She lowered her weapon and nodded at Holden. "Thanks for the assist."

"Nothing but each other in the wilderness," he said and tipped his hat again. "What about the lady of the cloth?"

The strode through the doors to see a bike screaming into the cloudy distance, dark rider slumped over it. A town strewn with debris pulled itself together in their wake.

"Well, whoever set them on you is going to hear 'bout their failure real soon," Holden said with disappointment.

Sam swung the railgun up. Her right hand dropped back, from the normal forward hand grip to a specially crafted wooden hold right near the receiver. Her body formed a stable tripod to hold the gun on her shoulder.

"You're not serious," Holden said.

"Wind about five kilometers an hour coming from my three. Range…" she sighted down the scope. "Seven hundred meters and growing." Her voice whispered on her tongue and no further. This wasn't for the whitebeard. This was a habit for her own mind. She aimed at a lone Sadie Tree, branches forming a red umbrella over a patch of road.

"No way," he said.

She aimed a centimeter high and half to the left. Her finger touched the trigger. A roar split the town down the middle length of mains street. Air burned down the gap. Children screamed and ran in terror, and every dactyl in sight took off.

A flash of red, and then a black dot falling off another black dot
She lowered the rifle across her chest, and breathed out.

"As I breath," he said.

She patted his shoulder as she headed back into the bar. No one was collecting that corpse. Time for breakfast.

∎∎

Sam stowed her bike in the furthest garage from the center of town and walked back. The sun had reached its height, yet the air was frigid and clouded at her breath. According to the preachers at the orphanage, she'd been born in a covered wagon, in the same blizzard that killed her parents. Cold was her home.

The preacher's corpse was freezing slowly in a barrow, with no one to collect the pretty young woman. Sam now had a name to who'd put the price on her head, and a fat crinkly billfold pulled off the preacher's shattered corpse before dumping her. And a week to find them.

A man in a towering hat greeted her at the bank's entrance. Twenty gallons had to be. "Hold there ma'am," he said and raised a hand. Two revolvers rattled at his belt. "Sheriff Gran Patterson. Coalville. You just killed three people in cold blood."

"They drew on me," she said.

He thumbed his massive moustache. "A woman with a weapon of forgotten technology walks into our saloon, and tears half of it down in the commotion. Sounds like she started it."

"Did you talk to the old fellows there?" Same shit as always, she thought. Every town wanted to shake travelers down in a different way. Just put a toll booth at your main street.

"I did. While one was a respectable man. The other is an outsider of a similar questionable character." She noticed a rifle aimed at her head. The wielder's blonde hair billowed out in the wind. Unprofessional of the girl to let that loose when fighting needed to be done.

"So self-defense is not a right given in this town? Alone on the frontier," she said.

"There was no self-defense against the common people of our town. I judge it so. Now. I'm going to need your name. And for you to hand over your weapons," he said. His eyes lit up as he stared at the protruding stock of her railgun

She looked around. There was a second deputy aiming at her from down the street. His hands shook as he aimed down the stock of his old muzzle-loader. That gun had seen high decades.

That was still three guns including the sheriff. The townsfolk were gathering at the edges of the buildings in curiosity. Dresses and heavy jackets among the wooden fence posts. Ruddy faces burying into their scarfs. Two little children clambered on a wagon across the street. They were directly in line from the idiot Sheriff to Sam.

"Names Sam, and that's all you get," she said as her fingers tapped her revolver. At this range, the little .32 was just quicker

"Don. Stop!" Salman stormed into the middle, jacket flapping open around him. "I told you they assaulted her, what are you doing man?"

"Sal, I'm protecting my town from an outsider and known miscreant," Don said. His confident expression cracked as the real estate mogul seized his jacket and shook him up.

"Well, you let three of them sneak in already. And this is my town, so I would suggest you halt," he said.

Don's eyes burned with embarrassment. He didn't look at Sam, but the railgun on her shoulders. "Fine." He stormed off into the bank. The rifles lowered. The children scowled disappointment. The rest of the townsfolk closed their eyes and sighed in relief.

Sam waved at them. "Go on, fuck off. All of you." Everyone scattered to their buildings. Except the two kids. The little boy waved. She blew them a kiss. Cute little buggers.

They convened in the bank. A couple old armchairs and a thick rug cut from a massive black pelt provided frontier comfort. "Thanks a lot, friend," Sam said to the old man.

"I'm just doing what's fair, before I die," Sal said as he rang the teller bell. "Don's a slimy shit. I'm guessing he wanted that railgun on your back."

"Seemed the way of a robbery," Sam said.

"A weapon like that is a treasure. No powder needed, maximum ammo, range longer than a kilometer. You're attracting trouble just by carrying it and being…" he shrugged sheepishly.

"Hence why I lug it with me at all times," she said.

Salman shrugged again. "Don's just alive because legally Coaleville needs a sheriff for taxation reasons. I have a couple private eyes to do the real police work here. I appreciate you coming in and settling that business. You see, I noticed the new bartender and was keeping them busy out front while my eyes investigated. They found the normal bar owner and his wife tied in the back, alive fortunately. Now, whatever business these people have with you, they attacked some good folk and endangered my investments. So I have an investment in you finding who hired them."

"And I thank you for it," she said. She pulled the billfold free. Pale blue hundred-bills were stacked thick in the swollen leather. "I got this off the lady of the cloth. Bills fresh as can be. Wanted to ask the bank teller if he'd issued them."

"Good sense in you," Sal said. "You ever worked a common business before?"

"No. I just add up the days of food in my bag," she said.

The bank teller cowered when he saw her, but returned shakily when Sal leered over the counter and rapped the bell with his knuckles. He pored over the notes. "We didn't issue these, but every bank makes a little note when they put bills into storage. In case they get stolen. Check here, this white box on the back," he said. "These were issued by our branch in Coalmont."

"That's about five kilometers down the road," Sal said to her. "Will you need a room for the night?" he said.

"I'm going right now. I'm in a rush," she said.

"To get this solved before you meet your son?"

"Exactly." She opened her own waterproofed wallet and showed the picture. His eyebrows went up when he saw the pale teenager next to the dark-skinned woman.

"He's got your eyes," he said gently.

"And his dad's nose, fortunately." She tapped her own long one. "He turned seventeen and flew off from school without waiting for me. Fortunately, we taught him a good deal about living out here. But he's still my boy. And still an idiot for ditching school four months before graduation."

"I know how you feel. I've got kids all over the region, and every winter I send care packages to all of them," Sal said. "Good luck. Send me a card when you get that bastard."

■■

Coalmont was fair bit different in the evening light. While Coaleville was a worker's town stretched on open plane a short walk from the mine, Coalmont sat in the gully around the mine itself. The buildings formed a half-moon around the open pit of the strip-mine. It looked like a defensive wagon fort against the rolling hills beyond. Sam liked the design. Raiders and large beasts occasionally roamed eastward from the wilds to here.

Without a straight main street, she took a minute to find her bearings once she passed the border fence of the town proper. A coven stood on a knoll across from the water, boards rotting and a single woman of the cloth painting the perimeter fence.

"Blessings to you," she called. Paint dripped down her cloak.

Sam ignored her. On the other side of the street, was a string of shops with apartments on the second floor. Fresh boards creaked in the wind. She rode down the row, until she came across the bank. She locked her bike down at the pole outside and stepped up to the front door.

A young man in red met her at the door. He tipped his hat. "Good evening, my lady. Shouldn't you be home at this…" he saw the railgun and his jaw dropped. Sam shoved past him.

The young woman at the teller's desk rose in a flurry of skirts. She wore a heavy dress of pale purple, and a blue scarf around her slender neck. She placed a hand on the table, showing off nails painted to match her scarf.

"Good evening ma'am and welcome to White River banking. How may I help you?" She eyed Sam up from her trousers to the railgun and had a more muted look of shock than the door guard.

"Hello," Sam said. "Three people tried to kill me and Salman in the next town over. One of them was issued these fresh notes from your bank. I was wondering if you can help me," she said. She produced the actual notes.

The girl scooped them up and counted them. "Five thousand. Normally, the White River Bank does not reveal customer information, but if old Salman's involved, we can assist. I issued fifteen thousand such notes a week ago. There was a man—he had really plain features. Light brown jacket, ten-gallon hat. Everything kinda new. That's what I remember; he was so completely normal I couldn't forget it."

"Is he staying in town?"

She chewed her lip. "I saw him yesterday. I was getting the news from the radio station and he was in the little cubby, reading the paper. Every time I looked at the radio, he started staring at me like a candy bar." She rolled her eyes. Sam nodded in empathy because even wearing pants wouldn't dissuade the hungriest of eyes.

"Well, thank you," Sam said. "I claim salvage over this money."

"Not my problem," the girl chorused. She returned to her stool and picked up her book.

Sam returned to her bike. She field stripped her railgun on the spot and checked it over. Magnetic coils, solar battery, receiver, magazine feed loaded with eight-millimeter slugs. All in good shape. As she did that, she planned.

Whoever this man was, she'd never seen him before in her life. Unless the girl's description was off. Always possible. He had money to pay three assassins. Fifteen large was enough to buy a house and full furnishing out here, and he was spending all that to kill her. She squeezed her eyes and searched her memories. There were a few people who'd want her dead, but not enough to travel all the way across the frontier. She'd caused a lot of death. Most were rotting in some wilderness, but a few had definitely been brought home and buried.

With three deft strokes she snapped her long arm back into place. The magnets hummed a moment as they connected to the battery. Her gun was alive again, and ready to kill like it had for the last century. She returned it to its sling.

Now to scour the town. Stuffing her cold hands into her pockets, she trudged down the cobblestone street. She tried the two saloons. Each had a bare handful of ragged visitors. It was too late in the year for casual travelers. Only the over-winter trappers came in for their last pints, plus a few other wayward souls. Then the two restaurants. Then, she resorted to roaming the back alleys, scanning every building.

Nothing. She leaned against the frost-coated side wall of a house. A pair of teenage boys ran by. A girl trailed after, struggling against woolen dress and jackets. One came back and scooped her up, then carried her away, giggling on his shoulder. She considered asking them and drew a copper five-chip from her pocket. She ended up toying with the coin, flipping it over and over in between her fingers.

A snowflake dipped onto the tip of her finger. She looked up. The sky was black. Even the three moons were smothered by storm clouds. For the past month, the cold winds had surged down the mountains and battered themselves against the hot, fast currents of the remains of autumn. Now, they'd finally broken through. Flakes began to glow in the streetlight. In seconds they'd grown to a slow but steady curtain of white flecks.

Sam ground her heel into the grass and found frozen dirt beneath. The flakes would stick and hopefully there'd be a fine white coat by morning. So she could track whoever this fucker was by their footprints. Not because the world was far prettier in soft white. Definitely not. She smirked at her own joke.

Sam wrinkled her nose. Having failed in her search, she needed room for the night. And space for her bike. She turned up the street and trudged towards the coven.

A restaurant burst open and a dozen people emerged. Most were adults, but a dimpled girl flitted through them despite her mother's attempts to reign her back to her side.

Sam walked amongst them. They parted when she was a step away and hushed themselves.

Then, over the last bonnet, she saw a man. His skin was pale, his hair a neat black. He wore a heavy brown winter coat and an equally brown ten-gallon. He was the most average man she'd ever seen. She'd have forgotten his presence if she hadn't been looking for exactly him.

He saw her, and she stopped. A larger man bumped into her from behind and bounced off with a shout of surprise.

They were in a crowd. Sam raised her hands halfway and stepped towards the curb. Away from the innocents.

Murder twisted his face. His brown eyes blazed, coat billowing as he reached back. The long draw saved her. He'd kept the pistol there, as a hidden weapon. That was good for sneaking around, but now they drew.

She pulled the trigger fast as she could and the .32 thump-thumped. Blood splattered twice out the back of his head. An empty spiteful insult, his cannon roared once. Someone screamed and sent a chill racing down Sam's spine.

She walked over to where he lay sprawled in the cobblestones. A third round made sure he stayed dead.

Another ten thousand sat in his pockets waiting for liberation, along with a dozen .357 magnum cartridges and a small notebook. She took it all. Then turned around.

The young girl was on her knees, pink dress crumpled in a heap. She sobbed over her mother. An arm reached up and took her shoulder.

The rest of their group had circled and went still. They all stared together as the woman's pale features twisted into a gasp. She shuddered and went still. The girl let out a wail that split the night.

Sam rode off down the road towards the next cluster of frontier towns. She didn't send Sal a card, and she didn't stop by the coven. Twenty-five thousand in bills made a heavy lump in her jacket. Her bike had a heater she'd installed. As long as the engine kept running, she'd be warm.

Chapter Two

Sam parked her bike under the Dome and wedged her kickstand into the gravel of the riverbed. She leapt off and splashed into ice cold trickle that maintained through the winter. The ankle-deep water moved just fast enough to keep from freezing solid. It still sucked the warmth from her toes through her boots and two pairs of woolen socks, as she crossed it.

The Dome was a piece of the continental bedrock jutting a thousand feet into the air, round like a defiant fist shaken at the sky. It was utterly bare of clinging plant life, though even now she saw a collection of raptors clambering over the shallower scale of its lower levels. With the morning sun low in the sky, the dome cast a vast abyss of darkness before it. Leaving the bike to catch any intruder's eye, Sam entered the shadows.

Working off memory, she found the elbow in the river where it met the base of rock and turned hard to give way. At the elbow, she found a seam of rock like a knuckle. She traced it down until her fingers reached the heart carved into the Dome's feet. For a moment, she closed her eyes and pretended twenty-four years could fall away like snow in an avalanche.

She leaned on the rock above it and waited. The void shrank but never reached her, as this late into the year the sun couldn't climb that high. She popped the stopper on her canteen and drank deeply, then refilled it at her feet. The filter caught a film of dirt and left clear water behind. She banged it against her hip and cast the dirt back.

Around noon, a low whine rose into the cold air. The trees rustled as it burst through their wicker basket of empty branches. Sam snapped her railgun to her shoulder and aimed down the long sights at her own bike

With a whir of electronics, bike and rider burst through a gap in the trees and raced along the riverbank. They swerved around her bike and came to a halt with an unhealthy rattle of an old engine's fan belt giving its last effort. The bike looked just as old, with a stubby frame and a mismatch of handlebars too long, a seat too far back, and a fat battery back for a much heavier duty ride. All squatted awkwardly atop an oversized hover cone. Sam had to stifle a giggle at the poor state of the equipment. The rider dropped his kickstand and slipped off the bike.

He was a boy, tall and pale with barely any muscle on his bones. His duster was two sizes too large, to make room for layers of sweaters underneath. As he approached her bike, he slipped a rifle off his back and held it loose, finger over the trigger long before he was ready to plug.

After circling her bike, he looked around. "Mother. I know you're aiming at me!" his voice cried out across the forest. It bounced off the dome and echoed down millions of years of unyielding rock to her ears.

"I am, Deck," she said. Deckard jumped. Once he recovered, he snapped his rifle to his shoulder and swept the shadow. Sam waited as frustration grew on his face, then took a deliberate step forward. He heard the splash and his eyes settled on her.

"Hello, mother," he said.

"Hey." She studied him. He'd definitely grown a few centimeters in the last year. His jacket and saddle bags were brand new, which was good. Meant he wasn't dumb enough to go off without proper gear to survive. "You ran away from school a month before university exams. How come?"

"Academics isn't for me, mother. Like you and dad I feel the call of the wilderness." The confidence in that voice twinged anger inside of her. Stupid.

"And look where that got your father," she said and spat into the running water. "I sent you back to school so you'd become someone more than a rider wandering the frontier in search of work. Like a lawyer or an accountant."

"Fuck would I want to do that for?" he said.

"You could live comfy and have some fun. Maybe eat three meals a day. You could've listened to me for the first time in your life."

"Mom, I came out here to see you," he said and dropped the rifle from his shoulder. He grabbed the butt with one hand and hugged it against his body.

That sad voice called to her. She lowered hers and sloshed forwards. He was shivering there along the bank. His lips had gone purple. "Hey, son," she said. "How was the trip over?"

"Cold and hungry," he said sheepishly. "I got my first game a week ago."

"Anything left of it?"

"No, I was really hungry."

"How'd you get the bike?" She stopped; her soles still wet.

"I worked odd jobs after school to get money, and bits of machinery. I cobbled this together from scratch in our school's garage." He patted the steering bar with pride. The entire frame sank down and bounced back up. "The day before I left, I learned there was a big-name salesman who needed an extra hand. I bargained and he paid me this here fresh out of the factory Marinelli Rifle and forty rounds of ammunition." He held the rifle up with pride. It was fresh off the factory line. The wood stock still shined with polish and serial number was freshly cut. The weapon had a massive frame and a long loading slot in its side that indicated a substantial bullet.

"A new rifle like that's about three hundred dollars. You got that from a day's work?"

"I pushed him a bit," Deck said.

"Definitely should have been a businessman," she muttered.

He rolled his eyes and the defenses came back up. "I don't want to, mom. There, we met. Now what are you going to do?"

"Follow you around."

His jaw dropped in utter horror. It was almost hilarious to witness. "Why?"

"Because it is my job to make sure you don't hurt yourself," she said.

"Don't you have something else planned after this? You're usually working in the winter" he said.

"I was going to go into Springham City and rent a proper dress so I could watch you graduate from school, and see you off to university," she said.

Deck sagged in his oversized coat. He stared into the grainy water. The defenses fell away again and she was looking at a sad teenager. The dark river reflected them both back in blurry flowing portrait. Their sadness was identical. "Mom. This is where you met dad, right?"

"That it is." She backed into the shadow, heels scattering water and pebbles alike. Deck cringed at his own shoes, and then splashed in after her.

Sam was delighted to focus on the past. "The stupid orphanage I was in brought us all out here on wagon ride. They claimed we were leaving civilization to find solitude to focus inwardly on ourselves and our relationship with god. Well, the morning we got here, Sister took her Laudanum and nodded off, so we snuck off.

Your father had come down with a bunch of other boys from Springham. In the summer when the river's high, there's a type of fish that swims upstream from the Slave River to that lake on top of the Mount Baron." She pointed at the more naturally sloped mountain rising to a peak on the far side of the valley. "So, there we were in those church smocks and stockings, seeing a bunch of shirtless boys casting lines. Their muscles were glinting in the sun," she said.

"Mom!" Deck said. They reached the carving. Deck stood back lest the water climb over his ankles and flow into his boots.

"What?" she said, grinning. "Don't you dream of having a pretty girl come wandering out of the forest?"

"Yeah," he said. "But…"

"They fried us up some fish that night. We went home in the morning. Sister beat us all senseless with her switch and promised us a week each in solitude. Apparently her going on a trip and nodding off was meant by god to test our character and we'd failed." She shared an eyeroll with her son. "I ran off soon as her back was turned. Found your father. Begged him to take me home. He showed me how to shoot on the trip back."

"How high was the water?" Deck said.

She pointed over her head, where the frozen brown moss ended. "We came back a couple winters later to make the carving. It's our secret only visible to the few who come here in the winter. I think I had you that next summer."

"And then you sent me to school, over dad's objections," he said.

"Yes, I did." Her voice hardened. That had been the right choice. Still was. Damn teenagers and that fucking delusion of invincibility. And damn all the adults who egged them on.

"So." He splashed a step forward and studied the heart at range. A tiny, two-legged lizard slithered past his boot. He reached for the knife on his belt, but Sam stayed him with a shake of her head.

"Too small for eating. All the big ones are downstream for the winter."

"So, are we going there?" he said, pointing back the other way. The stream continued down the wide plain of the valley. In the cold blue distance, two mountains parted in a V.

"You know where we're going. I'm just following you," she said with a gentle smile.

Deck sloshed back to his bike. "I grabbed a couple bounty warrants."

That ideal died on her lips. "Deck, bounty hunting is the lowest, most miserable profession on the fucking planet. This better not be one where we take them alive. Do you know how much of a struggle it is to get some angry fuck back home to jail?" she said as she walked after him.

"No, mother. This is a big one." He pulled the scroll from his side bag and unrolled it. She stopped and read.

"You're serious."

"Ten thousand dollars, dead."

"I've hunted him before. Twelve of us went in. Four came out."

"Well, he's killed hundreds before. But we're going to kill him," he said. "You said you'd follow along and I'd lead."

"And first, I said it was my job to keep you from getting yourself hurt," she said, crossing her arms. "No."

Deckard sloshed over to her. "Mom. You don't let me do shit. Don't go trapping over the winter with you. Don't take that canoe ride down the rapids with the outrides. Go back to school."

Sam pinched his cheeks and felt skin loose atop bones. His jaw dropped. Now that she saw, his eyes were sunken, and his clothes were even looser on him than his wide shoulders should have allowed. "You didn't successfully hunt anything, did you?"

His eyes dropped to his boots. "I herded Bergers for a farmer in Loveyton. He paid me in spoilt food cans. I didn't notice until two days out."

"When's the last time you ate?" she said in a hurry.

"Three days past."

She walked back to her bike and pulled out a quarter-kilo of steak jerky. She shoved it into his hands. "It's okay mother, I saw some tracks on the trail. Fresh and still wet." He tried to grin at her. She saw anger.

"You're going to starve yourself because you don't want me helping you." She smiled at him.

He took the jerky and dug into it.

"Can we at least go down river? I hear there's a beautiful town where it drains into the bigger one," Deckard said between bites. He pointed down the river, where the two mountains formed a V.

"That will work." She stepped out of the water and keyed her bike. The engine hummed along, perfectly maintained.

He keyed his own bike. A rattling sent dactyl flocks scattering from the trees, screeching into the cold air. That was definitely the fan in the hover saddle rattling away as improperly aligned machinery slapped itself on the fan housing over and over. The bike wobbled appropriately as he hopped into his seat and slipped the rifle into its saddle holster. He wrapped his hands around the steering bar.

"That needs work."

"I built this thing from salvaged parts. It got me this far," he said.

"Well. Let's hope it gets you the rest of the way." She hopped onto hers and stuck her feet into the stirrups. The railgun was too long for a proper saddle scabbard and so was strapped across the back of her saddle. The .32 Guerrier on her hip would have to do if she needed to shoot fast. She kicked the heel trigger and her fans roared to life.

She led and he hugged right on her heels as they raced between the dormant trees.

Chapter Three:

They camped at the riverbank, on a patch of frozen mud. The dome was a black monolith rising into the evening sky The sun was behind the rock now, and as the sky turned to grey its white rays traced the outline like a leviathan rising from the deep. Sam watched Deckard gather sticks and build a proper fire. Then the time came to strike a match. He held the first against the sticks, but it sputtered down to his fingers and died. The second, he ground into dust striking it over and over. He grabbed a third.

"You need a lighter. You can't just put a match to those branches and expect shit." She reached into her saddle bag and found the roll of newspaper she'd read months ago, then stuffed away. She tore a chunk from its frayed edge.

Deckard lit the match and a tiny flame shivered in the night. His glasses reflected the light like a pair of dying headlamps. He touched it to paper, and fire sprang forth.

"Lower it gently," she said. He did. And fire spread. Soon they were warming their hands. She pulled off her gloves and let her bare skin breathe for the first time in weeks. Deck did the same.

"Where'd you get that scar?" she tapped the white crescent across his thumb.

"I fucked up when installing the hover fan in there. Didn't cut the power and barely got my hand out before I lost it," he said.

"At least you lived to learn."

Branches crackled behind them. Deck leapt up, drawing his rifle.

"Relax," Sam said, still warming her hands. "If it was coming to kill us, you wouldn't hear it," she said.

"Seriously?" he said, aiming into the trees.

"Whatever it is. We'll hunt it in the morning. I'm in the mood for some fresh meat." She rolled onto her bedroll and wrapped herself in blankets. Frozen ground and rocks deposited by the swollen summer river dug into her back through the thin fleece padding, but she was too tired to care. "Sooner you sleep, the sooner we can wake up and go kill it."

The next morning, grey clouds choked the sky, a blanket coming to smother the earth. The air had gone from making her breath fog, to pinching her exposed face. It clawed down her open collar and into her chest, until she buttoned it shut. Sam frowned up into the white sky. "Snow's coming."

"Well, that sucks," Deckard said as he scoured the tree bed. "I found tracks!"

Sam packed both their bags up. Only then did she draw out her railgun and follow her son into the brush. She found him crouched behind an overturned log, peering over the brown veins of the dead wood beneath.

She tapped his shoulder, and then dropped beside him.

"Found it," he said with a grin. She patted his shoulder again and pressed a finger to his lips. Then, hugging the dead log, she peered over the top.

Grazing on the broken branches was a four-legged reptilian creature coated in dull brown feathers. Its head was wide and square with a large eye placed far to either side. Heavy teeth crushed the branches up. It stood waist-heigh on its four legs, thick with accumulated fat for it to survive the winter cold. It was a Garzelle. Out awfully late in the year.

"Aim for the junction where the front legs reach the body," she said. "You cocked, right."

"No." He squeezed his eyes shut in frustration.

"Aim, then pull the hammer back.

He levelled, left arm shaking just above the treacherous drying wood as it held his rifle's front handgrip. Then, he reached up with his left and pulled the hammer back. A click rang through the forest in its artificialness. The Garzelle's head snapped up. That beady eye twitched in its socket, searching for movement.

"Breath out," Sam said.

"I know mom." He sucked in a breath and exhaled. His left arm steadied and so did his barrel. His finger slipped over the trigger.

The entire rifle jolted as he pulled the trigger far too hard. A flame burst from the barrel and a millisecond later, thunder crashed. Trees shook. Feathers puffed off the reptile's back.

The garzelle hopped into the air and took off on its springy gait. Deck screamed a curse and yanked the lever back.

Sam leapt to her feet and levelled her railgun. She saw her prey's head bobbing, body undulating in its sleek running form. And knew where to aim immediately. The garzelle came down as its front legs hit the ground. Her sight settled in the open air above its right eye. Her trigger finger twitched.

The garzelle was dead by the time it pitched forward into the ground, spilling its brains all over the frozen dirt. Sam breathed in.

"Holy shit mom," was the first thing she heard. Deck stared up at her, leaving his jaw behind on the log as he gaped.

"You pulled the trigger too hard, and didn't adjust for recoil of that absurd thing," she said. "But we have time to practice. And prepare our kill."

They spent the morning plucking their kill down to the gray skin and dressing it. "You want the legs the most. That's where all the fat is stored," she said, as she carved one off with her knife, holding it up by the taloned ankle so the last of the blood drained out. She laid it on the specially oiled tarps they'd spread out.

"How about the intestines? I like jibblets," he said.

"We don't have the means to properly prepare them out here, so the intestines go."

Deck sighed and tossed the tangled rope of organs out. He ran over to the river and washed his hands. "What do we keep from the main body?"

Sam stripped another leg and dropped it beside the first. She still had to remove the claws. "There's some nice meat around the ribs. And. On the underside of the torso, there's a strip of pure muscle. It's about two inches thick and goes from its head back to the tail. If you can get it, mmm they pay top at fancy restauraunts for that," she said. She finished the legs up and got them salted.

"Mom, like this?" drew her attention. Deck held up a ribbon of steak, long as his fingertips to chest and thick as his fist. Perfectly cut.

"Outstanding, son," she said. "Now we salt this."

"How do we cook it?"

"Stick it under your saddle. We'll each take two legs and some ribs. The heat from the bike's engine housing will cook it nice by nightfall," she said.

"I never knew that."

"Most tenderfoot don't. It gets them killed when their food rots and they poison themselves," she said. "Now, wash your hands in the river. This why we do this barehanded."

Sam hopped onto her bike and kicked her feet into the stirrups. She hit a lever on her handlebars, and her bike switched to leg steering. Her hands were numb from the river. Circulation had never been great. Deck seemed fine at least.

A snowflake drifted across her vision and landed on the bike's front axle. It melted and steamed off instantly. Then, following the opening berserker a flood of white poured down. The skies broke open and the deluge landed around her. The cold ground was white immediately. Her bike hissed as the bare axle steamed.

They rode slowly, sticking to the river bank. Water didn't offer enough resistance to just fly over the now waist deep river, and it hadn't frozen into friendly ice yet.

At sunset they hovered through the two mountains. The already dim light went dark as the sun vanished behind towering black cliffs. The bikes hopped over the snowbank and stayed up as they passed through ten feet of snow. The headlight vanished into the snow, until suddenly they showed a black wall of rock. Sam twisted her hips and turned away. "Deck!"

"See it." He fell in pace alongside her. "Mom, can we just keep running through the night? I'm too warm to get off."

Snow still poured down. "Let's do that. Just stay by me," Sam said.

So, they went long into the night. Sam kept the throttle low. She wound through the valley; eyes peeled for the flash of rock that marked certain death. She wondered how hard the river had gotten and searched for the bank. Finding the uneven mounds of rocks beneath the snow, she turned right and headed straight into the middle. Her bike held up fine. Grateful, she stayed in the middle of the blanket of deepening snow, leaving a trail of slush behind.

The ground dropped away and her bike fell with it. She jolted into her seat. Deck cursed as he fell behind, his bike adding a deeper whine as it struggled to catch him. A crash and a scream announced his landing.

"You good?" The sound didn't get beyond her lips. "You good?" she said again.

"I'm fucking fine. Damn bike needs a new stabilizer. I smashed my balls."

That was an old injury. The biker's saddle, Sam thought with a laugh. It warmed her cheeks. She caught a second drop ahead and cut the throttle.

"We're on the bounty rapids. By morning we'll be out of the valley," she said. She steered them back to the left.

The valley wall met her. Shit, she'd forgotten that the trail broke from the river and wound up the side of the valley on a treacherous shelf. So they'd have to deal with the rapids. She throttled down the rockets and keyed up her fan until it was huffing, blowing snow around her. The next drop she took with ease. Deck winced behind her.

Going downhill on a bike meant leaning forwards into her steering bar. With the stirrups holding her frozen legs in place, it was a rough contrast between stably seating on the saddle and peering over toward the ground.

She'd killed her first on a night like this. They'd needed to eat on their first winter together, so they'd found a caravan escort gig. Get a gold shipment from one big city across four hundred miles of wilderness to the next. Thirty people, ten wagons.

The blizzard had been blowing right in their faces when the horn trumpeted. A section of logs crashed aside onto the ice and something rumbled forth, almost swallowed by the glaring white.

He'd brought up the railgun and fired fast as the magazine could feed. She took aim with the old single-shot rifle she'd been given. While he fired, and cursed as he missed, she held and aimed. Waiting, sight picture hovering around the front wagon and the two women crouched behind it.

A figure filled it. A man, shirtless, chest scarred by a dozen wounds. A curved sickle in one hand, double-barreled shotgun aimed at the two victims below. She didn't feel the trigger beneath her finger. Her old rifle crashed with a puff of white smoke. And his head vanished into a red mist, jawbone flapping as he tumbled free.

When the snow had cleared half their wagon train had been dead. Along with over twenty attackers. She'd counted three, with her old single-shot rifle. Her husband had only gotten two with the railgun.

The ground dropped away and she snapped her hips. The bike swerved to a halt, blasting snow out into forever, where it joined the steady fall. Deck pulled up beside her. Working from memory, she led him to the side of the valley and threaded her way down the narrow stream that looped past the Barrow Falls.

She twisted her head to check the ground, and a chunk of snow slid off her hat and right down her collar. Freezing turned to pain but she didn't move, lest a twitch send her careening off the edge. It burned until it became an annoying sceptic wetness against her throat, an invasion vector for TB or a host of other illnesses people died from in the winter.

The slope levelled off. She sat at the base of a wall of ice. The waterfall had frozen solid as it fell. Her breath condensed and froze against an icicle thick as her waist.

"That's it," she said.

Whistling wind answered. Shit. She swung about. Deckard wasn't hugging her tale. His headlights had vanished. "What did you do?" she muttered as she hauled her bike around and crawled back up the slope.

She found him barely a hundred feet back. He lay pinned beneath his bike, sprawled out in a crater of snow. "Deck." She leapt off hers.

"Mom," he muttered. "I slipped on the throttle and hit the wall."

"Fucking worry about it later." She dug under his bike and caught the forward bar. The hot metal sent pinpricks racing through her fingers. "Help me. Push." She heaved and rolled the bike over. It crashed down on its other side, hanging over the edge.

"My ride."

"We'll get it tomorrow. There's a cave around here." She hauled him up.

"I need it."

"Don't worry, dumbass. Get on my saddle." She shoved him until he gave up. He just draped over the side, and she had to maneuver him into the saddle. She paced around, sliding his feet into the saddle. There wasn't room for two, so she grabbed the front fan and led him back down. She just kept walking along the wall until the headlights warped in the round shape of the cave. She parked the bike across the front and turned the engine off. Then grabbed Deck and hauled him off.

"Can you walk?"

"Maybe." They settled on hobbling together, into the bare rock, over the softness of rotting blankets and crunching bones from long ago meals. She set him down in the alcove in the very back, atop a bed of fleece. The plastic would never rot. He curled up tight.

"Sleep," she said.

"My bike."

"You probably had the throttle too sensitive. We're not on open road. We'll look at it tomorrow," she said. She dragged her blanket off and threw it around him.

"Thanks."

"Welcome." She went back to where her bike sat. With it in the entrance to the cave, the heat radiating from the frame drove some of the cold air off. A few flakes drifted over the saddle but that was all that menaced her as she curled up against it. She let the warmth roll over her and closed her eyes.

The advantages of sleeping on bare ground were that it was better than sleeping in the saddle by virtue of being flat ground to lie upon.

The disadvantages were her aching back, frozen clothes, patch of frostbite where her cheek had touched the rock and thinking about the bed at least a hard day's ride away. She stood up. "Deckard."

He stirred. "Is it morning?"

She stuck her head out and snowflakes landed on her forehead. The sky had grown grey again. "Yep. Let's see the leg."

His right leg was the correct size and angle, which was encouraging. Him standing up on it and complaining was even more.

"You're fine, eat." She handed him a leg of deep brown grazelle. Then, took her knife and stripped half the meat off.

"Hang on, need to piss." He stumbled out the door and clambered over her bike. He vanished with a plop and came up red-faced and covered with snow. "Shit this stuff's up to your bike seat."

Getting his bike out required a lot of digging, then prying open the engine covering and breaking ice off the power belt. Then, Deck unfolded a crank charger from under his seat and spent fifteen minutes hand-charging the engines until they were warm enough to start. They sped off. The snow had not abated at all. Sam only knew they were out of the valley when the distant shadows of the walls fell away, into a wide plain.

On the completely flat river snow, they made good time through the day, and into the next. Sam strained in her saddle, searching for street signs or any sign of Crownport.

The town found them. The snow peeled back to a light drift, and the dark shape of the hill burst through to meet them. It covered half the horizon. A wall stretched across its crown. Peaked roofs of houses emerged over the top and dozens of threads of black smoke rose from their chimneys. The church steeple stuck straight up in the middle like a bishop's hat.

They cut the throttle and rode straight up the hill toward the gate.

The gate remained shut when they pulled up. A woman appeared over the top. Her hat had a gold star on the top. A massive weapon was cradled in her arms, barrel long as she was tall. This was a gun for mounting on the wall and firing at attackers, not carrying anywhere outside.

"Who goes there?" she said, voice like whiskey.

"My name's Samantha Lavarro. This my son Deckard Lavarro. We're here passing through."

"That your son? By marriage?"

"I wish. His nine-pound ass damn near killed me," she said. Deckard snickered. "Are you the Marshal?"

"I am. What's your business?"

"We're here to not freeze to death ma'am," she said.

"Why not build a fire? Forest across the ice. You seem well kitted for someone worried about death," she said.

Sam stiffened. Bitch was serious. "Rather spend money on some comfort. No point in having money if you can't use it," she said.

"You may enter. Any trouble and you go out without the bikes." She disappeared. The gates swung open.

"Fuck was their problem?" Deck said.

"Guess," she said. She touched the throttle and slipped through the gate.

Buildings spread out in a circle of houses across the hilltop. The inner circle was shops and restaurants. The church was still hidden behind it all, but the steeple cast a long shadow. The streets were empty save a crew of women shoveling the streets in their calicos and furred jackets. She looked back at the wall. The marshal and two other gunmen stared at her through the narrow slit between hat and scarf.

Crownport had two thousand permanent residents on the hilltop. In the summer, another five thousand generally came to work the docks or just live in the sprawling houses and warehouses on the river and wait for barges to come down from the cities upstream. In the winter, the town retreated to the high ground. Beneath the dirt a massive cellar held years of stored up food, a school, and the hospital. Last time Sam had been through, there'd been talk of building a furnace and heating the streets, but the town had run into the problem of getting fuel.

"Morning ma'am," one of the shovelers said. Sam looked up. Younger woman, clean face still shining beneath its woolen scarf with dimples. An old rifle dangled across her back. It was a single-shot, with a heavy bolt that had begun to rust. Like the one Sam had used to defend that convoy years ago.

"Hello," Sam said. "What are all the gunmen for?"

"Last month someone hit the last coal barge heading up the river. Picked off most of the crew from the shore. Pilot and engineer made it up hiding in the middle. Couple weeks back farmer Dayve's house was shot up. Killed him and his wife, left the kids. Country wants to get dangerous. We'll get dangerous."

"You hiring?" she said.

The girl stopped digging. "Don't think marshal likes outsiders. Most of security are port commissioners who town council paid to stick around with their families."

"Well, shucks," Sam said.

"You need directions to an inn? We have a couple," she said.

"No, thank you, this isn't my first time through. Is Valentine's Hotel still open?"

"Of course, miss," she said. Sam tipped her hat and puttered off. She looked back and made sure Deck had done the same.

Valentine's was the 'city folk' hotel. A wooden building three stories high and painted in brilliant red in contrast to the grey and brown boards on either side, sitting right in the center of town, next to the church. The front sign was in massive, gaudy gold that shined even with the backing lights turned off for the off-season. Inside, a receptionist's desk sat on one side of the lobby. On the other side was a wall-to-wall bar stacked with more bottles than she'd ever seen in her life. The air got toasty the moment she stepped onto the thick carpet, dripping grime.

The receptionist wore a dress of pink silk that showed off her figure. The girl smiled. Deck smiled back and leaned an elbow on her desk.

"Welcome to Valentine's. May I help you?" she said.

"We'd like a room, a bath, and laundry service," Sam said.

"Mother, I don't think we need to…" Deckard trailed off as he doubtlessly pictured the cost of separate rooms.

"Any floor you have in mind?"

"Ground is fine," she said. Ground floor was cheapest. Top floor had vast, insulated windows too look out across the entire valley. On clear days they could see all the way back to the dome. Ground floor was still cozy, with two beds separated by a partition. The living room had two couches curved around a fireplace. There was even a radio sat in the corner.

The girl dropped two sets of sheets on the couch. "I'm sorry but water's out right now due to the temperature. We can still do baths and laundry, but it will take a full day."

"Then I'll put in the order right now," Sam said.

Room was ten dollars for the night. Bath and laundry added another five each. The feeling of getting dinner in clean clothes, able to smell one's own skin again, was priceless. Sam had half a steak and eggs. Deck ordered a salad with eggs. Since Sam had last visited, CrownPort had dug an underground chicken farm and eggs were unlimited.

They were finishing breakfast when she heard heavy bootsteps and smelled tobacco. She stood up, dropping a hand to her revolver. The marshal stood before them, with that stern stare. Up close, Sam noticed her right ear was a scarred hole in the side of her head. Her blonde hair was tied back to show it off.

"Miss," the Marshall said and removed her hat. Under her leather jacket she wore a tightly cut calico. It was slim enough for easy riding, but still met the fashion standards of civilization. "I have a job for you, if that's what you're looking for."

"Well, always. What do you need?" Sam said. Money was at stake; she could ignore earlier transgressions.

"With the marauders unseen but active, the mayor's worrying about our outlying farms. We have three down the southern road. First is a corporation owned by Mister Libbs and his family. They keep a few hands to look after the animals in the winter. Make a nice contribution to the summer's eve festival, too. The next two are individual homesteads, families with kids. I don't want to risk any of my guns going out there. So, I'll give each of you thirty dollars to check them out, plus tomorrow night paid at the hotel. Compliments of the mayor," she said.

"We can leave first in the morning," Sam said.

The Marshal came up with sixty dollars right there and handed them out. "Deal." She left without a word.

Chapter Four:

Sam stepped out the front door at dawn and was delighted that the snow had stopped. The sky remained a rolling gray, a breeze ruffling her coat around the waist. She started her bike in the hotel's garage, gave it a quick charge, and headed out. She was saddling up when Deck stumbled out, weighed down by sleep as he tottered through the snow. By the time he was saddled beside her the cold had begun to bite.

Marshal opened the gate a crack and Sam steered through. An endless plain of snow spread before them, only a few lamps marking the roads. She gunned south and threw up snow in her wake. A clanking clatter told her Deck was right on her heels.

The Libbs corporation appeared as a black smudge on the horizon and grew into a small village unto its own. Three smaller houses clustered around a single large manor. Two barns and several smaller farm buildings spread around the nearby hills. Smoke rose from the manor house.

Sam pulled right up to the stairs and hopped off. The stairs had been shoveled, and then buried in several fresh centimeters afterwards. A trench had been dug out into the fields, towards the barns. "Looks normal. Let's give them a knock just to be sure," she said.

"Should we be worried?" he said.

"No." Snow crunched as she climbed. The door had a bronze knocker, frozen straight to the wood. She knocked with her elbow.

Half a dozen footsteps pattered through the house. The door swung open.

She guessed the man in front was Mr. Libbs himself, by his deep blue trenchcoat and luxuriously thick fleece under shirt. Two boys stood behind him, carrying double barrel shotguns.

"Who goes there," Libbs growled through his grey beard.

"My name's Sam. The mayor sent me to check on y'all," she said. "This my son, Deckard."

His eyes got predictably wide as they bounced between them. "Well, much appreciated then. Glad to see a face. Boys, lower the street howitzers please."

"Those your sons?" she said.

"Nay. I moved all my hands into the main house since we've got actual fireplaces that don't break in the cold. My three kids are still upstairs with the wife."

"Very kind of you," she said. Both young men behind him smiled.

"Just my job," he said.

"You need anything?"

"Nay, we're good through the winter," he said.

"Any sign of marauders? Apparently, they've been taking shots at the town."

He scratched his chin. "Yes. A day ago, the boys were shoveling out to the barn to look after the sheep, when they heard gunshots in the distance by the trees. That's where our two neighbors live on their own. Both have young kids, and only mom and dad to look after them. So, we're worried. Could you take a look out there for them? Let us know if they need anything," he said.

"They sounded like pistol shots," one of the hands said.

"You sure?" Sam said.

"Yeah. They were all high and quiet. Rifle's a roar," the dark-skinned boy said.

"Alright. Well, marshal included them in our job. So don't worry, we're going there," Sam said.

"Good. Have a good day miss." He nodded.

"Well, sounds like we're getting some action," Deckard said. He smiled beneath his scarf.

Sam steered out around the farmhouse and roared off. The trees stretched in a wall of brown across the horizon. Branches reached out to them and swayed as they tried to work closer. A slight gap in the wall marked the road. Aiming for it, she slid inside and carried on. The snow vanished into a dirt trail.

Sam searched for the usual signs of movement—footprints in the mud, and curved sprays of dirt on tree trunks as bikes maneuvered—but saw none. When she burst from the trees and into the clearing, she saw a farmhouse and a barn that sat a bare hundred paces apart. Smoke rose in a black ribbon from the farmhouse chimney.

As she approached, the front door opened. A tall man emerged. His rifle was aimed straight at her. She pulled up the steering bar and skidded to a halt. Deck bounced off her and cursed as he fell straight into the snow.

"That's close enough. Now give me a reason not to shoot ya," the man said. His forward sight was still folded down. The weapon was an old single-shot muzzle loader. The belling muzzle tip shook so much, he aimed at the sky half the time.

"Well. When you miss and take the ten seconds to reload, I could just draw and kill you. Except, my job, as assigned and paid for by the Marshal, is to come check on you," she said.

"Hell does the Marshal care about us?"

"It's her job to," she said. "Also, your front sight is down. What are you aiming at?"

He dropped the gun to the ground to fix it. In that time, she drew a revolver in her right hand and rested it on left forearm. He saw it and froze.

"I take it no one's died in your house?" she said.

"No. Wife and baby are fine."

"Libb's farmhands reported gunfire. That you guys?"

"No. That came from Charlie's house another klick down the road. That's when I got the old rifle out."

"Can I get details? I'm heading there next."

He leaned the rifle up against the wall and raised his hands. Sam lowered the pistol. Then, from the corner of her eye noticed Deckard aiming over her bike. "Deck, drop the weapon."

He slipped it back into his saddle harness.

"It happened near sunrise, two days past. Heard about seven or eight shots. I went running out and got halfway there before the snow was too much. I lost my way on the way back. If it hadn't been for Mary running out with a lantern, I might have frozen a hundred paces from my own front door."

A baby howled, and he looked back in the front door. Said a few soft words and a smile. He turned back. "Charlie's got four kids. Eldest is Sarah at thirteen. Youngest is Tal at four. Please make sure they're okay."

"Of course." She rode off without another word.

The last house was wedged between two massive trees, sheltered from snow by their spreading branches. At the corners, the veins of living wood merged with the dead as the trees grew. The chimney was stopped up by ice.

"We'll circle the house twice. Tell me when you see bullet holes," she said.

"Yes," Deckard said.

This was a typical cabin for homesteaders out here. A square floor and a half with a thatched roof. Inside would be a single living room with kitchen, dining and an oven heater, a bathroom, and the second floor was sleeping. The storage cellar would be buried underneath the house. For three months that little box was their entire universe, with only a fraught trip outside per day to care for the animals.

That was stifling. Sam would have gone mad stuck there, which was why she rode around in the dead of winter and froze to her bike instead.

There were no bullet holes. The windows were shuttered. Snow piled around the house but otherwise it looked like a family could still be huddled inside.

"I don't think I saw any bullet holes," Deckard said.

"Neither did I." She pulled up and pondered the front door. Fear tingled in her stomach at whatever darkness hid behind that simple wooden rectangle. The weapons at her belt didn't help because she had to know what she was looking at to shoot it. Something greater, more inhuman waited. "We'll knock, and if there's no answer, we'll force our way in."

"Yeah. Who's going in first?" he said.

"Me. I've got the pistol," she said. "Watch my back, in case this is a trap."

"Yeah."

She hopped off right there and sank up to her waist in the snow. "Fucking hell." She surged forward, forcing her way through. Deckard trudged in her powdery wake. They stacked up on the front door, Deckard with rifle up and aiming back towards the treeline.

Sam knocked. Silence followed. She kicked the door a few times. The log cabin shook. No one answered.

She grabbed her knife and drove it into the gap between lock and door. It clanged off a solid deadbolt. Good. That was an easy lock. She wrenched the knife out, took aim just to the left, and drove it straight into the door. It stuck deep. She stabbed again and again until the wood had chipped away. And with a clatter inside, the bolt fell clean off. She wrenched the door open.

The sweet stench hit her like a wall. "They're dead," she said, and stepped inside the dark room. The temperature barely rose in the shadows of the house. She saw a dining table tipped on its side, wooden dishes scattered across the floor. A chair lay on its back. A small foot in woolen socks lay across the headrest.

It was a boy of about ten, blonde haired and frocked in his own blood. Deckard saw him and staggered back. Jars toppled off the shelf he hit and clattered off the floor. One rolled across and came to rest against a slender hand stretched to its fullest, like it reached for him.

The oldest daughter looked so cold, even while dead. She wore only a white shift around her skinny shoulders, her blonde hair billowed out around her. She was frozen in wide-eyed terror. Tears had frozen into glittering streams on her cheeks. Two bullet holes had gone through her chest. Right over her heart. Her youngest brother was under her, a tiny ball of a boy.

Sam shut her eyes and moved on. She saw a figure in a calico dress slumped against the kitchen. Behind, a ladder. She clambered up and saw three neatly made beds. "Do you see a cellar door?" she said.

"Yeah. Yeah, it's right beneath you."

She clambered down and opened it. Rotting wood stank up at her, nearly as strong as the decaying corpses above. The cellar door threw a square of light down onto the earthen floor, and she saw mud.

"Looks like the cellar flooded. Probably rotted a lot of their food supply overnight," she said.

"Yeah, well, the mom's got a bloody knife."

"Fuck, really?" she leapt up, letting the door slam shut with a crash to wake the dead. Sure enough, she had a massive carving knife, caked to the hilt in dried blood. "Well. She didn't kill the kids. That leaves." She turned around slowly, sweeping the shadows. A dark figure lay on its back, by the bathroom door. A curtain draped over him, torn wide. As she approached, it groaned.

"You," she said. She spotted the revolver against his fingertips. A pool of red blood surrounded it.

He groaned again. "Are you the demons?"

"No. you're still here. What the fuck did you do?" She stepped down on his chest. He moaned in pain. Her toe found a scratch of stab wounds.

"Food was gone. Betty was screaming at me. We fought all week. Kids were crying. I just saw…" He gasped in pain. "Red."

"So, you killed them all," Sam said, anger rising in her throat.

"Betty was the real parent, she tried to protect them. I…send me to the pits of hell so I can burn for eternity. I have no recourse. Can't roll back time."

"We're one kid short. Where'd you put them?" Sam said.

His head raised up. His face was a gaunt grille of agony, eyes sunken into the shadows and stubble growing in tangled tufts over everything. "Liz must have locked herself in the bathroom. I hope…" he fell again and closed his eyes. Sam aimed her revolver straight down. She pulled the trigger twice. Then, grabbed the body and dragged it away from the bathroom door.

"Mother."

"I know," she said. She grabbed his shoulder and stared him in the eyes, until she felt his trembling fade. "Let's get that door open."

She tried knocking first. "Liz. Hey, we're marshals, can you open the door?" she said. Nothing. "Elizabeth, please we're here to save you. You're safe."

She shook her head. Then stepped back and kicked the door. It snapped right open. A high screech rang out. The little girl was huddled atop the toilet in her nightie. She buried her face in her hands and remained frozen there.

"Hey, Liz?" Sam said. The girl looked up. Pale face like a mouse. She squeezed her eyes shut. "Come on." Sam grabbed her shoulder. The girl spun and bit down. "I'm wearing leather gloves, you're not getting through those." She hauled the shivering kid up. "Keep your eyes closed, okay?"

No complaint. She grabbed a chair and turned it to face the stove with her boot. Then, deposited the kid in it.

"Deck, go upstairs and find the kid's clothes. I'll fix her something to eat."

"Nah, I'll feed her," Deck said.

"Alright."

She clambered upstairs. This wasn't a room, just a loft with the beds and a single wardrobe. She ripped it open and dug through the clothes. She found a small dress in bright pink, a ribbon tied into a bow around the waist. Slinging it over her shoulder, she dug out a pair of heavy woolen stockings, a bonnet, and a heavier woolen jacket of deep purple.

She clambered back down, ready to rouse them to action, and stopped herself. Deckard was crouched on his bootheels, holding up a can of dried fruit in one hand, and a glass of water in the other. He laughed as the girl dug fruit out and dropped it into her mouth.

Sam left them and checked out the window. The sky had gone grey and a few flakes spiraled down. "We need to go, I'm not getting snowed in here," she said.

"Are we ready?" Deck said, not to her, but the little girl.

She nodded.

"Good, I've got your clothes," Sam said. They got the kid dressed. Sam wrapped an extra woolen blanket around her just to be sure. The kid pointed upstairs and whimpered. "What?" She went back up and looked around. "Deck, she saying anything?"

"No."

Sam saw a small bear tucked into the sheets. Eyes of black buttons. It squeezed up in her hand as she clambered down the ladder. "Hey, Liz." When tapped on the shoulder, the girl snatched the bear up and squeezed it in her arms.

"Better?" Deckard said.

Kid nodded.

"Cool. I'll carry her."

"You sure?" she said.

"Yes. Where are we taking her?"

"Right back to town." She checked at the door. Snow was still in light flakes, but the swollen clouds promised another deluge.

"We can't leave her with her neighbors?"

"We were hired to find out, and report back to town. We're doing that," she said. She pulled the door open. The temperature didn't drop, as snow poured in.

"Those folk know her, at least," Deckard said. He took the girl's hand and bowed. She hopped after him.

"And they're dealing with winter just as hard," she said.

Sam brushed the snow off her bike and mounted. She took a last look back at the little square farmhouse. It would be a tomb until spring. A grave marker, slowly rotting by the seasons. Keying the ignition, she put her head down against the wind and rode forwards.

Looking to her right, she saw Deckard had zipped Liz into his jacket. Her head stuck out, leaning on Deckard's arm as the wind tugged her bonnet back. Those little blue eyes were open and sunken, watering up from the wind.

Exactly how Deckard had ridden in his dad's arms years ago.

The gate to town swung open upon their arrival. The Marshal met them. "Since you're back in one day I take it nothing bad happened?" she said. Then, she saw the kid. "Is she sick?"

Sam hopped off her bike and waved the Marshal away. "First two houses are fine. No marauders. Third. They had a problem with the cellar, looked like it flooded and spoiled all the food. The parents got to fighting and dad pulled out a gun. She's the only one left."

"Where's the father?" Marshal's voice dropped to a growl.

"Mother stabbed him a couple times on the way out. I sped up his trip down to the inferno," Sam said.

Marshal nodded. "Damn tragedy. We've been losing farmers for years. Everyone coming up just wants to do river work or pleasure work. Mayor was planning on subsidizing farmers for next spring, and now this…three kids gone."

"What do we do with the kid?" Sam said.

"Well. We have a church running. They could use a kid," she said.

"I grew up in a convent. I'd rather take the kid myself than send her there," Sam said.

Marshal raised an eyebrow. "Well. We also have an orphanage. They've got a few kids. It's a private endeavor. An old merchant left the money when he died."

"I'll give them a look," Sam said.

The orphanage was a three-story house with a peaked roof. Purity white paint peeled off the boards. A circular window stared down from the third story, cracked wide. Sam knocked on the door.

A woman in a brown dress answered. This wasn't a calico, but a wrapped gown of silk. Something Sam had looked for when planning to see Deck's graduation. "Hello," she said. She released the door with her right hand and took a lantern. Her left arm ended above the elbow. "We don't hire them to coal mines."

"I'm here to deliver," Sam spat. "Deck."

Deckard approached, little Elizabeth staring out from the collar of his jacket, head pressed to his chin. The woman's stern stare softened immediately into a smile.

"Why hello, what's your name?"

Liz stared back.

"Elizabeth," Sam said. "Her family lived outside of town. Can we come in?"

"Of course." She held the door. "I'm sorry, miss. About once a month during the summer, we get barge captains coming around looking for coal mine workers." She spat on the floor.

"For a price I'd take care of them for you," Sam said. They passed a kitchen. A teenage boy simmered up soup on a massive cast-iron stove. His right leg ended in a wooden peg. She smelt hot tomatoes.

"You would?"

"My job is to kill people, ma'am. Not raise kids. That's why I brought her here." The kids were all sat on a woolen rug, hand knit and covering every color on the rainbow. A younger woman scratched their letters on a blackboard as they recited. Sam strode up to her.

"Excuse me?" the teenager said. She shrank back, but Sam persisted. She checked the belt of her dress. "Do you want something?"

"Are you carrying a switch?"

"No, heavens no that's cruel," she said, aghast.

"Good." Sam returned. She tipped her hat to the old spinster. "What's your name?"

"Georgina. I take it you've seen a few church orphanages."

"I grew up and ran away from one. If I could go back, I'd rescue all the kids and teach them violence. We'd burn all the churches down," Sam said. "You've got lights, why aren't they on?"

"We had to choose between light, or heat. It's always like that in the winter. The old man, he was kind to us. So was his son. Now his son's died and his wife moved back to the nearest city and took most of the money with her," Georgina said, and shook her head. "We have the beds upstairs if you'd like to see."

They passed a closet full of little jackets, and a bathroom with a shining brass tub and sink. Upstairs was divided between a room for the adults, and a couple rooms for the children. Each kid had their own hammock and night table. Sam had shared a bed with four other kids and had stuffed her clothes into a single locker underneath.

She continued on her own up to the third floor. It was a single library, with old leather seats and a couple older kids reading in a corner. The windows stuck out from the sloping ceiling. "Jeez. Was this the old man's private collection?" she said.

"It was," Georgina said. "The daughter-in-law wanted them back, but we had that contract in writing."

"Cunt," Sam whispered, so the kids wouldn't hear. She walked over to a shelf and studied the spines. The letters were vaguely familiar. A lesson she'd forgotten in anger at the nuns who'd beat her over every misspelt word. Squinting, she tried to remember them.

"Voyage of the Night Flyer," a tiny voice said over her shoulder. Liz peaked from Deckard's jacket. Sam patted her head.

"Yeah," Deck said. "Liz. Do you like it here?"

"I want to go home."

"You can't go back. We need to find you a new one," Deck said. That only made the kid shrink into his jacket and tear up. "No, no, hey Lizzy. It's okay." He looked between Sam and Georgina, confused.

"You can't heal a wound like that with words. She needs time. And you're welcome to visit her daily," Georgina said. She reached out. Deckard peeled the kid off him, and she took her expertly in one arm. Liz huddled against her, eyes on Deckard the entire time.

Sam took Deck's shoulder. "Let's go."

"Mother." He looked at her with damp eyes. "Okay."

Sam stopped them at the donation box on the front. She counted out two thousand dollars and considered it. She still had eight thousand. That would last the winter and all the way until next winter. It landed in the box with a thunk.

At Valentine's, she ordered chicken wings and canned, dried apples to the room, then took a long bath to drive the burning numbness from her fingers and toes. She ate facing the ground floor window while Deckard got himself clean.

"Hey, mother." He slipped into the armchair beside her. "Nice view."

Snow swirled through the town streets, sticking to the frosted cobblestones. Already the roofs were white and fluffy. A dark shadow moving through the snow was the night watchman, his lantern swinging from his walking stick.

"Leaving that much money seemed a lot sweeter than what I remember of you," he said.

She pivoted on her elbow to stare at him and pushed the fruit can at him.

"Really, mother. You talked about your childhood before, but I've never seen you give money out like that. You paid for their winter heating." He fished a handful of crinkled brown apples out and threw them into his mouth. He chomped down with excess, drool running down his chin.

"I got that money off the body of an assassin. Someone hired three killers to come at me a week ago. I killed them, took their pay, and then hunted down the guy who hired them," she said. "It's blood money."

He swallowed with a gulp and stared at her with wide eyes. "Who was it?"

"Don't know. I killed him, took his money, and left. I've ended a few people in my time. Could be anyone's relative. Point is, I only got that money because someone came to me, and I killed them." She reached into the can and popped a couple chips into her mouth. She closed her eyes to enjoy the flavor; it was the perfect combination of salty and natural fruit sweetness. Deck still stared at her when she opened her eyes. "What?"

"Everything seems so brutal out here. That kid's going to grow up alone now because her dad was an angry fuck. Why do you need to make things sound even more brutal," he said. He grabbed a wing. It remained clutched in his fingers.

"Son, I'm telling you the truth about the life you chose. We could have died in that canyon. I could have spilled us over a frozen waterfall, or I couldn't get you out from under the bike and we'd frozen out there. Or hell, we could have just frozen in that cave."

"Mother, stop."

"Out here the land is your biggest enemy. It always kills the weak, and sometimes it kills the strong too. It's a matter of plain luck. You chose this life. I'm just preparing you for what's out there."

"I know you're just trying to scare me back into the city. So, stop trying to hurt me. And we're snowed in for the winter so I'm not fucking going anywhere. Didn't think that through, did you?" he stood up and glared at her.

"You don't listen," she said.

"I do. And you're just making me wish it would be spring already," he said. She caught the second meaning behind that. She spun her chair around. Deckard turned his back and strode back to his bed. He tossed his jacket on the floor, kicked off his boots, and flopped down, burying his face in the pillow.

"I can teach you to shoot at least," she said.

"Can you?"

"Yeah. Tomorrow," she said.

Chapter Five:

Sam roused Deck at dawn. "Hey. Son. Get up." She poked his shoulder.

"What." He rolled and fell right out of bed. The boards whined like they were cackling at him. "Ow. What do you want?"

"Sun's out. We're going shooting."

In twenty minutes, she had him riding out through the front gates and toward the forest. The snow had melted just enough for the top layer to become slush, then it had frozen over before receiving another layer of fresh snow. Sam pulled up to the treeline and leapt off the bike. Her boots jarred as they smashed through the glistening ice layer, then crashed through layer upon layer until she hit frozen ground. Pain flew up through her knees. She gritted her teeth. "I hate ice."

Deckard dropped off beside her. He fell half as deep. "I think I landed on a rock," he said.

"Probably the stone fence. We're on the edge of Mr. Libbs' land." She pointed to the wooden posts sticking through the snow every fifty meters or so. Then, she swept her eyes over the trees. A broken tree trunk, fingers of thick branches sticking up met her gaze. Range was about a hundred and fifteen meters. The trees around it formed a perfect box. She trudged through the snow until she was directly in front. She snapped her railgun up and took aim. Perfect sight picture. "Deck, get over here."

He crunched through snow until she heard his raspy breathing beside her. Then, with a tortured crinkling of jackets, pulled out his Marinelli. Side by side she was able to get a closer look at it. The barrel was six centimeters shorter than her railgun's. It was burly and rugged but paled before the complexity of her railgun's magnetic rails and box magazine. The deep brown wooden handguard was very square and formal compared to the railgun's curved stock. The massive receiver connected to a finely curved lever, and a hefty stock. The barrel itself was hexagonal down its length. "Son. Your shooting is trash, but you sure know how to pick a good rifle."

"Thanks mom. I know people. Including small children apparently," he said with a laugh.

"Well, now you can provide for those small children." She lowered her railgun and studied his form. She grabbed the rifle and jammed it further into his shoulder. Then, moved his grip up so his trigger finger didn't have as far to pull.

"Mother, the receiver will give me a shiner," he said.

"Not when you hold it tight," she said. "Aim it straight. That thing kicks like a mule. So, at a hundred meters to that tree stump give it about a centimeter of space between the blade of your front sight and what you're aiming at, for recoil," she said.

"How do I know the distance? Mr. Marinelli does have a range knob on the sights," he said.

"You'll learn to judge on instinct with time. Right now, take aim properly." His whole body shifted as he lowered his aim. Good, he was moving right. "Where are you aiming at?"

"Center of the log. Right at the junction of that stupid Garzelle's legs and body," he said.

She smiled. "Your finger is too strong on the trigger. That's why I moved your hand up. Don't pull with your whole hand. Use just the finger, on a gentle touch," she said.

He took a few practice pulls, hand shivering. She grabbed it in both of hers. Now he couldn't.

"Fire when ready," she said.

"Your ears."

"I'm half deaf with this cap on, don't worry," she said. She breathed once, twice, three times.

The Marinelli roared and the barrel jerked straight up. Deckard shivered as he held the bucking gun but held fast. She hadn't seen the log. She had to whip up the railgun and study through the scope.

A large hole was blown into the heart of the tree, up a few inches and to the right of the target. "You broke the poor lizard's spine. It's messy and requires another shot, but that's a kill," she said.

Deckard exhaled sharply in delight. His breath hitched up and ended gravelly with pain. She looked at him.

"I'm good mom. I'm just glad I hit in the general area." He yanked the lever forwards, then slammed it back with satisfaction. A steaming cartridge burst out and dropped through the snow, leaving a melted hole.

"It's a good shot. How many bullets can you jam in there?"

"Eight."

"Forty-five seventy, right?" she said.

"Hell yeah. Biggest that can fit into a lever action," he said. Those bullets were made to kill much larger things than garzelles. "Now. I'm aiming just to the right of the bullet hole."

"Good. Don't hurry it, just tighten your grip, exhale, and steady yourself," she said. She waited. The rifle roared and splinters burst from the log. She snapped up her rifle and took aim. "You actually got low and directly under. You were overcompensating."

"Yeah," he said with disappointment, then wrenched the lever back and loaded a fresh round. When he aimed, the gun shivered. It was jammed too far into his shoulder. Instead of resting comfortably on the stock, his cheek was right near the sight. That would give him a black eye when the rifle recoiled into his face.

"Deck. Let go," she said.

"What?" he snapped and loosened his grip. His finger remained on the trigger.

"First, let go of the trigger the second you're not about to shoot," she said. "Second. You're too tense. Look. You're going to be a poor shot at first; you're just learning how. The more you shoot, the better you'll get. As long as you learn the fundamentals and get them down, you'll only improve. That means cheek on the cheek rest. Keep a tight grip but don't pull your face up the gun." She slipped in behind him and guided his hands along the stock. She shoved it into his shoulder.

The last time she'd hugged Deckard had been three years ago, roughly. He'd been nearly as tall, but skinny as a wire. She'd lifted him off his feet and embarrassed him in front of all the hospital staff, including the young nurse he'd been chatting with the entire month of his stay. Even though she'd been engaged. Deckard had filled out at school, hopefully eating well and living in a safe, insulated dormitory.

She released him and stepped back to her son's side. He was still a kid. Face clean of scars and wrinkles, chin devoid of facial hair despite not shaving in over a week.

The rifle roared.

"Level with the last shot and a hand's breadth to the right," she said.

"Whose hand, yours or mine?"

She poked him under the ribs, and he laughed.

They fired off sixteen rounds. Ammo being expensive and all. By the end, she was sure he had some natural shooting skills, and was starting to refine them.

"Mom," he said as he slipped his empty rifle into its saddle holster. "Can you fire a few shots?"

"Like, how many?" she said, intrigued.

"All of them." He laughed sheepishly.

"You mean a mag dump?" she said. That term she'd learned from the father-in-law. Whose grandfather had been issued that railgun a century ago.

“Yeah, whatever.”

“Ammo’s expensive.”

“You only need to mint the bullet. Railguns don’t need powder.”

“Fine.” She snapped her railgun up. “I’m aiming for that tree behind the log we were shooting at. Do you see it?”

“The real thick one.”

As a final thought, she pushed in the pin under the scope and folded it to the side of the receiver. The thin blade of the front iron sight slid into focus, between the two posts of the rear sight. Perfect. She fired. A hole punched through the center of the tree, throwing out splinters. The lever slid down and back, loading a fresh bullet. She caressed the trigger, just thought it and the railgun cracked. Another hole blew out, level with the first. The rest was automatic. Lever, settle, trigger. Lever, settle trigger. The lever pumped over and over, and the barrel cracked.

She lowered her empty rifle. The barrel had grown warm.

Wood groaned. The remaining splinters snapped and the tree toppled forwards, throwing up a spray of snow as it landed.

Deckard leapt up and down on the spot. “Holy shit mother. Fuck!”

“What? I could do that at half a kilometer.”

He stopped short.

That night, he coughed deep and wet. She ran to the pharmacy in the morning and bought some of the expensive city drugs. The cough deepened to a fever, then it was gone by the morning.

Sam spent some extra money on fresh vegetables, grown in the town’s tiny underground garden. She stood in line as workers installed piping for a second garden.

“I never recovered,” Deckard muttered as she served the steaming vegetable stew Valentine’s senior cook had come up with. Vegetables were thicker than brown broth, green and red and chunks of pale potatoes.

"Of course not. Wounds like that don't," she said.

"You're going to lecture me about going back to school," he said.

"Since your father died, I've grown less fond of words," she said. He avoided the conversation by lapping up his soup.

Three days and he was fine. The next morning, she walked with him down to the orphanage and knocked on the door. He vanished inside. She stepped back into the street and watched. He appeared in the third-floor window by the library, his back to her. A little blonde head was tucked under one arm, and a braided black one under the other. Smiling, she went off to find some work.

The lived that way for months. She could do it all winter. Until the eighth of January.

That night the gates opened. A caravan of three wagons and a dozen outriders. A fuel convoy, because the last fuel boat was still moored in the docks after most of its crew had been shot down.

Sam was awoken by a knock at the door. She grabbed her jacket and revolver and answered. Marshal stood there, alongside a younger man with a stubbly beard. "Do you know what time it is?" she said.

"Midnight," Marshal said. "We need to do this right now."

"Correction. The convoy lead wants to do it right now because everything they do is hurry up and wait," Sam said. Deckard groaned from his bed.

"She ain't wrong," the man said with a shrug. "Hello Samantha. My name's Hans Greer. Two of my riders have taken sick. Town doctor thinks it's pneumonia from riding all night to get here. Thing is, they're both going to be sick for weeks and we don't have that time. So, I'd like to hire you. Pay is thirty dollars now, sixty more upon delivery of the convoy, each. One of my guys served with you before. On a convoy about four years ago. Do you remember Valery Killmore?"

"Small man with a vast moustache?" she said.

"The one. He got excited when Marshal here mentioned your name. Says you could hit a running Garzelle at three hundred yards," he said.

"She split its skull through a forest," Deckard called. Hans smiled sheepishly.

"I can hit anything you can see, and with my scope, some things you can't," she said. "We going as far as Grentonville?" she said. Grentonville was a logging town in the height of the mountains, the furthest north organized civilization got.

"No. They're good. Just to Gramely, about a two hundred kilometers far north. I'd run as is, but someone took a shot at us two days back, and we know there's marauders out here," he said.

"When do you leave?" she said.

"Two days from now. At dawn," he said.

"Deal," she said. Hans offered a hand. She shook it.

He looked over her shoulder, out the window.

"Damn, does it ever stop snowing up here?"

"In May," Marshal said. "You might want to install the snowplows."

"We'll manage," he said in a way that made Sam's belly tingle. It was almost enough to recant on the deal she'd just shaken on. But the prospect of getting a move on was worth it. "If that will be all, dawn two days from today. And I mean from the current day because it is now after midnight, making it a new day."

"I got you," she said.

"Pardon the disturbance, ma'am." He plucked his hat from his head and swept it out across his body in a torturously long bow. Marshal shook her head. They shut the door, and Sam was done.

Deckard was propped up on an elbow, peering through his little half doorway. "We're leaving?"

"In two days."

"I promised Georgina I'd help out at the spring harvest. They're doing a play for the town," he said.

"Well, that's why you don't make promises. She'll understand. She knows the life. You've got two days to say goodbye to everyone," Sam said.

Deckard buried his head in his pillow. Sam ignored him as she shut her half-door. He'd chosen this life, and she was just living it.

It turned out to be more than two days. The snow came down in heavy, wet chunks that stuck to the ground and piled up in thick blocks, perfect for building. Such snowfalls were normally short and heavy, but this one lasted three days. The town ground to a halt as the walls gained extra height. Sam got to work shoveling, sending snow down to the botanical docs, who were setting their water recycling hydroponics system up. That was all based on designs as old as her railgun.

It was a full week before they met at dawn. They were twelve gunners, each on their own bikes. And three hovering roll carriages loaded with coal. Without a word in the frozen pre-dawn air, they set out.

As they left the gate, the Marshal came running out through the falling snow. A boy had gone missing from one of the innkeeper's tenants. Had they seen him? Name was Leyal and wore a sky-blue jacket, with a silver chain around his neck.

Act II: Spring

Chapter Six:

The lead wagon rattled as it crossed the summit of Subiya pass. Perhaps it was a celebration of finally hauling up four thousand meters lined by the vast drops of valleys and the bleak sides of eternally bigger mountains. A cry of delight up to the heavens those mountains reached. Or it was a final gasp as the front right fan that had given them trouble the entire way up reached its peak and began to give out. Because the wagon dipped a few centimeters. Its lead bumper scraped snow and it skewed hard to the left. The rattle grew as the fan threw up a stream of snow. The sound rolled through the mountains and then echoed back as the heavens laughed at them.

"Goddamnit," Hans said and yanked back on his steering bar, coming to a halt. He was a dark figure wrapped in deep brown leather, embraced by the vast black and glittering ice mountains all around him. "Fan's jammed again. Tow, Deckard, one of you."

"Yeah boss," Tow said and pulled tools from his saddle bags. He had the fan stripped, cleared, and back on faster than taking off a girl's dress.

Hans tipped his hat. His beard had grown long and curly. His eyes had gained some perpetual bags. Sam thought she saw dust on his shoulder. Until he rode on, and she realized that far away, an avalanche was tickling the mountain's belly.

She put her head down and coasted on. Ahead, she finally saw their destination at the end of the pass. Relief made her suck in thin air hard. They'd passed the peak. Like the wagon, she slumped a bit on her steering bars.

"Mother," Deckard said, coming around the first wagon to match pace with her. "Are we there yet."

"Say that one more time I take your rifle," she said without looking away from the view. The mountains split and green forest spread.

They'd made it in half the time Hans had planned. The wagons had been snow proofed, but the drivers kept taking turns too tight. On hard ground they'd have been fine but in softer snow the fans dug out divots and the bumpers caught snow. The passes had been snowed in when they shouldn't have been. And each town they'd reached had been a little hungrier than the last.

No bandits had set forth, but the last hamlet had a group of farmers park a wheeled wagon across the road and demand more coal. Hans had fired warning shots. Tow had simply shot two emaciated men through their head and laughed at the wails from the women.

The mountains had winded all of them. And slowed the bikes. Sam, half the riders, and the lead wagon had all been equipped with high rotation fans to maintain altitude, but the other half had not, and were now forming a lagging rear guard. Standing up in her saddle, Sam couldn't see them over the top of the valley. the winding trail crouched into a hump that obscured all behind the white peaks.

They camped for the night within a stone's throw of the forest. No one could sleep. The air was thicker than it had been in a week and everyone could just breathe. Hans and a couple of his fellow city folk shared a pipe by the fire, and the usual coughing did not accompany it.

The drivers cursed as they picked through the lead wagon's faulty fan. There were no reserve fan blades, so they'd make do with repairing whatever was wrong there. No one went to help them. The wagons were a far smoother ride than a bike and had room for extra blankets in the cold.

Sam disassembled her bike. She dug into her bag and pulled out a thick brush of fine white bristles. Then, she ran over every fan blade several times each, and threaded it through the motor head above. She did the smaller front fan, then the maneuvering jets. That done and the brush deep brown with dirt, she snapped back on the plastic dust shields, and went to Deckard's bike.

He was stabbing at his mismatched fan blades. "No, brush it like a painting," she said, and demonstrated. He adjusted without thanks. By the time he'd fiddled over every motor and fan on his bike, his brush was caked black in carbonization and dust. "Something's overheating in here, it's probably coming from the motors. I used two different models. They probably have different tolerances, especially in the high altitude," he said.

"Well. We'll get you a matching set at our next town," she said.

"I'll get it with my ninety dollars," he said with a hurt look.

"Alright. I'm going to bed. Wake me if someone starts trouble." She wrapped herself in her blankets. The last thing she remembered was the smell of burning wood mixing with the more acrid stench of pipe tobacco, and the laughing of a drunk Hans.

Deckard popped the dust cover back in. His bike might last until the end of their trip. That motor had been more charred than he'd let on with the brush. The central spindle had begun warping. That would only make his mother worry more.

They'd pushed him around at first. He was a boy, and these were seasoned men and women with disdain for anything softer than them. Same as school with the older kids abusing the younger to get off on that hit of power before the teachers came along and clubbed them back in line. Mother had always stood over his shoulder, a reassuring reminder that she'd kill them if they got past shoving him.

Then he'd started fixing their bikes, and at least they'd left him alone. He strode past Tow's sleeping bag. The mountain of a man stretched across half the fire, forcing several more riders out to the periphery.

"You got a sweetheart back at your city?" Tow said.

"No," he said and stopped.

"Really. I thought you were going out to take her picture out and admire." He burst into giggles.

"Fuck off."

"I'll buy her off you when we get back. Show her what a real screwdriver does."

Deckard kept walking. Tow had just gotten more irritating, instead of grateful someone else could shoulder the burden of keeping the bikes running

He had one target tonight. It wasn't for repair. He walked out past the warmth of the fire and down twenty paces. Seated atop a felled tree was a lump of a man in a woolen cap. He had a round face rimmed by a heavy beard. Seated across his voluminous lap was a rifle longer than his own. Deckard knew the bullet was smaller, but the cartridge longer. There was a seal on the buttstock but he'd never gotten close enough to identify the making arsenal.

Valerie looked up when Deckard sat down beside him. He lit a cigar and hunched his shoulders up to block him.

"Hey," Deckard said.

Silence, which he was used to when he tried to talk about something other than the quality of their bikes.

"You knew my mother," he said.

Valerie puffed away.

"I said, you knew my mother!" his got an echo back on his voice.

"Boy. There's a term out here. You earn your own respect. That means don't lean on your sure-eyed mother, or the moment she's out of sight you'll find yourself dead on the trail." Still, he stared straight ahead.

"Your word about my mother is the only reason I'm out here, bothering you. So, I will be bringing her up," Deckard said.

Valerie's grimy cheeks inflated, and then puffed out a perfect ring of smoke. "Let me guess. She's refusing to tell you the truth about this wild world and you feel infantilized and left in the dark. You're hoping I'll give you some wisdom." He blew another ring.

"No, she's told me everything. I watched my father die. And I butchered his killer. That's disrespecting both of us."

Valerie turned his head to peer at Deckard from the corner of his eye. "You've killed a man?"

"With a rifle bayonet. I opened his belly and when he went down just kept stabbing him. He murdered my father in cold blood," Deckard said, grinning the vengeful memory.

"If you'd let on you've killed, then you'd have been treated better from the start."

"Perhaps you should just be decent to anyone you're working with instead of being an asshole until they meet your criteria," Deckard said.

Something changed in Valerie's dim gaze. He dropped the condescending little look of his eyebrows. "What did you want to ask, son?"

"What's the most dangerous thing out there?" he said.

"Including people?"

"Yeah."

"Filibusters," he said. "Ever heard the term."

"No…" he shook his head at a flash of memory. "Wait, I did. A man and woman in fancy military outfit were waiting outside school one day two springs ago. They told us about all the glory we'd earn and the pay and the riches. A couple of my friends went off. I almost signed on, but decided they sounded a bit too gilded at the last second."

"Well, you have some brains at least. Filibusters go out to drive local settlers off their land. There're the cities, then there's the territory between that they all want to control. Filibusters are entrepreneurs who do it for their own profit. There's no humanity in their leaders. They kill and rape for a living. Normal folk with warm flesh and red blood are just sources of fun and profit to them," he said.

Deckard breathed in. He enjoyed how the air filled his lungs so easily. "Like marauders?"

"Worse. Marauders live out here and grow hard to survive. Filibusters get fat in civilization and then come out here."

"Can we shoot them?"

"I have. Came upon a few picking over a farm after their main brigade had moved on. Father and son had been shot on the spot. Wife and three daughters…" he spat into the frosted dirt.

Deckard nodded.

A high howl boomed out of the valley ahead. A second and a third joined it, chorusing together like wailing ghosts, running shivers down his spine.

Valerie shifted his rifle up across his chest, ready to aim. "Speak of the devil, that's the second most dangerous things in the wilderness; greywalkers."

"I read about them in school. They always travel in packs of three. Two females and a male. They're the apex predator because they're the smartest thing out here," Deckard said.

"That they are. They're also inhumanely quick, and they see perfect in the dark. If you camp without a fire they'll be on you in an instant. No disemboweling." Valerie raised a curved blade to his own throat. "Just a quick snip at your throat, or your wrist first if you get an arm up to fight."

"My textbook said they're optimized to kill and travel and that lets them hunt anything and go wherever they need to hunt," Deckard said.

Something screeched in the dark. Three wails chorused, yelping their wet delight over and over. Though sight was impossible, Deckard stood up and peered into the blackness. The wails ended as something out there died cleanly.

"At least they haven't learned to use rifles," Valerie said with a nod. He rapped his pipe on the log. Red ashes fell to the ground. "Sam shot one of those off me about three years ago. We were chasing the leader of a bandit gang into the brush after we'd wiped his hideout. He started screaming and stopped. That's when we ran. Except, one of them got atop me. She made the shot in the dark at a hundred yards. Hit the beast square in the right eyeball." He burst into laughter.

"She's a good shot," Deckard said.

"She's the second best alive. And I'm not too sure the Beast of the East still lives. Hasn't killed anyone in five years." He slapped his belly. The entire man rippled as he stood off his log. "Watch my back, I'm taking a piss."

Deckard drew his rifle and aimed the hefty barrel into the night. He jammed the stock into his shoulder and sighted properly, straight down the road. Nothing moved until Valerie returned.

"Don't sight until you've got a target. It narrows your vision too much. See your target, then snap up and take the shot."

Deckard pulled back. "Thanks." His fingers went numb on the cold barrel. His bed roll called, but one more question nagged at him. "How dangerous is the Beast of the East?"

Valerie put the cigar to his mouth and his entire face seemed to inflate as he sucked in. He blew two rings out, and then descended into dry coughing. "Beast is the third most dangerous thing out here. The only reason he's third is there's only one of him."

"How many has he killed?"

"Hundreds. I've never seen him in person, but I came upon the aftermath once. Beast uses two railgun pistols. A stagecoach had been robbed. All the guards had a neat little hole in their forehead, and massive chunks blown out their backs of their heads. They'd fallen while running and shooting back." He shook his head. "Divine comedy that a monster with a monster shot like that gets ahold of two of the most dangerous weapons around."

"Anyone know where he's from?"

"Apparently he started as another farmer. Survived a filibuster raid. After that, not much is known except he's been raiding for thirty years and apparently fathered a son." He shrugged. "Just hope you don't run into him. Fifty thousand ain't worth it."

"I'll believe you," Deckard said. "Goodnight." He wrapped himself in his bag and curled up to savor every little bit of warmth.

They saw the remains of the greywalkers' prey the next morning. A skeleton of a Garzelle, picked clean overnight. Deckard pulled up his bike and studied the results. The bones were red with blood, scarred by hundreds of tiny teeth marks. They were deep, but thin. Those were razors, he thought with a shiver.

"I'm thinking their next meal will be you." A deep voice whispered. Tow stood over him, towering on his massive bike. He was utterly hairless and pale as the mountain tops.

"Sure," Deckard said. If only he could fight the man.

"Imagine lying down to bed. You think you'd wake up before they killed you? Come out of your wet dreams and suddenly you're drowning in your own blood. Maybe they'll give you a kiss."

"I suppose you know how to survive them?" he said.

"Yeah, cross a river. They can't swim well. Did they teach you to swim in that fine boarding school you came from?"

Deckard hit the throttle and buzzed ahead. Tow followed him, battering insults until they came in sight of Sam. And once again, Deckard ran to her side and hid.

They rolled through the valley. By noon, the trees were revealed to be but a brief copse of cover as they gave way to a rolling hellscape of moss-covered rock and narrow ravines filled with rushing water. A low rumbling never faded as meltwater ran under their feet. At least the temperature was warm enough his sweat didn't freeze to his forehead anymore.

Passage was granted by a handful of rope and wood slat bridges. Each with a date placard over two decades old. The bikes made easy time first. Then, the wagons rolled over. Deckard's stomach dropped as the road wound along the ravines.

By mid-afternoon there was a fine mist in the air. He stuck out his tongue and tasted the water. It was cold but refreshing

A crack roared behind Deckard. He snatched his rifle up and spun around. Then had to grab the handlebars as he nearly throttled into the ravine. Screams rang out.

No shot had been fired. Racing back, he saw the last wagon had turned too loose and caught its right fan bumper on an upturned ledge of rock. It swung wide.

"Shit!" Lambel bellowed and gunned his engine. He latched right onto the left bumper on the fly and gunned his engine. "Cut the engine, you fool!" he screamed, voice barely audible over the whine of motors and fans, and the water roaring beneath.

The driver wasn't at the wheel. She'd slammed into her steering axel and Deckard saw her picking herself up, blood trickling from her jaw. He hit the throttle and surged towards the doomed wreck. If he could latch on besides Lambel, he could just…

The thin sandstone broke in sheets. A ledge became a divot and the wagon scraped over it. Without resistance, it kept going until it flipped over and vanished. Lambel and the driver screamed together as they fell until they ended in a crunch.

Deckard kept going until he reached the edge. Lambel was dead. His head and legs flopped in the fast current, chest smashed between wagon and rock. The driver had vanished beneath. Black petrol leaked out, tainting the clear waters as they coursed through. The wagon's fans still spun down and threw out great sprays of foam where they aeriated water. Vomit rose in Deckard's throat and he clamped his sleeve over his mouth. Shame fell back down to burn him.

"Fuck!" Hans bellowed. He grabbed his revolver and fired a shot into the air. "God damn whore of a driver. There goes a third of our profits." He hopped off and stood beside Deckard, staring into the oblivion.

"Look. The ledge on the other side is over there. Let's see if we can salvage some of the oil. Bring the lead wagon up there and pull out a hose," he said, pointing.

What about the dead? Deckard wanted to say. That would only earn him angry shouts. Helplessly he sat and watched as the rest got to work. Until Hans grabbed his arm roughly. "Let's go. You're the mechanic—see if you can help out."

"Come on boy. Make that ass useful," Tow said with a snicker.

Hans turned about. "We are exposed out here if any man or beast wants to take a shot at us. Samantha and I will ride ahead and scout the way. For now, keep working on that."

Sam threw him a nod. And they rode off.

Deckard and the other drivers got another wagon backed up to the stream A driver leapt onto the wagon's belly and found the hose. Deckard threaded it to him. Oil pumped immediately.

"Tank's not filling," a driver said. Deckard bent down to check the gauge. A massive hand grabbed the bottom of his pants. He leapt up and spun around, rifle stock in hand. He found Tow giggling.

"I am doing company work. Stop," he said.

"Sure, boy. You just want to bend over like that and expect nothing to happen?"

Deckard bent over. And spun around again. Tow was still laughing.

"You're the repairman, aren't you going to help?" he said.

"Here." A driver leapt down from the wagon and got to work. "Fuel line is pinched. Hang on…and fixed." Deckard stared at Tow. The mountain of a man giggled as he walked away, blending in with the jagged ravine wall.

The rest of the guards looked away as Deckard steamed. Could he murder the man?

Deckard headed back up and joined the group of riders.

"Here's what I think," Tow began. Everyone gave him a wide berth. "I think Hans is going to fire three of us right now. He's only got two wagons. He will not pay the extra guards. So. I think two will be Miss Samantha and her boy." He jabbed a finger like a pistol barrel at Deckard's nose. "Why not save him the trouble of dealing with them."

"Nah," Deckard said.

"Your opinion is not valid, boy."

Deckard looked left and right. No one had directly sided with the giant, but none were moving to stop him either. "You could just walk away and not cause trouble for everyone. Just live peacefully and let everyone else live."

Tow's face sullied raw red. Something in that statement had deeply offended him. "Out here in the wilderness we live on the knife's edge. I've got my place and I've spent thirty-five years building it with these hands. Then you come along, you little shit, and you try to do my job. I'm just living out here and you're chipping away at it. There's no room for both of us on this payroll. So, I'm giving you a chance to earn it."

Deckard stepped back, out of Tow's shadow. He grabbed the stock of his Marinelli.

"If you pull that rifle out, I'll draw." He patted the massive revolver on his belt.

Deckard raised his hand in a fist and slid the rifle off his back. He laid it on the ground and straightened up. "You're insane."

"Spoken like a true soft-bellied city boy." Tow balled his fists and lunged forwards.

Deckard had learned boxing at school. He faked left and buried a right hook into the muscle-bound jowls of Tow's head. Something broke and the massive man snorted blood. Encouraged, Deckard followed up with two punches to his belly. It was like hitting an iron wall.

Tow's first punch screamed at him like a locomotive. He stepped right, then kept stepping right as he landed blow upon blow on Tow's shoulders and side. He caught him right on the eye.

Tow grunted and kicked him. Pain cracked through his knee, and he stumbled. Instead of hard rock his boots landed on moss and slipped. Tow grinned and punched.

Deckard landed on his back. His left arm flopped over the edge. He opened his eyes against the pain and saw a mountain of a boot crashing down. A scream left his lips as he rolled right. The ground shook. Deckard clawed his way to his feet.

Tow hit him again, then stepped on his chest. "There. Not so bad," he said.

Valerie slammed into the giant. He came in low and threw his body like a bowling ball. Tow vanished with a crash and groan of pain. Then he was up and the two slammed into each other. Deckard lay there and gasped for air. Every breath made his ribs cry out, which only made him gasp the next deeper.

A wet crunch filled the air. Valerie cursed something and came stumbling back. Tow drove him into the ground and clamped his hands over Valerie's throat.

■■

Sam stood up in her saddle, keeping her bike at a low hum. She sat down and hit the throttle to max acceleration. Hans shouted something that was lost in the wind. She roared back across the trail, to reach the scene unfolding before it finished.

She hit the break and swung the bike around to a halt. Tow was grinning as he strangled Valerie. Deckard was sprawled out beside them, mouth open like a fish. His right eye was already purple and swollen shut.

Sam didn't bother with fists. She hefted the railgun and swung the butt into Tow's head like an axe. The mountain didn't budge as blood poured free. "Let him go." She flipped the gun around and slammed the butt into his right arm over and over, until it folded. Tow collapsed to the ground.

"You too, the weak teaming up to bring down the strong," Tow said and leapt up. He swung for her head, but she'd already darted around. He spun about and she caught an elbow to her shoulder. The rifle slid from her fingers.

She spun and punched him. As she hit, she jabbed her thumb straight into his eye. He swatted aside.

"You're not much bigger than your boy."

Deckard leapt onto his shoulders and clamped his hand around his throat. Valerie slammed into them and toppled the entire pile.

"Get his right arm," Sam said as she knelt on his left. Deckard stomped on his right. Valery jammed his knees into the man's chest. Bruised, black-eyed, and bleeding from both nostrils, Tow just laughed at them.

"Well look at all of you. You've gone and banded together. Like all the fucking factory workers trying to tell the owner what to do." Valerie kneed him in the belly and he coughed hard.

"Stop. Right now, all of you," Hans said. Sam ignored him, until she heard the click of a revolver hammer being cocked.

"He tried to beat the shit out of me," Deckard said. "He made his intention clear and the rest of you did nothing." He jabbed a finger at the rest. Sam glared at them.

"They only need one mechanic to finish the trip. I'm saving them the loose ends of firing you," Tow said and laughed. As he did, a chain slipped from under his jacket. A silver L glittered in the light. Sam stepped forwards to study it, taking her weight off him.

Tow shifted under her feet. Inexorably, he rose.

"Stop!" Hans bellowed and pressed the gun to his forehead.

"You're not shooting," Tow said. He kept rising until they were forced off him. Only then. Hans kept the gun pressed to his head

"We are here on company pay to do a mission," he said. No one was listening. Sam snatched up her railgun and aimed it between Tow's beady eyes. "Samantha, stop it now!" The revolver shivered in his grasp.

"That boy. The one missing when we left Crownville. What did you do?" she said.

"I saw Tow leaving the last night, and he didn't come back til morning!" someone said around them.

Tow leaned in so her muzzle pressed to his brow. "I enjoyed myself. Same you'd do in my position."

"Same as you were doing to my son." She looked at the glittering L around his neck. More pendants were on the chain behind it. There was a 'G.' then a little heart locket, then a P, then she couldn't count them all amidst his greasy collar. "Damn you."

"Sam. We'll drop him when we get to the end of this trip. We still need him," Valerie said. Like hell she trusted him.

"You are all on company pay," Hans said.

Tow shrugged. "Shoot me or put it away. You're wasting time."

His head exploded, blowing a fan of blood and pink brains across the snow behind and the rider on either side. A single eyeball remained in its half socket, staring at her as if in surprise. Tow hit the ground. She lowered the railgun to her side. Blood hissed and vaporized off its barrel.

"God damn," Hans said.

Samantha knelt over the massive corpse and yanked the necklace off. She tucked the pendants into her pocket.

"That was uncalled for," Hans finally said. Mutters all around.

"It's the most called for thing I've ever fucking done," she said, and stormed off towards her bike. As she passed, she patted Deckard's shoulder.

Chapter Seven:

They camped a few miles down, atop a ridge that cut through the ravines like it had been rammed up into there from the deep planet itself. There was little wind, but a cold rain rolled in slowly and drenched them. Sam huddled under her waterproof blanket, arms tucked against her body to leech every bit of warmth out of her chest. The rain pattering on her blanket drummed a steady rhythm. It lulled her into sleep.

The rain had ceased when she emerged in the morning, though a gray sky reigned overhead.

"Everyone over here," Hans said. "Get up." Someone told him to shut up and quit wasting time. "Get up. I'm your boss!"

Valerie offered her a cigar and a light.

"This is ending badly," she said and took a puff.

"Yeah, you sealed your job by killing Tow."

She stared at him. "Should I have let him continue on after threatening Deck?"

Valerie shrugged. "We're at the limit out here is all I'm saying."

"Get over here!" Hans snapped. The echo across the mossy rocks was nature laughing at him. Slowly, the group closed in.

"Okay, listen up," Hans said. "I was paid for three wagons at four escorts each. We now have two wagons. So, we only need eight escorts. Samantha, Deckard, you are our newest hires. You're fired."

"You owe us for getting the wagon this far," Sam said.

"No, I don't. Our deal was pay upon completion," Hans said. He looked about. "Unless you want to attack our convoy."

Six gunslingers glared back. Six dissenting voices merged into a wall of universal contempt. Sam was impressed with how fast they'd rounded on her.

"You fuckers are serious. He'd fire you just as easily," Deckard said. No one budged. "Fine. Slaves."

"Damn Hans. You're letting go of our best marksman," Valery said.

"Shut it, Val. If she hadn't killed Tow, you'd be getting fired for your part in that fight."

Valery stepped forwards. Sam waved him off. "Relax. We're leaving," she said. Deckard's jaw dropped.

The convoy started up. Fans whined, water sprayed.

"Mother, I need to know what are you god damn thinking?" Deckard said soon as they were out of earshot.

"I'm thinking about waiting until they hit that next ridgeline and struggle over the snow, then setting up at half a kilometer and picking them off one by one," she said, arms crossed.

"Wait. What would we do with the wagons?"

"Who cares. We go through the pockets of the dead and empty their wallets, their food supplies. Leave the rest for the greywalkers." She lowered her gaze to him. "That would end with us as outlaws, fleeing from civilization. So we're not doing that. Come." She stalked over to her bike. He tagged at her heels like a puppy.

"Well why didn't you fight them? We had Valerie."

"We didn't have Valerie. He was going to step back and sit it out. They all got attached to Tow because he fixed their bikes and was the biggest monster in the wilderness. Valerie was siding with him, even if he did nothing," she said.

"Is that why you shot Tow there instead of waiting until he got to civilization? I think you got us fired doing that," Deckard said.

"Yeah. I shot him because I didn't trust anyone to bring him to justice. And because he wasn't going to leave you alone." She leaned over and grabbed his shoulder. He nodded back, frustration fading.

"Where are we going?" he said.

"This valley is a crossroads. At either end, it actually widens into a fairly fertile plain, fed by meltwater. Like the Slave river. Plenty of folk got this far and stopped there for good. We'll find a farm. We still have a fair bit of money," she said.

"And then?"

"There's always work in my profession," she said. She hopped on her bike and keyed the engine. The fans buzzed with the smoothness of perfectly maintained machinery. Beautiful. Water sprayed off the rocks beneath in a halo, splattering Deckard below the waist. He scowled and leapt onto his own bike. His let out a cough and spun up. She cast a worried look, but it held steady.

They threaded through the ravines, taking routes wagons couldn't. A touch of Sam's throttle slid her between raging water and black cliffs. Months of leading trundling wagons left her with a thrill for open terrain and she sated it now. A few amphibious leggers splashed into the water as they raced past. A couple Dactyls squawked from a cave carved overhead by rainwater.

With a hand signal and sharp jab on the steering bars, Sam ducked right and slipped under a vast arch of rock. Water sprayed off like a curtain, dampening her clothes as she went past. Deckard whooped behind her. In the corner of her peering eye, she saw him swing wide and swipe the spray with his hands. She looked ahead and saw this ravine continued uninterrupted into the hazy distance. So, she gunned the throttle and they raced on.

After hours the sun was high and the ravine came out onto the ridge, except now it had widened and hosted topsoil with small bushes, whose bare branches rustled in her bike's wake. A look at her compass told her the ridge pointed in the right direction. She continued.

"We're safe from Greywalkers," Deckard shouted over the wind.

She raised an eyebrow. "What makes you say that?"

"They can't cross rivers. Don't swim well." He pointed at the water running past.

"You sure?"

"No. It's what I heard." He laughed.

Deckard weaved through the brush behind her. He snatched a gnarled red branch off a bush and held it out. The boyish smile on his face was infectious. Sam swung out behind him and grabbed her own branch. She saw him turning his head for a quick glimpse. She evaded his vision, until she landed a tap on his shoulder.

"How the fuck do you do that?" he said.

"Get a racing bike," she said. Hers was built for cobblestone city roads and the maintained dirt between cities. With a few modifications it had turned into the absolute highest performance bike you could find for the open country. So long as she didn't crash it.

"Hell no. You're crazy driving that. I never told you that, mother. Your bike is crazy."

She responded by doing a loop around him and then ducking between two large, moss-encrusted trees. Too late, she saw the translucent fibers running between them.

They caught her and snapped. "Deck!" she yelled over the rumble of earth. The moss snapped off the tree. Had she been a slower earthbound dactyl it would have landed around her shoulders. Instead it splattered over her coat tails and landed on the baggage behind her bike. A hissing rose up as leather melted. She came to a stop and leapt off.

"Deck. Help me get this shit off." She drew her knife and scraped her own jacket, yanking off green and dissolving leather. "Just cut if off."

Deckard tore chunks off plant and dissolving plastic the bike. He used his right hand and yelped in pain, then grabbed his knife in his other hand. She ran over and joined him, tearing through her sleeping roll as she worked. Fuck it. She grabbed the entire hissing sleeping roll and hurled it off. It lay in a dissolving pile on the ground.

"Light a match." She grabbed the newspaper from a now exposed satchel. Deckard lit it up, and she dropped it on the pile. The hissing increased in intensity until it felt like an organic scream.

"What…" Deckard withdrew.

"It's a predatory plant. Sits on trees like normal moss. Catches Dactyls and small reptiles coming through. Dissolves them in acid and eats them. Then over a few days slithers back up to the tree," she said. She stomped back to the tree. A fair bit of green clung to it. "Fire. Now." Another hissing screech went up as it all burned. "You want to fuck with me? I've lived forty years out here and you haven't killed me yet." She spat on the burning trunks.

Her bike had a few fresh gouges through the dust cover, perfect for letting moisture in. Her sleeping roll was ruined. And her coat had been reduced to ribbons below the waist. "Let me see your hand," she said and grabbed Deckard. His fingers were raw red and bloody. "Let's get that patched up before you get infected."

Antiseptic and bandages made him bite his tongue and groan. "Why does this even exist? Who on this planet wanted flesh eating moss?"

"It exists because god either doesn't, or doesn't care about us," Sam said. "Come on. It's probably going to rain tonight and we need to find some cover.

Cover came as the ridgeway widened out. The ravines gentled into streams. The water pooled into a lake on either side, the water lapping against frigid bedrock. Moss became grass. Like breaking a curtain, they spilled into fields of pale blue grass dotted with trees.

Sam had forgotten it was mid-March, and spring had arrived in the lower elevations.

Then the sky broke open and rain poured down.

Sam kept them driving in search of shelter. Water wormed its way through her poor brutalized coat and poured down her trousers. It pooled in her boots and soaked her long johns into wet slicks freezing her flesh to her bones. It poured into her bike and hissed in the internals. Steam billowed up.

A light shined in the distance. She put her head down and pushed the throttle. A three-story farmhouse with a peaked roof emerged. A porch ran around the sides of the building, supported by wooden columns. Lamp light flickered in every window. Sam pulled up and looked around. Several barns and various other farmhouses spread around it. Winter had beaten the paint off the wooden boards.

"This it?" Deckard said. He'd pulled his sleeping roll out and wrapped it around him like a blanket.

She leapt down and walked ahead. A wooden footbridge crossed a stream up to the wooden front gate.

Barking rang out. Dogs burst from under the porch and charged straight to the wood, where they snapped at the fence.

Sam drew her revolver and fired into the air. The front door opened. The dogs kept barking until the man pulled on his jacket and hat and limped up to the door.

"State your intentions," he growled in a voice like aged whiskey. Two other figures on the porch took aim. One in a dress and poncho and one in a man's dressing gown.

"We've been on the trail for three months. Can we spend the storm in your hay loft?" Sam said.

"Who's he?" he pointed at Deckard.

"My son. He's a good boy," she said. The man's eyebrows barely wavered.

"You're welcome to the hay loft in our main barn. Don't expect food or fire. And don't touch the Blergs. We moved them in because the cold rain gets them sick"

"Of course not. Thank you, Mr…"

"Sansford, Miss…"

"My name's Samantha," she said.

The barn was well-made and warm. The Blergs huddled comfortably in the straw, and didn't even rouse themselves as Sam and Deckard parked their bikes and clambered up the ladder. Piles of fresh, golden straw greeted them with open arms. Sam flopped right in and stretched herself out.

"This is real comfy," Deckard said.

"That it is." She was asleep immediately.

She awoke in darkness, felt her way to her canteen, and drained it. Then went back to sleep.

She was awoken by the stamping of clawed feet and grumpy complaining from a dozen large, reptilian herbivores. Then the sharp cracks of whips, and low chatter of a pair of farm hands. They trod off into the morning. Grey twilight filtered in through the door, casting them in fog.

"Mother." Deckard rasped. Sam plucked his canteen off his belt and handed it to him. He tipped back where he lay and finished it. "I need to piss."

"Well. Go in the barn. I changed your diaper," she said. He disappeared over the side, then was back in a minute.

"What now?"

Sam checked her kit over. Jacket still ruined. Pants now soggy and clinging to her. Everything else seemed fine. Or it wasn't broken at least. She disassembled her railgun and pulled out the cleaning kit. "You should clean your rifle."

"Okay, but what is our new course of action?"

"We'll see when they come for us."

As she spoke, the barn door creaked open.

"You still up there?" Mr. Sansford said.

"Still here," she said.

"So. Now that we have no rain bringing urgency I'd like to know how you ended up out here. There's a fair few people in this area, but we don't get many outsiders this time of year."

"We came as part of a winter convoy. Sent by the Walticon company to get fuel up north. One of the wagons overturned, so the convoy leader fired us and we decided it was enough misery dealing with him and went off," she said.

"Well. Ain't you at a low point," he said.

Sam clambered down. Sansford was average height. His beard was gray, but there were flecks of brown under his hat. He had a round, gentle face, but she saw all the violence she needed in the eyes. And the rifle over his shoulder. A squat carbine with a round receiver and unusually thick stock

"Is that an Engram?" she said. Engram had been a gunsmith with a zealous belief that enough bullets simply weren't enough. His Engrams Carbine had a tube stuck straight through the stock. The shooter would load rounds into the revolving magazine, which had far more room than any other weapon, even her railgun. The standard carbine had twenty-eight, if she recalled correctly.

"Load on Sunday and fire all week," he said with a gentle grin. The look was just as dangerous. He'd definitely used that thing on humans before. "Ain't quite that monster you carry. I saw that and figured you weren't some common outlaw." He pointed a crooked finger at the railgun.

"No. We ain't wanted for anything by anybody."

"Well…" someone screamed outside. Wood snapped and a blerg howled. Sam looked outside just in time to see the footbridge pull straight from the muddy banks, taking the last blerg and the young man bringing up the rear with it. Ropes wrapped around both of them as they splashed into the water.

"That's my son," Sansford said. Farmhands and a couple women grabbed ropes, a walking stick, whatever they could and tossed them in the water. No one went in. Sam understood. They were hundreds of miles from real water, why would they be able swim?

She shoved the railgun into Sansford's surprised hands. "Don't lose that." As she walked, she stripped her jacket and ripped off her boots one by one.

The Blerg's head burst from the water. Its massive mouth yawned and howled in shock as cold jabbed at its tiny brain. Tied to its side, just out of the water, was a tiny white hand grasping at pale skin. It rolled to the side, struggling to regain the wall. A bearded face emerged and gasped a breath, before disappearing back under the dark water.

Sam grabbed her knife and leapt in feet-first. Her feet hit mud and cold drained her as hard as an uppercut to the jaw. The surface was way above her head, a ceiling of light an eternity away. All her strength vanished into the water. Her heart shuddered.

She breached the surface and pumped hard for the Blerg. At its side she dove and felt for the ropes. A hand grabbed her wrist and her hand grabbed a thick rope. She saw the young man up close. And she sawed away at the rope until it broke free.

The Blerg rolled and dragged them up. Sam slipped off. The bulk of the beast poised over her, gasping for breath. And splashed back down. It slammed her into the bottom. She kicked and found enough room under the mud to scrabble out. Instead of clawing for the surface, she felt around the man until she found another rope. She sawed through it, too. As it broke, an arm snatched out and grabbed her wrist. Fingernails dug into her skin.

She threw punches until the hand loosened and kicked for the surface. Gasp of breath. A lot of screaming people over her. Then back down. Pale face. Bubbles rising as the idiot screamed his air away. She found that grasping hand again and cut it free. The entire man inched upwards and caught on a rope further down. She dove deep. The blerg shifted again and yanked her away. She followed it until dark boots emerged against its flank. A full wooden slat pinned them down. They twitched. Nothing more. She was running out of time.

Her lungs burned, which was the only warmth to be had. She ran a hand along the board until she hit more rope and got to work. It split easily. As it did, the knife jarred from her numb fingers and sank.

She grabbed it by the blade and didn't care as she hauled for the surface. She gasped air in. And vomited back up. Then sank back down. Her limbs wouldn't work.

Some farmer isn't getting your railgun. She dove back. The man hung by a single rope around his chest. His fingers twitched, eyes vague. She cut him free and saw blood in the water. He floated right into her arms. And she dropped a shoulder into him. Then he was out of the water and weighing her down. She spluttered one breath.

Something bumped into her shoulder. She turned and saw a hoe sinking down, a rope attached to it. She grabbed it and wrapped the rope around idiot's limp arm. It snapped taught and he was hauled away. Someone yelled and a second dropped. Sam grabbed it and let herself be hauled up, too.

She hauled herself over the side and landed in a shivering heap.

"Hey." She looked up and saw a woman in an emerald green dress, faded by a year of wearing. A white bonnet obscured much of her face. "Here." She bent down. A slender girl, not a woman. She offered a blanket.

"Thanks," Sam muttered and wrapped herself in it.

Chapter Eight

Sam huddled under a vast blanket. With the fire roaring close enough to shower cinders on her, and half a bottle of bourbon in her, feeling was prickling back into her fingers. Staring into the fire made it better.

Bootsteps and a heavy thunk. "I brought you your railgun. The rest of your clothes are being washed now, though the jacket might be finished."

"Did the kid live?"

"He'll live. Thanks to you." Sansford laid the railgun down behind her.

Slipping a hand through the blankets, she laid bare finger on the wooden stock. "Good."

"Where'd you learn to swim?"

"Husband. I can't work a field or read a book, but I can swim long as you need me," she said.

"That's enough, miss," he said. He placed a steaming mug. "Fresh coffee. My daughter in law makes it the best. We've got another mug for your son."

"Put cinnamon in his if you can," she said. A log popped and the entire pile collapsed in a spray of cinders. Sansford tossed another on. Sam scooted back a step. She poured coffee into her mouth, then poured bourbon in after.

"It's good. Thanks, Mr. Sansford." He grumbled behind her.

"Anything's good with enough liquor put into it."

"Except milk."

"Except that. And you can call me Wyatt. You're welcome here for now," he said. She heard the danger again in the harsh undergrowl in his voice. It was comforting. Small, light footsteps scampered across a neighboring room in a tide. "That will be the grandkids chasing the cat. They've gone crazy with being cooped up inside."

"Oh yeah. That's why you're seeing me riding through the winter instead of sitting pretty in safety," Sam said. Wyatt pulled up a spindly wooden chair. They talked the rest of the day away. Wyatt had moved here with his five kids thirty years ago. A wagon train of twenty-six families had come through the pass. They'd delayed past the end of travelling season and it was now New Year's Day. Wyatt decided to winter here. The rest continued on. A few starving, desperate men returned, carrying their children. No one else made it out.

Wyatt hadn't been the first to settle here, but he'd been the most successful. A degree in ecology helped him irrigate the fields the best and grow the most. Soon he was the unofficial leader of this farming valley, where two of his children remained with their families. A third, his youngest, who Sam had saved, had been driven from his old town by poverty and hoped to build a homestead here next spring.

And yes, Wyatt had used that Engrams he still kept slung over his shoulder. As a young man, he'd been a ranger for a smaller city. Often outnumbered, they'd been all issued with Engrams to deal with the odds. He'd bought his off the rangers just before leaving.

"Were you ever an agent of the law?" he asked.

"No. I was hired to run with rangers and marshals a few times, but I've always rode free," she said.

"Teaching your son the road?"

"Not by choice," she said with a shake of her head. "He should have stayed in school."

"Well. Sadly they don't learn until they've experience it themselves. Wisdom wasted."

"Yeah." She was wearing some woman's lacy shift and woolen jacket. "Are my clothes dry?"

"I'll check." He came back with them in an armful. "Like I said, the jacket is ruined, but my wife took a look at the rest."

Sam went over the work. Her shirt and trousers were good as new. "Jeez she did a great job."

"Her eyes are going, but her hand is steady as ever. At your leave, miss."

She dressed and left the donated garments strewn on the chair. Without her jacket, she still felt the cold through both shirts. The railgun went over her shoulder.

■■■

Deckard wandered around the farm. No one bothered him, but none approached either. The blerg had drowned and lay dead in the stream, water lapping around its leathery grey back. A few hands were outside, discussing what to do about replacing the bridge. He saw a woman with snow-white hair sitting on a swing on the porch, watching him trek across her lawn. He tipped his hat. She waved.

From a lean-to on the side of the house he heard the whir of a bike fan, like music. Then guttural profanity.

He slipped through the door and the air grew warm and turgid with machine oil. Half a dozen bikes were parked in the back. The subject of profanity stood in a stand, its entire primary engine housing lying in picces on thc ground.

A woman bent over and hit the ignition switch. The engine whined to life, too deep to be healthy. The fan whirred a bit, then choked and died.

"We might need to just replace a motor. It's not the fans and it's not the intake," the woman said.

"Fucking hell that's going to be money. Might need to shelve this and wait for the bridge to be paid for," the man said. She tried the motor again, with the same results.

Deckard strode forwards. He bent and read the serial number along the long front axis of the bike. Now both stared at him. "The oil line is jammed. You need to clean it and change the oil," he said.

"Who the fuck are you?" the man said.

"My mother just dove into the river to save one of you," he said. "And the engine sounds too deep. It's not getting any oil."

The man stepped between him and the engine housing. "And we're supposed to listen to a city boy on this?"

Deckard stared incredulously. The man was actually barely older than him. His beard could only get halfway across his chin. "I mean, you've tried everything else."

"Well, we're not trying that."

"So you're not going to fix the bike just because a gunslinger suggested it," Deckard said and stepped past him.

The man raised his hands.

"Mat you idiot. You need to get over yourself." The older woman shoved past him. He stormed off without a word, slamming the door hard enough to knock a couple wrenches off the shelf. She rolled her eyes at Deckard. "Sorry. Since he could grow a beard he thinks he's fucking marshal of this valley."

"It's okay. He's not the worst I've met." Deckard pointed at his black eye.

They stripped off the engine housing. Deckard dug a hand into the hot engine and pulled out the tube. The woman found a tube brush and yanked out a massive plug of solidified oil.

"As I breathe," she said.

"This is a Revellier bike. They've got a special tube feeding oil in, separate of the entire engine housing. You have to clear it separately," Deckard said.

"Hell would they do that?"

"It gives the oil a longer life because it's not being heated as much by the engine. However, when it needs to be cleared, it's an extra headache," he said. She grabbed an oil can, and together they emptied the last few drops, then re-oiled the entire bike. When they were done, their hands were black and slippery.

"I'm not going to ask you to reassemble the bike, I'll make Mathias do that later," she said. "I'm Mattie by the way. Mathias is my brother. So is Mathew. Mathew's the one your mother saved, so thank you for that."

"Deckard." Their hands slapped together in an oily handshake.

"You eat?"

"I had a bite of biscuit for breakfast."

"Mother's cooking for lunch. I'll make sure you two get some," she said.

"Got any more bikes in the meantime?" he said.

She cast her eyes about. "Yeah. That one there. Fan blade's busted. It's easy to fix, but this is a working bike and that's a leisure bike used by the hands mostly," she said. "Fix that. I'll think up something suitable for you, okay kid?"

"Yeah, sure."

Eagerly, Deckard gathered a pile of tools at his feet and stripped the bike open. He'd felt alone and terrified for months. All that vanished as he worked the engine at his fingertips and breathed in fumes of oil through his nose. He didn't notice the shadow over his shoulder until she crouched beside him and picked up a wrench. "You fixing my bike?" a girl's soft voice said.

"Yeah. Just got to replace the fan motor and it should be good," he said. She helped him remove the fan blades. "I hate models with those individual blades.

"Makes it go faster when it works," she said. He turned his head to see her and was struck dumb by how beautiful she was. The girl was about his age, maybe a year older. She had a sharp face like a hawk's, with a peaked nose and green eyes. Her hair was tied back into two wavy black ponytails that went to her waist. She wore a billowing calico of emerald green, though legs peaking through sheathed in white stockings hinted at her slender body beneath. She wore tan moccasins, and her stockings bunching up around her ankles where she crouched on the ground.

"Hey," she said and dragged his attention back to her eyes. They were beautifully wide and inquisitive. "We have a spare motor. I'll get it. You get the old one removed." She scampered off. He was still distractedly working on the motor when she got back. Realizing time was wasting, he yanked it out with more force than necessary.

"There."

"Yeah." She slotted the new one in and together they fastened it. By the time they were done, her hands were as blackened as his, and sweat dripped down both their foreheads. "

"I need a bath," he said.

"Well, we bathe nightly out here. I'd like to talk to you when you don't smell like the trail," she said with a snicker.

"What's your name?" he said.

"Claire Dollarrow," she said. "You?"

"Deckard," he said.

"You got a surname to go with that?"

He shrugged. They finished reassembling the bike. Claire had brought a bucket of soap water and they washed their hands together.

The door burst open and a tiny boy stared at them with his huge brown eyes. "Mommy made a bath for you, Decky," he said, and sprinted out.

Deckard grinned after him. "Reminds me of a little girl I met at an orphanage in Crownville," he said. "I gave her a ride on my bike and she curled up in my arms."

"How cute." Claire had a narrow, petite smile. Her entire brow bent up at the corners like her eyes were smiling too. "Are you going back to see her?"

He thought it over. Crownville was six weeks of hard riding away. If he wanted to go back to school, that would be months away. "I'd like to if I ever go…home," he said. "You're really far from everyone out here."

"I didn't choose to be here. The most action we get is the festival on summer's eve," she said and shook her head. "Well, go bathe. You stink."

He did. When he came out, Wyatt was waiting, looking away and carrying a roll of clothes. "These belonged to my middle son. He's off in a city, working as a gunsmith. I think they'll fit you while your own stuff is washed."

The shirt was frilly and the jacket had a weird double collar and puffed sleeves. It fit. When he figured out how to wear it right and donned the sleek black trousers, he felt stylish, even. He was shocked when Claire met him at the door and the sight knocked him senseless. Her hair was still down, but she wore a pale blue bonnet now. A jacket of the same blue covered her up. She was stunning.

"Well. This is as fancy as my school uniform," he said.

"It looks quite smart on you," she said, and did a curtsey.

Deckard's cheeks burned as he nodded back. "So, when is dinner?"

They had two tables. The farmhands ate in an annex off the dining room. The family itself was seated around a long table, starting with Wyatt and his wife, followed by the children and their spouses, and then all the little grandchildren at the end. There was one seat open at the end of the table. Deckard let Sam have it and went to sit next to his new friend at the farmhands table. He'd assumed by how she carried herself around, she was a member of the massive Sansford family. No, she turned out to be a worker.

Halfway through the meal, Wyatt stood up in his seat. "Oi, someone needs to go check on the Blergs in the barn."

"I'll go," Deckard volunteered, eager to please.

"I'll come," Claire said and stood up.

A winter chill gripped the night, and they sprinted across the field. A couple of wooden planks had been mounted over the river and spiked into place. Arms held out to either side, they tottered across. Then they ran the rest of the way.

The remaining blergs were huddled in a corner with a low moaning cacophony, as if holding service for their departed number. Claire circled their pod, patting a few on the back. They mumbled through their massive mouths to acknowledge her presence. "None are dead, and none are bleeding. We're good. Let's check out their hay."

She clambered up to the loft. Deckard followed her, right to the spot he'd slept last night. They pawed through the hay for worms, fleas, or any damp patches that could rot and bring more disease, or god forbid a fungus. Everything was fine yellow hay.

"So, where are your parents?" he said.

"Mom died bringing me into this world. Dad's been gone three years now. I don't know where. Told me I wasn't ready to follow him on the trails." She knelt in the straw and spread her dress around her with her fingertips. Her white clad ankles poked out, stockings bunching up around them. "You're lucky you've got your mother with you. She seems tough."

"I don't feel that way. I ran away from school to join her, and she told me to go back." He dropped beside her, throwing up hay. He quickly brushed it all off his fine coat. "Back at school, any stain we got would get us beat with a switch."

Claire nodded. "Why would she do that? Your mother, that is."

"She wants me to stay in school and go to university. Mother could never stay still. When she was raising me with dad, we rode all over the country. I want to be like her, and she doesn't get it," he said.

"Can you shoot like her?" She leaned up on her haunches and stared at him just as intensely as he stared at her. The realization made his heart rush.

"I'm a terrible shot," he said sheepishly. He tugged at the little frill under his collar. "What's this for?"

"I am not certain. However, you do look dapper," she said.

"Thanks." His hands shivered. Whatever he was thinking didn't matter because he couldn't control his own smile. "So. Do you farm in the summer?"

"Of course. I am general labor."

"You are gorgeous general labor," he said.

She twisted sideways all the way, cocking her head and grinning at him from under her bonnet. "Thanks Deckard. What happened to your father? He must be a hell of a man to marry someone as crazy as your mother."

"I know. He was and I miss him. Mom got a lot colder after he died."

"You don't need to tell me," Claire said hurriedly.

"It's okay. Dad took me out to help him hunt a bounty. An outlaw chief who was supposed to be retired. Figured it would be an easy two thousand. Like, we normally don't do bounty hunting but winter was coming and we needed money bad. We got there, and he got the drop on us. Appeared behind us out of the snow and told us to drop the weapons and turn around real slowly," he said.

Claire clamped her hands over her mouth.

"So, we did. He told us to strip naked right there. It was November in the mountains. Snow was already half a foot thick upon the ground. We got down to our underwear. Dad asked if I could leave. Man laughed at us. He had a revolver out, and another at his hip. Dad dropped to his knees and pretended to beg. He was grabbing his knife out of his pants. We rushed him. Look at this." Deckard unbuttoned his jacket and shirt underneath. Claire gaped at the three scars stitched across the left side of his chest. "He killed dad. Shot me three times, hit a lung. I gutted him with my own knife as he tried to draw his other."

"How did you survive?"

Deckard closed his eyes. His face was buried halfway in the snow. Every time he breathed blood flowed between his teeth and spread around him. It warmed his face. It was the only warmth he had. "We were near railroad tracks. Train conductor going past saw us and stopped. I just remember being carried onto the train," he said. He buttoned up his clothes again and hid the scars away.

Claire clasped his hand. Her fingers wrapped in dark woolen gloves. "You deserve much more than this."

"I'm doing fine. I got what I need right here." He hadn't meant to hint at her. He totally hadn't. He grabbed her other hand. She was burning hot to the touch, fresh and energetic.

"And we're better for it here," she said. She made a movement towards him. He was so on-edge, he lunged forwards. His teeth clanked off hers and rebounded. As he recoiled, he left his soul behind, burning up in her confused expression.

Fuck it. He went back in, slower. The second time, their lips met in a gentle breath. Hers were rough with winter's dry bite, but soft and delightfully warm. She smiled into him, and it infected him.

They broke apart and he couldn't tell whose heart pounded louder. The corners of his face ached from smiling. "Wow."

The barn door burst open. "Deckard?" Sam said. Deckard clamped a hand over his mouth. Claire's hand was still in his. She giggled into her sleeve, which made him giggle. "Deck."

"We're just making sure the hay's clean. Barn leaks sometimes when it rains," Claire said.

"Great," she said. Her tone was dry as the hay.

"We'll be down in a second. Are they done with dinner?" Claire said.

"They are. You have escaped table-clearing duties, Miss," Sam said. A pause as they melted on their knees. "You know. blergs are kinda cute." The barn door slammed shut.

Deckard collapsed on his side, laughing. Claire flailed on the ground beside him, her face bright red. He laughed until his ribs ached.

"She knew," she squealed.

"Scandal, thy name is," he said. He leaned across and kissed her cheek.

"You missed." She caught his cheeks in a woolen grip and kissed him again.

They peeked out the barn together, still giggling. The coast was clear, and they slipped out.

"Deckard, we need to talk," Sam said, making him jump in his boots. She leaned against the side of the barn, arms crossed and hat pulled low against her brow. Looking at her, Deckard realized she could have been the greatest outlaw who ever lived. Or marshal.

"Yes, mom," he said, blood running cold. It froze him in place.

"Miss, it was my idea," Claire said.

"Don't worry about it. We just need to talk," Sam said. Claire sprinted back to the house, leaving Deckard very much alone as his mother bore down on him.

"Deckard. You hold her life in your hands and you need to be careful," she said.

"Mom we…we," he said. His tongue went dry in the moment he needed it the most.

"If someone finds out, that will be a scandal. This isn't the city where there's a hundred thousand people to hide amongst. There are maybe fifty families in this valley and they will all scorn her if they find out she's infatuated with a homeless gunslinger and not married to him. You can move on. She can't. This is infinitely more dangerous to her," she said. Her eyes burned hot like coals. Deckard had never seen her this angry. He'd imagined it as he wrote the letter declaring he'd left school. This anger should have been there on their first meeting. And now she burned at him.

"Mom. I'll tell her to go away," he said.

"I know neither of you will be able to. Remember, I ran off with your father the day we met." She grinned in a most terrifying way. "I'm saying to be careful. Keep it secret to everyone and be patient. Do you understand me?"

He nodded quickly, the stupid frill of his jacket bouncing on his shoulder.

"Good. Now get inside. We have a couple bedrolls waiting in the dining room," she said.

Claire was sweeping the dining room when he arrived. It seemed several more hands would sleep in the dining room, as they all unrolled their cloth beds. She looked up. Her mouth opened to say something, and she bit her tongue.

"We're fine," he said. She nodded quickly and resumed sweeping.

Samantha had been asked to walk the lawn fence and check for any breaks. The six-hundred acres of the farm was cordoned off by a barbed wire fence. The main house and barn sat on a little parcel of land guarded by head-height wooden posts. There were no howls from greywalkers, no scratches from any of the other predators. Sam strode back to the house and headed first to the dining room. Claire swept hard and fast, ponytail bobbing over her shoulders. Yet she didn't look at the growing pile of detritus at her feet. Instead she stared across the room at Deckard as he made his bed.

They were careful. Sam didn't catch them again that season. She knew from the little glances, and the insistence on doing everything together, they were still close, but nothing more.

Deckard repaired his way through every bike and wagon on the farm. The thoroughly impressed Wyatt spoke eagerly of him to everyone in the valley. So, out he went to repair whatever he needed, and brought back decent money with him.

■■

Sam volunteered for night watch every day. It wasn't hard work, but it made her feel useful and let the regular farmers get their sleep. Wyatt quickly trusted her not to fall asleep on watch and he paid her a decent salary.

Wyatt had twelve hands total, plus an old comrade he employed as a veterinarian and doctor. The hands made him the largest farm in the valley. The doctor made his farm the most important. So, there was a steady stream of visitors and customers from all thirty-two families and the dozen odd loners living on their own little houses. He didn't need to work anymore. He had everything taken care of in his retirement. Yet he was always in the fields, or fishing in the larger river that ran along his farm's outer border and bringing it home for Mattie and her mother to cook. Or herding the blergs and various sheep and fat flightless dactyls.

One night Sam got up from the dinner table and buttoned up her jacket for another night watch. They were in the part of spring where the days were too warm for a jacket, and the night too cold to go without.

"That will do, miss," Wyatt said with a raised hand. "I'll be taking your post tonight, because I have something I'd like you to do tomorrow."

"Oh?" she said.

"Normally, after the last snow Mathey and I will check the perimeter sensor posts. They guard the entire valley from larger animals, and any marauders who want to take from our homes. However, Mat hasn't quite recovered from his pneumonia. And my knees aren't as cooperative as they used to be." A few affectionate smiles broke across the table.

"I'd need their locations," she said.

"You're not going alone. Our next door neighbor, Mr. Jesse Crayton will be going with you. He'll be here at dawn. He's a drunk, but I trust him," he said. "That's if you want to."

"Time to get a little movement," she said and grinned. Already she was eager to get on her bike and take a ride beyond the barbed wire fence.

"Alright. It's settled. Remember to eat breakfast and bring extra water before going," he said.

"Yes, mom," she said. Laughter burst around the table.

At dawn she rose, blood coursing through her limbs at the full night of sleep. All the other workers rose in their dressing gowns. The sun burned white through the great window, jabbing them all awake without need of an alarm. Sam dressed and checked her railgun and bike over one more time. Breakfast was already sizzling on the buffet plates set out by the wives. She piled a plate high and ate, then chugged a small can of peaches for vitamins. Deckard stumbled to the table with half-closed eyes as she left.

The front door opened and Mathias came in from the night watch. "Morning, miss," he said and tipped his hat. His hideously scraggly beard was damp with morning dew.

"Morning. How was the night?" she said.

"I didn't see frost tonight, and there's still no greywalkers," he said with a relieved smile. He held the door for her.

"Cross your fingers," she said and ducked under his arm and out. The air smelt earthy like fresh soil, and wet from the morning mists receding before the sun. The ring of jagged mountains seemed like a giant fence protecting them from the outside world. She took off her hat and let the sun blind her with delight, as spring came out in force. A bike roared up from out of the glare.

She replaced her hat. A squat, burly offroad bike came to a halt. The rider slid off, kickstand falling behind him.

Jesse Crayton was a slick, skinny man. His hair was gelled across his head. He wore a pale duster and a red bandanna around his neck. He saw her and grinned widely. "Good morning to you, ma'am. I take it that the massive piece of artillery strapped to your back makes you my partner for today."

"I'm the one," she said with a nod. He wore a long rifle over his shoulder, almost the length of her railgun. It was a single shot weapon, with a lever on the trigger to drop the receiver and load fresh bullets. Most modern rifles had a hammer that slammed the firing pin forwards and fired the gun. Upon closer inspection of his rifle, she saw the hammer sat on the side of the receiver, instead of the middle like most rifles. "You're Jesse?"

"One of seven living the valley," he said. "Five percent of all inhabitants on one name."

"Sam ain't any better," she said. She noted his bike. It didn't have a direct fan to air vent. The fan was entirely encased in a shield. Thrust jets protruded below and to the sides. The front steering array was as big as the rear. The saddle was in the middle of the bike between the two fans. Heavily armored bumpers sat around the sides. "That's a monster of a bike."

"Goes up mountains as easy as roads," he said. "What about yours? Looks like a fancy racing bike you've modified for offroad. Why not just get a cross-country bike?"

"Cross country engine is less efficient. I got maximum trail per battery charge, and it's faster." She slapped the hood. She'd replaced the dust shield on a trip to the general store, and it shined fresh atop the weary bike's other components

"Less maneuverability and stability," he said.

"Well. Can't buy skill," she said.

He nodded. "Let's go. We do this right, we're done by nightfall."

They roared off. Sam had to throttle down to keep abreast of his bike. That made her engine rumble ominously. She zig-zagged gently to keep her forward speed down.

When she had first arrived, she'd driven right past the first beacon without noticing, distracted by rain and the ruination of her coat. It was a simple wooden post with a sensor wired on it. A small windmill sat on top, spinning gently in the morning breeze. Heavy vines had wound their way up the post. James hopped off and walked over. "These posts run on wind power. They can go forever unless they're broken. Usually, Wyatt just cuts vegetation free." He whipped out an ugly machete with brass knuckles built into the handgrip and did just that. "All good. Next two are on the slope itself in case anything ignores the trail and climbs from the ravines.

Each of the posts was covered in vines that seemed to fight James. Sam had to dismount and pull as he cut, tearing them off. "Any flesh-eating moss ever show up?"

"Oh. Those. Wyatt usually stubs a cigar out in them and the entire mass dies. They ain't too fond of fire."

"I torched an entire tree of them. Though I was pissed they'd just ruined my coat," she said. He winced.

"Justifiable."

They reached the edge of the valley and drove straight up the rolling slopes of rock and harsh brown grass. Sam had to go into a lower gear but she still kept up easily enough.

"You ever leave the valley?"

"I used to be a bit of an outlaw myself. Blerg rustling only. Never shot anyone. Which is why they only gave me three years in the coal mines when they caught me," he said. "After that I called Wyatt up. He's an old war buddy. He leased me some land and I settled down."

"How did you put your boots up?" she said. They passed a sheer cliff. Far above, guano-encrusted caverns marked the dactyl caves. The sun had just crested the mountains and the sky was pure white. The next beacon was at the base of the cliff, guarding a rocky gap between it and the next.

Jesse didn't answer until he'd gouged a pebble from the windmill's blades with his knife. "I thought it would be impossible. It was at first. I just stuck around because I knew Wyatt was my last chance at a free life. Once I got to working though, it took over. I run a distillery. My liquor's been sold in cities far away. It's just given me something to do. Why? You looking to settle down."

"I'm trying to stop my son from following in my footsteps," she said.

He shook his head. "Hot blooded is hot blooded. My mother and father used the whip, boarding school, and a locked bedroom to keep me in line. And I left at thirteen anyways."

They worked their way across the western side of the valley. Two ranges of mountains intersected, and the world wrinkled. Sam stood in her stirrups and pulled up on the throttle to take in the spires of rock. They stretched hundreds of feet to stab the sky, taking chunks of brambleweed and cactus up with them. Shadows hid from the sun in the gaps between, like gaping holes torn out of the world by these vicious mountains. Beyond, the spires simply grew higher until they capped with snow as they reached their heavenly target.

She exhaled a long, slow breath of mute shock. These didn't look like nature could have made them, with their utterly horrific shapes and the brutal rage with which they raced up to chomp the sky. She stared upwards into the sun and searched for the top fangs crashing down to finish the bite. Clouds billowed dark grey in the distance as it came.

Jesse pulled up and circled around her. Flakes of sandstone sprayed out into a cloud of ruddy dust. "We have two mountain ranges colliding and chaos results. Those are Johbert's fangs. Johbert went in here a century ago, with about a hundred men and women. He thought it would be a shortcut to the southern cities. They never emerged."

"So. Is it haunted?"

"No. I've traversed it. It's not impassable if you're a veteran guide. It's just we've never found what happened to Johbert. Not a wagon nor a skull," he said.

She breathed a sigh of relief. "Well. Let's go."

The fangs began with a shock of rock, hundreds of feet high. Jesse led them to the right and into a seam between that and the next. It was like night fell, even as the white sky hung bright and clear overhead. She followed him out and into a patch of sun. the land rose on the shoulder of another spire. A dark crack became a seam another hundred feet deep and she swerved away. They continued up the spire until it merged with another. Jesse didn't slow as he approached the darkness, and she followed with confidence.

They emerged into a canyon lined by teeth. At the end, another spire rose to the frozen heavens. The post was just ahead, up a hill. Sam's bike stalled out. She hit the lowest gear and dumped all power into the thrusters.

"Yeehaw, dirt power!" Jesse whooped and burned straight up the sheer slope, hat waving behind.

"Asshole." She took her time zig-zagging up the slopes.

"Fuck!" rang out across the mountains. Dactyls screamed and burst from their caves with a rush of wings, framing the echo back. "Fuck!"

"Jesse!" She hit the throttle and burst up the last few yards.

Jesse was on his feet, looking unharmed as he studied a post. "I'm fine. Hold on to your boots," he said.

"Then what the hell was that about?" She leapt off and drew her railgun.

"Check out the sensor." He pointed at the crater blown straight through the heart of the electronics. "Now either one of our own did that for shits. Or someone outside did it. I know a few bad seeds who'd do it. Those sensors were built from tech ordered from the cities over passing caravans. They took years to assemble and we don't have many spare parts," he said and kicked the post. The windmill toppled off with a catastrophe of clanging metal.

Sam circled the post, studying the scene. "The hole is pointed straight ahead, over the canyon. Either the shooter learned how to fly, or they came from outside." She pointed into the rugged but level terrain ahead. She pawed over the ground. Metal and splinters stuck in the dirt. "If this were old then the wind we had last week would have turned everything up."

Jesse stared back and forth with wide eyes. "Makes sense."

"Would the sensor have picked it up?"

"No. They only report when something trips the sensor beam. Saves power that way," he said. He pulled binoculars from his jacket and took aim. "We need to get out there and see if anyone's been in the area."

Sam surveyed with her scope. "I can pick out three locations. Between the two halves of that boulder, under the tree a hundred feet off the ground, and that spot twenty feet ahead with the three cacti. See them?"

"Yes, yes, and gotcha ma'am," he said. They took off together.

Between two cacti, they found a single brass shell casing. Jesse scooped it up and gave it a deep kiss. "Forty-five seventy. Someone with a big rifle took that shot."

"And a taste for smokes." She kicked at the pile of white butts curdling on the ground, then circled the area. Enough footprints for multiple boot sets. They covered each other in dirt and ruined their own tracks, but she saw a couple different sets of boots and the wide spray of a couple bikes running down from the cliff face above. "Multiple people. You were the outlaw. Think we're getting hit?"

"No one would come out this far just to rustle blergs. You rustle them to sell them, and you're not getting them back alive through the fangs," he said. The canyons rolled and his voice bounced back in a deep baritone. Sam's hair stood on end as she looked around.

Then the rumbling of bikes b ehind them. Sam turned around and lowered her railgun to her chest.

"Mother," Deckard yelled. His voice boomed back far louder, from all sides. He emerged in a cloud of dust, followed by Claire on her touring bike. Their clothes were all array and dust caked their skin through sweat. "You're needed back at the farm, now."

"Hell's going on?" she said.

"Big wagon train is coming down to visit us. Wyatt wants everyone back just in case they aren't settlers. Or they're the greedy kind of settler," Claire said. Her hair was half out of her ponytail and everywhere.

"If they're going this far off the beaten trail to visit us, they ain't friendly," Jesse said and hopped on his bike. He didn't wait before coating them in blowing dust.

Sam took her time with the kids on the way down. Then, she floored it.

The cloud of dust rose from her left shoulder. It spread more vastly than the pitiful smoke trail coming off Wyatt's farm.

Chapter Nine:

The standoff was on when she rolled up. Wyatt stood on the edge of his fence, Engrams dangling by the receiver at his side. A couple hands were aiming at the lead wagon, upon which stood a man in a vast hat. Sam leapt out and unsheathed her railgun.

"Who the hell are you?" the newcomer bellowed. There was movement up and down the wagon train. She saw a few more rifles emerging.

"My name's Wyatt Sansford. This is my farmstead and these are my people," he said. "Who are you?"

"The maps said this valley is uninhabited." Behind him, a small face appeared behind the entrance flap. Two feminine hands snatched the inquisitive boy back to safety. The man looked back quickly. He reached for the long rifle across his lap.

"You didn't answer my question. I cannot negotiate in good faith without knowing who you are," Wyatt said. "You see that rider who just arrived. She's carrying a railgun. That is what you risk if you push me."

Sam swung the railgun up. She aimed at his right shoulder, away from the entrance flap.

The man dropped the rifle back into his lap. "My name is Thomas. This is my party. We're heading for the Arigan plateau to settle on Arigan lands."

"And what are you doing this far off the open trail?" Wyatt said.

"We had a fast start, but burned through our battery supplies quickly. We were hoping to graze our stock and spend time recharging. There's still plenty of traveling season," said Thomas. He leapt down from his wagon, leaving the rifle behind. "Look. I apologize for stumbling onto your land. I did not know anyone lived here. I would like to find a way through. Last summer my brother plotted a trail through the Fangs."

"What's your brother's name?"

"Lackon Langerman."

"Well why didn't you say so? I knew him. Didn't think he'd spend a week under my roof and buying a new saddle from the general store and then tell you this valley was empty," Wyatt said. "Is he here?"

"Nay. He fell ill and promised to follow us later."

Sam did not track his aim but searched the convoy. Most of the men and women visible were crouched on their wagons. A few had rifles out in the open. There were no shadows creeping from under the wagons, and no recessed hatches for heavier weaponry disguised war wagons loved. A few bikes pulled up alongside the front wagon. The riders were a girl with dimples, an old man in coveralls, and a younger man with a rattling old revolver.

"They don't look like raiders," she said to Jesse, who fidgeted with his rifle's strange side-hammer.

"No. They look like your average folk."

Wyatt and Langerman put their hats together and talked.

"Should be go down to them?" Deckard said.

"No," Sam and Jesse said. He nodded and withdrew. "At least move a bit to the right, so we don't form a single target on this hill," she said.

They circled twenty paces out. On the third wagon, and older woman raised a rifle and took trembling aim. The rifle's hammer rustled on its rusted screw, hovering above the primer and doomsday. Sam lowered her rifle, agape.

Wyatt split and walked back.

"Jesse. You're going to guide them to the pass," Wyatt yelled.

The old woman lowered her gun. The muzzle struck her steering bar. A puff of white smoke blew off. The gunshot rolled through the valley and drove everyone back to the triggers.

"Hold fire!" Sam yelled, waving her arm. "Lower your arms, that was a misfire." Deckard froze, finger on the trigger, rifle aimed into the lead wagon. Claire was aimed lower, probably at one of the riders on the ground.

The rifles lowered. The settlers retreated to their wagons. And Jesse stormed down the hill. "Hey boss. We got a problem with the pass."

"What now, friend?" Wyatt said, taking his shoulder.

"Someone shot out the sensor. Forty-five seventy from the Fang, straight through the pass. And it happened within the last week."

"Shit. I'll go warn them to get back out onto the trail," he said and turned right around. He went right up to the knot of settlers and pulled Langerman aside. Sam watched until he returned. "They ain't budging. They're insisting on being the first to the new land. Apparently, there are several more caravans coming."

"Goddamn it," Jesse said. "At least warn them."

"I did. You know what? They're a big party. They'll lose a few livestock, but they'll make it," he said.

"I hope," Jesse said, shaking his head. "Damn city folk."

Wyatt turned to Sam. "How did you know that was a misfire? I was about to unload. Thought someone had sprung an ambush."

"I saw an old gal with a faulty rifle. Accident waiting to happen," she said.

"Well, good thinking. Saved a few dozen lives there," he said.

A rumble went up as the wagons started their engines. Jesse hopped back on his bike and headed off. Sam, and everyone from the farm stopped and watched as the great metal serpent stretched itself and lurched forward. Women and old men and children leaned out of the windows on their wagons. Drivers leaned onto their throttles. A couple waved at them now that the danger had passed.

A cloud of dust blew over Sam. She pulled her jacket up over her mouth and nose and squinted through. The dark shapes churned past one by one. When they were gone, the dust remained for a long time after. A blerg howled from the farm.

"That could have gone worse," Claire said.

"It could have," Wyatt said. "Speaking of it. Did you finish loading the planter?"

"We did," she said. "Deck helped me."

"Well, that's enough excitement in the fields for a day. Go wash up. Harriett probably needs some kitchen help."

Dinner was a pair of freshly slaughtered lambs, pit roasted and served with a vast pile of canned vegetables taken out, rubbed in barbecue sauce and baked beans, and fried until the metallic aftertaste was driven out. Water was served alongside the deep brown amber of freshly pressed apple cider, bought from another farm and stocked with ice. Sam tore into a lamb leg and picked the bone clean.

She looked up and saw all the little kids at the family table staring at her with wide eyes. "Rawr," she said, and snapped it in half. They burst into giggles.

"You know, the summer fest is coming up," Mathew said with a grin her way. She caught the heat wafting off.

"Is that a dance?" she said.

"It's a three-day festival. We have prized animal contests, a talent show, and then the dance. Every year someone proposes."

"What do you guys dance?" Deckard said. Laughter ran through the table as the light left his eyes.

"We start with a waltz, then do the foxtrot, then square dance," Wyatt said. "As an eligible young man, you do know how to dance, right?"

"Of course, I learned at school," he said.

"Really?" Claire said and stood up. She shucked her apron and rolled up her green dress. "I need to know in advance. In case I have to teach you"

"You challenging my dancing?" he said and leapt up. "Someone. Music, please."

Mattie fetched a gnarled fiddle and threw herself into a straw armchair in the corner. She touched bow to string with a puff of resin and a pale twang ran through the air. Claire advanced to the space between the tables. Deckard plucked off his gloves and met her. And didn't know what do with his hands. Smirking, she raised a hand to head height and opened her fingers. He slipped his slender fingers between hers and they locked together.

They spun about. Boots slapped the floorboards. Her skirt flared out like a green sail. His brow creased as he twirled her about. Sam was delighted to see him keep up, and soon she clapped along with the mischievous beat. They caught each other and rocked across the floor, in a tight embrace.

A smile burned between them. Their gazes locked on each other, fixated only on the light in each other's eyes. They stopped and reversed direction, reversed grip in each other's arms, and kept smiling right into each other's eyes. They switched again and his jacket fluttered as her skirt swooshed out, brushing the table. She dug a boot heel in and swung him around. Except he was too big to stop and they stumbled an extra half step. The children giggled, but the fiddle was clambering into its steepening pitch and there was no time to stop.

He grabbed her and spun her about, twirling her over and over. Until with a final screech he caught her and tipped her back. Their lips stopped just a breath from a kiss.

The room burst into applause.

"Another?" Deckard said.

"Save it for the festival," Mattie said. She went to put the fiddle away, but now the crowd demanded more. So, she put out another song even as the couple sat down.

After dinner, Sam buttoned up her jacket, slung her railgun over her shoulder, and headed out into the night. A couple men were setting up to smoke on the porch and tipped their hats at her.

She strode towards the perimeter, boots squishing in the spongy sod. Another set squished deeper behind her.

"Claire's at that age. He'd better watch out, she's man hungry," Wyatt said.

Sam snickered. "Do you think he's any better?"

"No." Wyatt's pipe glowed red as he puffed. "What do you think?"

"Maybe he'll settle down."

"Well. He's got a trade he learned all on his own. Mechanics are needed anywhere. And so are farmers like her," he said.

"Where did she come from?" Sam said.

"Her father was a rider who came here a few years ago, a young girl clinging to his saddle. I'd been asking passing caravans about hiring a new hand and I guess he heard. He offered her to us. Said he had dangerous work and couldn't take her. So, I did," he said. He blew a cloud of smoke. "My bleeding heart and all. He might have been a wanted man for all I know."

"Well. She seems like a decent girl. Works hard, very pretty."

"She is. And it speaks to his character and looks that she's gotten his attention, despite having no dowry but what I'd donate, and no family," he said with a shake of his head. "How's he?"

"Arrogant. Thinks he's ready to take on the world. He's not," she said. "Still. He looks like his father, and his father was a handsome bastard."

"He's got your eyes, and those are some fine eyes," Wyatt said.

She grinned. "Thank you."

"That's all I wanted to discuss," he said. Yet, he continued with her for the next hour, on one long loop around the immediate farm area.

∎∎

Deckard awoke still hot and buzzing from the previous night's dance. Closing his eyes again, he saw Claire flitting before him, and felt her soft hands steering him around. Then, everyone else started getting up and he had to open them again.

Work for the day finished quickly. There was no machinery to fix, and plowing had proceeded at such a prodigious rate they'd finished it all. By noon, the little smoking circle was strewn on the front lawn in the warming sun. Deckard found Claire scrubbing the dining room floor, working over a wine stain from last night. He grabbed a rag, dipped in the soap bucket, and got to work beside her. They scrubbed across the house without word and washed their hands together when they were finished.

"Done, you're free," Mattie said as she walked past, carrying a butter churn and chased by a couple toddlers and a dog.

"So," Deckard said. "Want to go for a ride?"

"Yes, actually. I've got an idea." She was already off towards the garage.

"Where?"

"Just follow me," she said.

Deckard stopped short before the Fangs. Shadows reached towards him as if the ominous mountains wanted to drag him in. The turned-up ground of the caravan party made his skin crawl, as he imagined them vanishing down the drain of the mountains. Gone forever. His skin crawled as he peered into the shadows in the gaps.

"What's wrong?" Claire said.

"Nothing. Have you been in there before?" he said.

"Yeah. I used to go with Jesse to help when he hunted in there. I've navigated on my own a few times. It's beautiful," she said.

"Okay," he said, unconvinced.

"I've got a spot I want to show you." She hit her throttle and hummed gently into the rocks. He followed. They went to the left of the opening in the mountains and trialed through the hills. He lost his way immediately in the maze. Mountains, impossibly tall and thin, leered over him. They were all granite. A hard, dark rock coated in brighter dust. While the lighter sandstone had eroded, only their spires had remained. He grew cold in the shadows and warm in the heat. Claire hit a steep ridge and his bike struggled up after. She came to the top and stopped.

"Look. That's where the party went."

They overlooked a thread of a canyon, thin enough he was tempted to jump it to the lower ridge on the other side, but longer than he could see. Down the middle were a scattering of dust and footprints from all sorts of animals. Specks of man-made refuse glinted angrily up at him. He just stared and stared into the vast view.

"This way," Claire said and slapped his bike. She sped off. They went around another spire. Now he heard a roar in the distance, punctuated by the occasional thump of something heavier.

They ducked under an enormous archway of rock, eroded into a bridge by the wind.

The waterfall plunged from somewhere mossy green hundreds of meters ahead. It was a ribbon of foaming white, raging into the sun until it splashed into a pond. He hopped off and walked his way right up to the lapping edge. A couple small crawfish clawed away from his shadow.

"Where did this…" he trailed off as he tried to follow the waterfall to its source and got dizzy.

"Jesse showed me this." Claire appeared at his side. She sat down right there. "Come on."

They shucked off their shoes and stockings into a pile and waded into the cold water. They tiptoed across the smooth bottom and laughed as the crawfish scuttled away from their toes and vanished down their burrow holes. They ventured close enough to the waterfall that mist dampened their skin and let them wash the dust from their faces.

Deckard's outer jacket was fairly damp, so he tossed it off on the pile. Claire removed her bonnet and shook it out. She pinned her hair behind her ears. "Jesse used to catch crayfish and bring them back for dinner. Like this." She lunged for one, only for it to scuttle away.

"Yeah, sure you've got it," Deckard said. He spied one near his left foot and went for it. Fucker *flew* back and straight down its burrow. "Now that just isn't fair."

Claire hiked up her dress and went for another. "Hell, they're fast. Get over here." She lunged dangerously off one leg. Deckard caught her just before she fell and hauled her up by the shoulder. "Thanks," she said and pinched his shoulder.

"How do crawfish get up here? Did some dactyl drop them?" Deckard said.

Claire giggled. "Maybe. I have no idea. Maybe Jesse put them here years ago for food," she said.

"I like the idea that some dumb dactyl dropped a couple," Deckard said and burst into laughter. She clung to his shoulder and giggled along.

Then they sat down on the shore and just watched the water ripple as they threw rocks. Deckard could skip stones clean across the narrow pond. Claire got frustrated and stormed off. She came back hauling the biggest rock she could carry and launched it with both hands. Deckard threw up a hand as it splashed the shore with a thud.

"Fuck you, too," she said and sat back down beside him. Her hand landed atop his. Deckard grabbed it without thinking, blushed, and doubled down when she grabbed it back.

"I can't wait for the dance. Do you want to kiss then?" he said.

"In front of everyone? Yeah. I really do." She flushed red. Her bony cheeks were red and even her nose was going red to the handful of freckles. He zoned in, because his face felt just as hot.

She kissed him on the lips and slipped her hands around his shoulders. He caught her by the back and leaned forward until he held her in his arms, her head resting on his palm on the ground, as they kissed.

She released. "I hope you never leave. I'd miss you so badly."

"Mom's the one who wants to leave. I promise I won't leave you," he said.

The air thrummed as something thumped in the distance. He stopped kissing her.

"Deck, what's wrong?" she reached up, and stroked his forehead.

"That sounds like gunfire," he said. She stared over his shoulder into the sky. "It does. Come to think of it, that banging earlier was gunfire too."

In a breath they were up and shoed and heading to their bikes. They drove towards the sound, until they reached an impassably rocky ridge crowned by dry yellow grass. Now the gunfire came in sharp blasts, before bouncing over the mountains like a cannonade. Deckard leapt down on his hands and knees and scurried up the ridge.

The wagon train had been circled around a black, bottomless watering hole. Someone had shot it full of holes, then ripped out the survivors. Except, all the rifles he saw were piled in a heap just outside the circle, along with powder belts and spare ammo.

The settlers had been lined up against a sheer cliff and shot. They'd fallen in neat rows, blood pooling around and flowing downhill towards the watering hole. Deckard buried his face in his sleeve.

"Oh god."

Claire buried her face in his shoulder. She shivered against him.

Deckard peered through his fingertips. Everywhere, he saw men and women in grey, with wide, circular-brimmed hats. The attackers rifled through the corpses and executed the survivors with revolvers. A young woman stood at the center. In her hands, she clutched a pole. Atop the pole was a silver statue of a Dactyl, wings spread. Its triangular face stared straight at Deckard. He scrabbled backwards and tumbled down the hill.

Claire helped him up. "Let's get out of here—we need to warn everyone."

There was a ridge between them and the watering hole, but they ducked low and scampered down the slope. The waterfall thundered past. They slipped down a wide-open slope, throwing up dust.

Deckard saw figures moving in the canyon below. He seized Claire, hauled her to the ground, and pointed.

A couple ran along the lip of the canyon, tottering on the sharp edge of forever. A figure in grey stepped in front of them, hands in his pockets.

The pair dropped down on their knees and begged. They looked his age. The girl had her hair down in a pair of pigtails, with pink ribbons. The boy wore the same jacket Deckard did, but reddish instead of blue. Four closed in on them.

"Can you reach them?" Deckard said, bringing up his rifle. The sight trembled so he couldn't get a clear picture.

"I can, just cover me." She leapt up. Dust kicked behind him. Then a bike whirred. His heart tightened in his chest until it ached. Why couldn't he aim? He exhaled but it didn't steady him enough. He exhaled again.

The girl was on her hands begging. The boy looked a bit small. Maybe he was younger. Deckard studied them. He aimed over the girl's shoulder, right into the first marauder's belly. And he hoped Claire could get there in time.

One drew a knife. He yanked the girl up by her ponytail.

Deckard breathed out. He didn't feel the trigger. His Marinelli roared. Fire burst from the barrel as the stock drilled him in the shoulder.

Red sprayed from the marauder's shoulder. He curled back, clutching at his arm. Deckard had aimed high. He jacked the lever, scraping his knuckles on the ground.

The girl threw herself to the ground. The marauders had ducked for cover, except for one, who swept his revolver about. Deckard settled his sight and fired without thinking. Rock cracked behind the man, who swung toward him and fired. Deckard levered another round in and fired again, missing as he flinched uncontrollably.

Claire's bike whirred along. Another marauder leapt up to meet her with a rifle. Her shotgun roared and he fell back down.

Deckard saw her circle around the kids. He kept firing. Until his rifle clicked. He fumbled in his belt for the extra cartridges. The first one sprung out of the loading gate and bounced down the hill. He jammed the next ones in as hard as he could.

Claire fired her other barrel into the bushes. The kids ran. She stopped in place and broke the shotgun open to reload. She doubled over suddenly.

Deckard screamed as he leaned out and fired fast as he could lever fresh rounds in. His rifle rocketed around his shoulder, tearing up rock and vegetation on the canyon below. Claire sat up and gunned the bike forwards. She reloaded as she went and fired both barrels after her.

Dirt kicked up around Deckard's face. He realized he'd been fired on. Muzzles spat fire from at least two spots in the growing dust cloud below. He felt them zip past and ran from them.

He was on his bike before he knew it, fumbling with the ignition until the fan roared to life. The metal steed under his feet hiccupped, and his heart dropped. Then it roared off, nearly taking him over a ledge as he yanked his steering bar at the last second.

The fangs sped past. He saw Claire, keeping pace with the two running children.

"Deck, let's go. Grab one," she said.

"I saw you get hit," he said as he closed and throttled down.

"Winged me." She held up her left arm. Blood seeped into her dress from a long, shallow gash beneath her armpit. "Come on. I saw them getting on bikes."

He grabbed the boy and hauled him up behind. The kid's arms locked around him, pinning his arms in place. "Let go, I need to steer," he said. No response. The kid was panicking even more than Deckard. Deckard had to wriggle an arm out and elbow him in the head to make him loosen his grip.

Claire raced along the canyon. He followed right on her exhaust pipes. When she steered into a twisting mess of shadow, he threw himself blindly after. They exploded out onto the open plains and churned air beneath their bikes. He had no time to think. Only the wind searing his face and grass snapping against his bike's bottom as its own thrust pushed it downwards.

A whirr behind warned him. He twisted back in his saddle and saw six bikes fanning out in pursuit. The riders were all cleanshaven, armed with rifles and revolvers in their pommel sheaths. They all wore steely stares of death. Like Tow as he towered over Deckard and laughed. There was no feeling in their hearts for the lives they were taking. He pushed the throttle down all the way. The bike beneath him bucked, then something in the engines caught the air, and it snapped straight as an arrow as it found form.

He drew even with Claire, her bonnet gone and hair flowing out behind. They looked back at the same time.

The riders were crouched low in their saddles and gaining. Deckard fought for more power to the engines. He turned on all the aft-slanted jets. Nothing. They had to carry an extra rider. That was double the weight the marauder's bikes had to carry.

He looked ahead. The farmhouse wasn't even visible yet. There was only grass, then rolling fields of greenish shoots, freshly planted. The barbed wire fence started as a necklace across the horizon. It grew to its towering size of weathered brown wood, the gate yawning before them. They fit through together and Deckard reached for the door, only for his fingers to go numb on impact, pain racing up his arm. Now they tore on, spraying fertilizer and unfortunate shoots

Deckard twisted in his saddle and stared over the boy's rustling hair. The distance had closed. He saw two of the marauders were women, slender faces as blank and even more terrifying then the men. They had shorter carbines instead of rifles. Perhaps they'd lean out of the saddle and take the killing shots with their nimbler arms.

He looked back. A string of smoke rose into the clear sky, just a thread at this distance.

A gunshot rang out. Claire had fired into the air. A signal, he hoped. He looked back and saw the range was down to a bare handful of yards. Close enough he could throw a stone and let their approaching speed make up the rest of the distance. He looked ahead, then at Claire. She looked at him. She shook her head softly. Tears sparkled in her eyes.

He nodded back. Then took one more look. The leading marauder hauled a monster of a revolver from his saddle pommel. The entire thing was nearly long as his forearm. The barrel gaped as he aimed low at Deckard's engine. The women drew their carbines.

The marauder's chest split open. Deckard saw the Fangs straight through the bloody gap before the marauder toppled from his saddle and was dragged along like a ragdoll in his stirrups. The marauders on either side swerved away. The women aimed high in search of the new target.

Deckard looked ahead. He saw two specks fast approaching and raised a hand to them. That had to be mom. Only her railgun could tear a man open like that. He looked back. One of the women's bikes burst into flames, shards of metal spraying off its engine housing and into her belly. Her face twisted in agony as she doubled over, short rifle tumbling to the ground. Her bike wobbled. Another marauder grabbed the bars.

The other woman shouted something and waved back towards the spire. The rest turned off and gunned their throttles away. Against a marksman with that range, they had no chance

Deckard punched a fist in the air. He kept the throttle on full until the specks materialized…into Wyatt and Matt. The two older men fell in.

"What did you fools get up to?" Wyatt said. "And who are they?"

"The Langerman party was attacked by marauders. They're all dead," Deckard said. Wyatt's jaw dropped.

"Get back to the house, now. Full speed." As they climbed the next hill, he saw his mother, another dark speck amidst the forest. She was leaned against a tree, railgun aimed through a fork in its branches. It was well over two and a half kilometers. An impossible shot. As he approached, she straightened up and slung the piece over her shoulder.

"You guys sure had nice picnic," she said as they walked up to the house. Her expression was stern. Deckard couldn't tell if she was angry. "And you met some new friends. Did you steal them from the caravan?"

The boy pushed forwards. "My name is Arthur Lameer. I had a mother and three sisters. Our party was attacked by a group of New Covenanters. They fired on us from the mountains while others attacked up close. We circled our wagons but there was no way to fight back and many of us were wounded, so Master Langerman surrendered. Then they killed everyone. Your hand and his lady saved us."

Sam grabbed Deckard's arm. "Did you hit anything?"

"At least one. In the shoulder, though," he said.

"They ain't fighting when forty-five seventy shatters their shoulder. That's good enough."

"You guys get in the dining room. Mat, get Mattie out of the garden and have her make coffee and food for them. I need a messenger," Wyatt said.

"I'll go," said Jesse.

"No. I need your rifle here. Arthur, how many were there?"

"Many. I don't know. Fifty, maybe a hundred," he said. "The woman you shot, she slit my mother's throat and took her wedding ring for gold."

"Fuck."

"I'll go." The old doctor hobbled up on his cane.

"Can you make it?" Wyatt said.

"I need my arms and an eye to see, not my legs," he said.

"Get to every house. Tell them marauders are coming. I want all guns at my place, meeting at four this afternoon," Wyatt said. "Jesse, bring him my bike."

"Are farm hands coming?" Claire said.

Sam stared at her employer, awaiting command. Wyatt's eyebrows furrowed.

"You two will remain on watch outside, on the hill where Sam took the shot from. You will make sure they don't come back for you," he said. Claire wilted.

"We saved them. That whole caravan would have died without anyone knowing if we hadn't been there. Why are you acting like it's our fault there are bandits?" Deckard snapped. Wyatt rounded on him, and he bit his tongue.

Mother came between them like a friendly barricade. She said something. And they were gone.

Chapter Ten:

Sam leaned her railgun against the armchair. She stepped around the other side and sat down. The gazes of twenty-five men and seven women went from the rifle to her and back again. She knew that feeling. She was just a body. Eventually she'd die, and her body would rot until the gun was left amidst a pile of her bones. Then someone else would pick it up and use it.

The two settler kids were led in by Mattie. They sat down in the middle and told their story. Then, they were led back out.

"Whatever you think, the fact is that the disciples of the Second Covenant are coming. They shot out a perimeter sensor days before the convoy even got here. They are filibusters, and our valley is the site of their next communion. They will burn our houses down and fill in our cellars, then build their own churches all over the land and help themselves to crops we spent thirty years planting," Wyatt said. He sat at the head of the room, opposite Sam.

A tall woman in a black dress stood. She wore a hat with a brim so wide it drooped around her. A mesh netting had been woven around the edges. She leaned on a walking stick.

"What price does the gunslinger charge for her services? We need every rifle."

"Room and board," Sam said. The woman looked at her railgun.

"That's all, for such a weapon?"

"You can get someone to pull the trigger. I hit a moving bike at twenty-six hundred meters. Weapon's ten times as effective with me."

"But it would still be effective."

"And you'd lack the range. Anyone can hit a shot at close range. When you start killing at long ranges, it terrifies the enemy. Nowhere is safe to them because they can't reach you before you reach them," she said. "So, look me in the eyes when you address me. The Covenanters could take this railgun just as easily with the valley."

She sat down gently, adjusting her dress on the way to the seat. "I've been here second longest of all farmers. Don't lecture me on defending the valley."

Sam sighed. This would be a long one.

"Anna, I brought Samantha here because she's been doing her job as long as I've been farming, and that's her professional advice," Wyatt said. He glared at Anna, craning his neck to see under her hat's vast brim.

"Well. If I'm not wrong, her and your hand started this. Why does the attack on a group of misguided travelers threaten the valley? Perhaps they should have left with the caravan," a younger man said.

Jesse stood. "Douglas, perhaps you missed the part where they'd already shot out our perimeter sensor days before the caravan showed up. These are Second Covenanters. They hail from the twin cities of Crater Lake and Deep Charity in the far east. They believe the soil of this entire world was gifted to them by god. They are filibusters and our valley was always their goal."

Douglas retreated into his seat.

"Covenanters took over my grandmother's farm and drove me and my husband to flee here. I will come myself, with my eldest daughter." The speaker was a short woman with deep brown skin. She carried a 45.-70 with a short barrel.

"Thank you, Regina," Wyatt said.

"You talk like your mind has been already made up," the man of the cloth said. He adjusted his black robes as he strode to the center of the room. "You shouldn't be so rigid. If we go to war against these wayward children, then we will not win. Even if they were all slain, our casualties would be many. Look around. Try and guess who would not be at the summer festival when the battle clears. We must negotiate. I will go. Any price is worth not fighting."

"They've already fired," Wyatt said.

"An entire party of a hundred or more, wiped out in cold blood. The kind of people who would do that cannot be reasoned with," a young farmer with black skin said, slamming the butt of his rifle into the floor.

"That's a lot of plunder, perhaps they've had their fill," Anna said.

"The land is their prize, the caravan was a bonus," Wyatt said.

Sam stood, taking the railgun with her. She stared at the preacher and let her childhood of hatred build up in her eyes, until he retreated into a corner with the upturned dining table. Loosening her grip, she let the railgun drop to the ground. The steel buttplate made a decisive thud that shut everyone up.

"Reasoning with bullies does not work. If any of you have been to school, you know they just want to hurt you. And they won't stop until you've either fled or beaten them bloody. Those brutes came through the Fang in numbers and happily murdered a caravan full of families. Do you think they'll stop? So, what's it going to be? We've got hours to decide before they get here. Are you going to stop them? Or not?"

Silence. There was nowhere to retreat from here. Sam leaned on the barrel of her rifle, arms crossed, waiting.

"We're in," Douglas said. "I have three rifles.

An older man stood and spoke in a booming baritone. "I have a son and a daughter I will bring with me."

Regina stood, as did the young farmhand seated behind her.

"We will not go," Anna said, not even raising the brim of her hat to address Sam.

"Then we will all remember you, who have never seen tragedy touch your family nor hunger, hid at the sight of danger," Wyatt said.

"You're punishing me for dissenting," she said.

"The point of farmer's council meetings is to decide for the whole valley," Wyatt said. "You've always abided. Now that you're against it, suddenly you won't."

"This is different. We're talking about killing," she said, and stood.

"Now we fight amongst ourselves. All fighting is an endless cycle that will consume everything," said the man of the cloth. Half a dozen voices shouted him down.

"Your family will be there, or as per the rules we all agreed upon, you will be punished," Regina said.

"Very well. If you insist on leading us to our deaths," she snapped. She stood alone, surrounded by the volatile glares of two dozen determined people.

"Jesse, go back to her house and make sure they bring firepower," Wyatt said. "Do we have agreement?"

All stood. It was agreed.

The sun blinded Sam when she stepped onto the front porch. So long had the meeting gone on, she'd assumed it would be nighttime. Atop the forested hill, a tiny figure emerged, and waved. She waved back.

"I have a strategy." Wyatt was at her side. "I want to set up a firing position on that hill. If they come directly from the Fangs, they'll have to go past it to reach my doorstep. A group of marksmen fortified up there would have clear shots," he said.

She studied the position. "Do you have heavy firepower?"

"Cannons? No. Or I'd put them atop the hill facing outwards," he said.

"Then marksmen will do. I recommend five. Who are you sending?" she said.

"You, Jesse, Regina, Dob's son Correy, and Allen. They were all top finishers in last festival's shooting competition," he said. He pointed along the river. "I want half a dozen in there, against the far bank as a front line. And the rest of us will fortify around the house with our wagons. I'll be right here on the front door with this." He hefted the Engrams and all twenty-eight rounds in its magazine. He walked off. "Matt. Get the farmhands and set up the wagons around the house. We're building our own fortress."

A few of their visitors ran over to the garage to help. The rest were speeding off on their bikes. Sam noted Anna climbing into a wagon, driven by a younger woman. As they huffed off, Sam turned her chin upwards and spat far as she could at them.

By the middle of the night, they were ready. Sam wiped sweat from her brow and lowered her shovel. Half a dozen men and women around her were down to shifts and bare overalls. They'd dug a ditch four feet deep, then cloaked it in tree branches and a single, heavy log to act as a firestop. In the deep night, all she saw were their outlines as they brushed the dirt off and withdrew. A lantern would give them away.

"Suppose this comes to nothing, and you scared them off for good," Claire said. She had her dress tucked under a dirt-caked arm. Her hair was everywhere.

"Then we wasted a night. No problem," Sam said. She looked at the bright lanterns by the garage. Deckard was clearly visible strapping extra wooden logs to the flanks of the wagons, now spread in a circle around the house. There were a dozen more men and women around him.

A bike whirred as it approached. Sam grabbed her railgun, even though it was coming from the direction of the house.

"Any work to do?" Jesse said as he leapt off.

"We're done, where were you?" Sam said.

"It took all that effort to get ole Anna and her family to budge. Five of them and two wagons just made it. I hate those arrogant fucks."

He spat into the dirt. "If y'all are done I'll take watch. Have we seen them?" he said.

As he spoke, lights flickered on the dark night, tracing the invisible horizon. Sam grabbed her railgun and snapped up to aim through the scope. She was aware the figure she cut, wearing an undershirt and rolled up trousers as she stood. Start a riot in any city. Through the scope she only saw more brightness.

"Can't see anything. They must be all the way out," she said. Half a dozen rifles filled the freshly made barricade beside her. She zoomed out. The lights climbed up into the darkness and hovered together.

"I think they're on Breen's hill, by the old chicken coop. Don't know what they're doing, but I'm tempted to take a shot at them," she said.

"Don't. I'll go in for a look," Jesse said.

"Here." Claire shoved her shotgun into his hands and added a dozen extra shells from her discarded ammunition satchel. "In case you get too close."

He was gone without a word. Sam followed him with her scope until his lightless bike vanished.

Then, just as soon, he came roaring back. "They're building a camp," he said as he went past, and stopped right at Wyatt.

Then, he was back with them. "We're holding our ground. Wyatt's posting a couple scouts further out," he said. "And I've brought water if you need a drink or wash."

There was a delighted cry from the hassled farmers. They all took washcloths and wiped themselves clean. Then, they refilled their canteens.

"Still got first watch?" Sam said.

"I do," he said.

So, she threw down her bedroll right there next to her trench, crawled into the bushes above it, and fell asleep on the spot, railgun across her chest.

Chapter Eleven:

Rays of gray light pierced Sam's shut eyes. They dragged her back with them. She sat straight up and looked around. Everyone was asleep amidst a messily dug, but still camouflaged trench. Except Jesse, who'd fallen asleep against a tree, facing the open fields where everyone could see him.

Branches popped and snapped before her as she tore out of her cover. He groaned as she snatched him under the armpits and hauled him back.

"What the hell? Get off me lady." He clawed free.

"You fell asleep in full view of our secret position," she said. His face went red and he opened his mouth. She turned around and walked away before he could blurt out some excuse to save his pride. Behind her, brush shifted. A check told her he'd sat back down in cover. Good for him.

She brought up her railgun and had a look, through the bushes. They had assembled a wooden platform of some kind. She couldn't tell what it was, except it had walls. A puff of smoke rose.

One of the farm scouts swerved in the field and fell a bit closer to the house.

"Hey mom." Deckard dropped to his hands and knees beside her. "I brought you something." He unwrapped a yellow honeycomb, and an apple.

"Jeez where did this come from?"

"Mathias found a beehive a few days ago and cleared it out. He wanted you to have this, as a gift of thanks," he said.

Sam bit down, and slammed her eyes shut. This was too damn sugary to take. She had to chew slowly.

"You eat it with the apple, I brought a wet towel too for your hands," he said.

"You've had some?" she rinsed her hands, then started eating. The apple tempered the sweetness a little.

"Claire and I shared a bite. She came down last night and we slept in the hay loft."

"Did you…"

"No!" Someone stirred behind them.

"Okay. I'm surprised you even know," she said.

"Well, I kind of went to school with a bunch of other boys and girls. Do you think she knows?" he said.

"No. From what I gather, they don't tell the girls until the day before the wedding," she said.

"Well…" he trailed off. "I want to marry her. It's been a few months and every day I see her, it's like the first time we kissed," he said.

"That's a good sign she's right," Sam said and patted his shoulder. She felt a lot more solid muscle there, than she last had. "Are you going to keep riding with me? You can't have a family on the trail. Even your father and I didn't," she said.

"I don't know. This wouldn't be a bad place to stay, but I'd get more machinery to play with in the city. We'll see after the summer festival, assuming we make it," he said.

"We will."

"You promise?" he said.

She looked him in the eyes. He really did have her pale brown irises. "I promise. I'm here this time."

He settled back in his seat. "You didn't want us to go. I was pretending to be asleep, but I heard your fight with dad."

"I didn't think it was worth it to go after that dangerous old coot on his home turf. Dad pointed out that none of our traps had caught, we hadn't seen game in months, and we were running out of money for the general store."

"You refused to go, so he took me as his partner," Deckard said. "I was so excited. Except. I'm just thinking. With both you and dad, we could have killed him just fine. Now, it's just you. Nothing makes this different," he said.

"I was the better killer. Always was. I didn't need the railgun to hit a moving target. Just a straight-shooting rifle. There's more to killing than that. He was good in a fight, but he didn't have that instinct. To know how to gut your enemy. How to flush them out, and where they're going. I could do that without breaking a sweat. Not going with you guys when he made up his mind was malpractice. And arrogance," Sam said.

"Then why didn't he give you the railgun ever?" Deckard said.

"I think it was pride. He gave it a couple times when a really long shot was needed, but most of the time he held onto it. I mean, it was his great grandfather's weapon," she said. "Anyway. I'm here this time. We'll be fine." She patted the back of his neck. "You cut your hair."

"Claire likes it better short and curly, and I like her's better in a ponytail," he said. "Mom. How many people have you killed?"

Sam rubbed her temples. "You want a number, or…?"

"Just give me an honest answer, please," he said.

"Possibly a hundred. I didn't start fights or just murder people for nothing like Tow and those sick fucks out there, but I killed a lot. Bounty targets, bandits attacking my caravan, a couple fights they started. Once I gutted a woman in front of her kids. That was self-defense. Dad and I were tracking a blerg rustler who'd gone a step further and murdered two hands. We tracked him to a house, and when we tried to apprehend him his wife went for his dropped revolver."

"Fuck," he said.

"Her problem. Dumbass," she said. Movement burst onto the distant hill. A mass of figures spread out at once. Sam raised her railgun and made sure. "Run down the hill and raise the alarm."

He sprinted off, crashing through brush until he hit the open hillside. "Get up!" Sam snapped.

Her sharpshooter cadre rose and concealed themselves. Sam took the end of the trench, closest to the open air. Jesse dropped in beside her. He dropped a round into his weapon, hit the lever beneath the trigger to seal the breach, and pulled the hammer back to cock it. Sam only needed to pull the charging handle back to accomplish the same for the twenty shots in her magazine.

Three bikes came forth. Two had a second rider on their backs. A white flag unfurled from the lead bike.

"Well shit, we might not do this after all," Jesse said.

Sam tracked them with the scope until they passed the hill, and then aimed her scope back to the distant enemy. She kept one eye on the group as they stopped in the front lawn and dismounted. Wyatt came out to meet them, a farmer in a blue shirt at his side.

She couldn't hear their words. Wyatt said something. The lead man turned away. And drew a revolver from his shirt.

Wyatt snapped the Engrams up to his shoulder and fired. The lead man fell, blood pouring from a gut wound. Then Wyatt threw himself onto his back as gunfire broke out.

Sam swung her railgun around, but the burst had passed and fallen to a ringing in her ears. A lone woman staggered from the haze of white and red, and leapt on her bike.

Jesse fired from standing, and she fell back off into a heap of grey calico. The rest of the riders were down, and Wyatt was picking himself up to his feet while jamming fresh rounds into his Engrams. One of the men on the porch was down, curled up and rocking.

A scream rose from the house. Wyatt sprinted inside.

"We missed the beginning," Jesse said. "Oh well. Next ones up."

A wave poured down the hill and rolled towards them on steel beasts. Sam counted forty bikes, and five wagons. These were dragging, wheeled beasts, weighed down by the logs strapped to their front bumpers to absorb bullets. They were manned by Covenanters in grey. She saw men and women, young and old alike. All with that same bleak expression of soldiers afraid but determined. They looked awfully human for a group that had just massacred a hundred civilians.

A distant weapon crackled, booming over the plains as shots poured in. The big farmhouse shuddered as paint and wood chipped off in puffs of white. The woman helping the wounded man vanished in a spray of red. Sam heard windows tinkling as they shattered, and porch columns smashing open. Looking forwards, she saw a cloud of white smoke rising continuously from the platform.

"They brought a gatling gun," she said.

"God in hell below," Jesse said. "Can you hit it?"

She raised her rifle and took aim. Range was over three thousand meters. The gun was a rotating thing poking through a slit in the wooden palisade. It disappeared in a growing cloud of smoke. "No shot," she said. She swung her aim to the bikers and settled on the leading wagon. A single eye slit marked the driver's location. She aimed on it. "Range to enemy is five-hundred yards." She counted down. "Four hundred."

Rifle fire crackled from dozens of different of weapons. Little puffs of white trailed after the advancing bikes. A rack of them blew off the tops of the wagons.

Jesse fired past her. She didn't see who he hit as she aimed.

The railgun thundered in her arms. She didn't see where it hit. The wagon slewed to the right and dug a trench into the ground. It righted again as someone else took the wheel. She fired again, and it resumed its rightward plunge, until it tipped over. Bodies poured out. Sam sighted back. Her snipers fired fast and ready, calling targets. A dozen bodies lay writhing or still by their shattered bikes.

She sighted down at a woman, riding past the hill, and took her head clean off. Her bike swerved right, still on full throttle. Half a dozen more had to slow down to evade. "There. Right under the hill, they've slowed!" she snapped. Jesse spun, throwing dirt onto her jacket, and fired. One dropped. A couple more fell. Sam found another target and hit them. Then another.

Fire rose not from the disintegrating houses, but the river. Waist-deep in water, the half-dozen rifles poured loose into the oncoming bikers, heedless of the fire splashing them black with mud and water. The bank itself began to come apart. One shooter was forced back as his armrest fell away. He shuddered as half a dozen rifle bullets struck him, and then fell into the water.

Sam fired fast as she could. There were too many. The Covenanters dismounted as they closed. Then they were in the water and fighting descended into a melee of frothing water and blood. One of the wagons rolled up, and Covenanters began tearing logs out and spanning the river.

"Go for the bridge builders! Stop them," Sam said and opened fire. She put two shots into the wagon's driver cabin, then struck a massive man handing logs down by himself. Her first shot blew out a chunk of his belly. He grabbed, not a rifle, but a blue pennant, and waved it at her. She hit him center chest, then pumped the lever and let recoil drive her third shot into his throat. He stumbled back and plunged over the side of the wagon, scattering logs. A smaller man grabbed the pennant before it hit the ground and began waving.

"I got you," Jesse said, and put a shot through his right eye. "Shit. Another."

A bridge was already across from two more wagons that had parked at right angles, blocking her fire with their full masses.

Sam put a shot through their back. Covenanters were climbing out of the river, clothes soaked black by the water.

"Aim at the porch. Hit them as they climb the barricade," Jesse said.

Sam had had an inkling of what the blue pennant had signaled. It was confirmed when trees and brush disintegrated around her. "Everyone down," she said. Jesse dove in beside her as splinters filled the empty space where he'd once been. Another young man threw himself over the log. He howled, caught halfway. Sam grabbed him and pulled. He fell and sprayed her with blood from the shattered mess of his lower half. His legs were gone. The log they'd used rattled and cracked under fire. Its supports gave out and it fell with a crash. Someone screamed. Sam looked up from the dying man, head sprayed by debris, and saw Regina slumped against the wall, arm pinned beneath the log.

"Jesse." She sprinted over and grabbed the log. Jesse lined up next to her. Another woman grabbed Regina's shoulders. Her face twisted up in agony.

"Get it off, don't matter if I scream."

The log smacked Sam's brow over and over as it was hit. She strained from the legs and pushed with Jesse beside her.

The log didn't budge. She couldn't poke her head out to see why. A tree fell forwards and slammed between her and Jesse. A wall of green branches tore at her skin, driving her back.

"Come on, I can't feel anything," Regina pleaded.

Sam left her with her flask of whiskey and ran up the trench. She dropped her near-empty magazine and jammed a fresh one in. There was a slit between the log and the wall of the trench they'd dug, filled with wooden splinters. She slid the railgun in and took aim. The bridge was down. Fire sparkled from the wagons on both sides. Twenty bodies floated in the river. A man in gray held someone under the water. She only saw the hands twitching. She put a shot through his head. He fell away, but the figure in the red dress remained floating limp, head below the surface.

She looked at the house. A stream of gray ran up towards the front porch, covered by the sheer size of the house from flanking fire.

She couldn't shoot them without exposing herself. Something sharp jammed through her coat into her shoulder. Somewhere in that house Deckard was crouched with his stupid oversized rifle.

A man with a revolver in either hand climbed the porch and fired through the front door. The return blew him off his feet. The woman behind him, then the man behind her fell before a barrage of bullets. Wyatt emerged, sneering like the devil to mankind beneath him as he pumped the lever on the Engrams fast as he could. Bodies fell around him.

In the window she saw Deckard's frocked city jacket. Then the massive blast of his rifle. Then another.

The forest stopped disintegrating around her. She leapt up, sighted the gunners on the furthest wagon on the end wagon, and opened fire. They fell one by one. She saw them, their faces concentrated in saving the lives of their comrades by cutting their enemies' rifles down. And each fell as fast as they appeared. One wagon down. She moved down to the next and cut them down, too. One gunner ducked into the driver's cabin. She put three rounds through the wall at waist height.

Half a dozen covenanters swarmed around one of the wagons and into the barn. A single man emerged, hat gone and rifle swinging haphazardly in his arm as he ran. She shot him at the river. Then swung back to the house. Wyatt stood strong, his sons flanking him with their revolvers.

She clambered onto the log and aimed into the distance. There were a handful of sharpshooters firing. They'd overturned their bikes for cover and sprawled out behind them. She sighted the first and fired.

She noticed Jesse when one sharpshooter suddenly grabbed their throat and keeled forwards. She watched as he killed the next three.

And the sharpshooters were picking up their bikes and leaving. A variety of Covenanters followed, running hard. She picked them off until her magazine clicked empty.

She yanked it out, then noted the silence and stopped. The last few shots echoed back from the distant valley walls. White gun smoke and black smoke from the burning wagons hovered in the still air, furling across the farm as it tried to hide the carnage. More substantial movement flickered beneath as the remaining defenders extracted themselves from their defensive positions. She smelled the gunpowder. It was like home. The calm after the end of the killing.

She lowered her rifle. Someone whimpered behind her. She remembered Regina and raced over. The squat woman had gone pale as she could. Blood trickled down the wall, soaking into the dark soil. "Help," she mouthed.

Sam clambered up. The log was wedged between two of its own supports. Sam dug one out with her own knife. Then she and Jessie pushed until it rolled free. Regina fell onto her side and whimpered.

Cutting her arm off would have been better. Regina's forearm had twisted into a curve, shattered bone protruding through her rolled sleeves in many white spikes. There was no recovering from that. Sam could only tie it against her body, then press the liquor bottle to her lips.

"Thank you," she muttered, eyes shutting.

"She's going to die if we don't do something," Jesse said.

"I'll go down to the cabin. Keep watch in case they come back," she said. He nodded. Then grabbed his binoculars.

The house sagged. There wasn't any one piece to replace. Every board had been holed through and each nail wrenched free, and they bent under their own weight. The porch ceiling leaned towards the ground, until the shattered teeth of its columns propped it up. There was nothing worth saving. Wyatt would have to rebuild it from the foundation.

The old man himself emerged from the door. The blood of a dozen people was sprayed across him in little circular stains. Impossibly he was unharmed. "Was that you shooting?" he said.

"Yeah."

"Well. Try to do more of that because we won't last another assault," he said, looking out through the white gun haze towards the enemy. A wagon sat dead center of the river, burning.

"Regina's going to die without medical attention. Arm got crushed."

"I'll send someone. Matt got hit in the hip. Mattie…" he trailed off. She saw when she stepped inside.

Sitting behind two walls with the medical supplies, a bullet had punched through and hit Mattie center-belly. She lay still amidst a bloody angel, blood spreading as she died.

There were wood splinters and wrecked furniture coating the floor like snow. The house moaned ominously.

"Get her out, get everyone out," Wyatt said.

No one else would touch the dead musician, so Sam did. Hauled her up on her shoulder and out the front door. Wyatt directed everyone to the largest barn. Five dead Covenanters were piled outside already, being stripped of valuables by a couple farmers. They saw Mattie swinging from Sam's shoulder and dropped to one knee. Sam pushed out a bed of straw with her boot and laid her down.

"Mother."

Deckard's eyes were wild with the fight between fear and pure adrenaline. His chest heaved with every breath he took. His hands were balled around the stock of his rifle, though its lever hung wide open and empty like an afterthought. Otherwise, he was fine.

"We made it. I told you," she said.

"I know." He looked about. There were no stretchers, so people were laying down hay and depositing dead and wounded. Matt groaned against a wall, a bottle of whiskey in hand. In the back, the doctor washed his tools in clear rubbing alcohol. Deckard winced as another man cried out when he was lowered to the ground. "Outside."

They stepped out. Gunsmoke drifted across the battlefield. Three wagons remained behind, pointed directly at them.

"Leona!" a young man screamed and sprinted into the river. He grabbed a girl in a red suit and pulled her out. "Not my beautiful wife, please, Leona wake up." He hauled her out soaking and cradled her in his arms. Her eyes were shut and limbs astray around him. His lips brushed hers, but she didn't react.

Deckard ducked behind a haystack. Sam followed him. Blood was sprayed the ground. A covenanter man barely older than him lay on his back. There was a look of immense surprise on his face, like the hole blown through his chest was a prank. "I'm marrying Claire and going back to the city."

Sam looked at him. "That's okay," she said.

"No, it's not. Men live their lives out here and they're the toughest around. Nothing scares them," he said.

"Sounds like Tow. Mr. apex fucking predator. And he died to a woman a third his size," she said. "Fuck cares how tough you are. Go be happy. Take your girl and love her and go to sleep in an actual bed with her," she said.

"I just won't forget how the west defeated me," he said. He looked down at his boots and remembered that his rifle was hanging ajar. Propping it on his shoulder, he jacked eight rounds into it, then closed the lever.

"This planet defeats everyone. It's a planet and you're one man. The people who survive it the longest…do you really want to live like that?" she said.

"No," he said. "But you do."

"If you haven't noticed, I'm a widow with no future prospects and no home. I can't settle down. Just don't want to. And your father. He was a bit more typical. Look where that got him," she said.

Deckard nodded and sniffed. "I love her, mom."

"I know." Someone gasped behind her in a sharp rush. She spun around and looked right into Claire's pale blue eyes. She clapped a hand over her mouth.

Deckard trudged past Sam and threw his arms around the girl. She hugged him back. A whimper escaped from their little huddle. Sam pretended to check over her woefully ignored revolver in the meantime.

"Mom." Each of them reached out an arm. Fine. Despite both being her height, they just felt so small and fragile in her arms. They could have just as easily drowned in the stream or vanished amidst the hail of gatling fire. Or starved to death one winter when the game wasn't around or the food was spoiled.

They found Wyatt outside the barn, staring over the farm. "You did well," he said. "I was in the last war. Luck. No matter how well you shoot at some point it's your time or it's not," he said. He shook his head. "Do you think they're done?"

"Not as long as they have that cranky demon sitting on that hill," she said. Maybe the gun had jammed. Being carried in pieces across an entire mountain range wouldn't have been good for it. Or perhaps they'd been dumb and not brought enough ammo. It had been firing for a solid five or ten minutes. That was an obscene number of bullets.

"No, they're not. If that thing starts firing again it will just keep going until we have to retreat. I don't know how many of them there are. This could be the first wave only," he said.

"So, we take the gun," she said.

"Exactly what I was thinking." He stood. "Everyone with a rifle who's not tending wounded. Gather on me!"

There were a bare fifteen of them. Everyone was blackened from service at their weapon. Most had the same wild look as Deckard.

"We stopped them, but we're not done yet. They still have that murderous machine on the hill and only the grace of god is keeping it from obliterating us right now," Wyatt said. "We need to take it. Now, while it's still morning and they're reeling."

Sam tilted her head back. The sun was still below the mountains, the sky still blending through the colors into white. What the hell? She'd be more convinced they'd fought all night and into the next day.

"Can we even do that?" someone said.

"We can. And we're sending Samantha to lead it. I need six volunteers. You'll take a circuitous route so at least you'll be out of the line of fire," he said.

Sam raised her hand anyways. As did Jesse, Deckard, and Claire. Douglas put his hand up. Then, a girl barely older than Deckard raised her burly arm. By the muscle in her arms, Sam guessed she was the blacksmith's apprentice

"Good. Grab what you can from the deceased. I saw some fine pieces on them."

Wyatt shoved his Engrams into Jesse's hands. "You might need a bit more ammunition than just the one. I loaded her up in the meantime."

Jesse turned the gun over in his hands, sizing up its oddly bent frame. "Thanks boss."

Chapter Twelve

They set out. Jesse steered with one hand and peered through his binoculars with the other. Their route ran north along the river until they came to another bridge and crossed. From here, the house was a small white smudge. Sam swapped to leg steering and took her railgun in both hands.

They spotted the platform atop the other hill. Bikes leaned on either side. From the side, the gatling unfurled to its full steel lethality. A solid frame of wood, atop which a brass receiver sprouted into half a dozen long, heavy barrels. More firepower than any one man could ever carry in their arms sat right there.

The gun spat fire. Its roar followed the flash over the plains. The bullets shot towards the farm. Everyone pushed the throttle forwards.

Jesse tapped Sam's shoulder. "I'm thinking we sit back and keep their heads down with our fire, while the others storm in. Put some rapid fire to good use for once."

She nodded. As they closed, she saw half a dozen figures in grey around the gun. Someone sounded the alarm and they dropped behind the palisade. Muzzles flared. Rifle fire hit the air all around. Sam took aim at the wooden boards themselves.

Rifles kicked hard. The railgun tapped her lightly, assuring her it had fired. All its destruction went the other way; far more efficient than a gunpowder-driven rifle could manage. Wood splintered. A cloud of fragments rose into the air. She pumped the lever fast as she could. Tree logs cracked under the impact. She saw bark fly apart. Should she have just shot at the platform from her covered trench during the battle? Maybe with the weight of the gatling, she could have just knocked the platform right over and saved so many lives.

"Goddamn I want one of those," Jesse said. He rose up and fired fast. The carbine made a heavier crack as its black, chemical propellant ignited. Fire spat forth.

She and Jesse stayed straight. The other four raced to the right and swung out of their line of fire. As they looped around the rear of the hill, a lone figure in a grey hat rose impetuously from the palisade, a long rifle in his hands.

Sam and Jesse fired simultaneously. The figure jerked back as his body and head split open and fell from view.

"They're running!" Claire shrieked. Gunfire rang out. Sam heard revolvers, and the massive boom of the .45-70.

Then, silhouetted in the sun; another covenanter stumbling from cover with splinters digging into their face. Claire clubbed him with her shotgun stock. He spun and raised a revolver.

Deckard jammed the barrel of his rifle under the covenanter's jaw, and blew his face across the palisade. Claire added an extra shot in case he had the misfortune of still living.

When Sam reached the summit, she saw two riders racing away. She put one down with a shot between her shoulders. Jesse hit the second on his right side. The bike swung out, wobbling precipitously. Jesse chewed his lips and waited until the covenanter found his balance. The Engrams fired again, and the rider fell free, his bike continuing on into the growing daylight.

Now the gun. The gatling crouched, streaked in black residue and waiting for their loving tenderness. A pile of loaded magazines sat on one side, along with a bunch of brushes. "I bet it jammed from dirt accumulation," she said. She aimed her railgun at it. A few shots would demolish the receiver, leaving six barrels attached to a box of scrap metal.

"Wait, wait." She had to point her piece at the sky as Jesse leapt past her. He pawed over the gun mount and the platform. "Covenanters just stuck this in on its travelling mount. We can steal this in a few minutes."

"Yeah, let's do that," Deckard said.

Sam sighed. "I'll watch for hostiles."

"Take these." Jesse tossed her his binoculars.

Sam set up on the back of the platform. She switched between the scope and the binoculars and settled on the binoculars. From here, she saw the Covenanter's camp. It was a collection of tents and wagons sitting under the jagged shadows of the fangs. A yellow banner flapped from each tent. She slid down to the ground so she was leaning against the wood, arms resting on either knee as she held the binoculars.

"They screwed the damn thing in," Deckard said.

"No worry. There's a screwdriver right there," Jesse said. A string of grunting and metallic scratching followed.

"I hate screws," the blacksmith's apprentice said.

"Well that's the last of them. Now, everyone, get a corner. Cassandra, you get the middle. Everyone, three, two, one, lift!"

The platform shook. There was no movement in the camp in response. How many were left alive? Sam wondered as she aimed into the distance. Did they still have a leader, who could make the call to go save their most powerful asset?

"Deckard, get the maneuvering trailer."

Metal crashed like a gunshot.

"Fuck, did that work?" Deckard said.

"It did. Douglas and I will get our bikes. Douglas, you'll turn it. Then Claire will latch onto the other side."

A flash illuminated all the tents in black silhouette. They were heavy, wood-frames over cotton. The kind of tent for a season-long stationary camp. Not trekking through hostile terrain. A low boom rolled over the plowed fields.

"Hurry. Hook the winch in," Jesse said. Muzzle flares flashed hard and fast from all over the camp. Gunfire rattled from many different cartridges. She heard lighter pistol rounds amidst the deep booms of rifles, and the occasional boom of a shotgun.

"They're not shooting at us. All that fire is coming from within the camp," she said.

"Are they turning on each other?" Deckard said eagerly.

"I'll find out," she said and stood. She handed the binoculars up to the mounted Jesse. "Do you need me?"

"No. Now we just need two to tow and one to trail. Never thought I'd be a father but this is quite the girl," he said, and patted the gatling's barrels

"I'm coming with you, mother," Deckard said.

"No," she said.

"I'm promising to watch your back, now," he said.

"I'm coming too," Claire said.

Their party split in half. Sam leaned low on her steering bars, staring into the gunfight. She saw movement flicker between tents. Accompanied by the occasional scream. It continued as she rode right up to the wall and front gate

A body laid between two wagons. Sam dismounted at a run and sprinted into cover beside them. Gunfire crackled all over. Someone screamed. The body had been shot in the face as he tried to enter the camp.

Claire and Deckard dropped beside her, and both tried to peer into the gap. She grabbed handfuls of their jackets and hauled them out of sight. "You two. Shh," she said. They nodded and clung together like the most adorable little attack dogs she'd ever seen.

The gunfire dropped in volume. As it slackened, she heard a single weapon above all. A fast, low gun firing too fast to be a lever action. Was that a revolver? Could be. Unless.

"Mom, it sounds like your railgun," Deckard said.

She nodded.

Footsteps. A single gunshot. Silence.

Gunsmoke drifted out of the gap. White haze met Sam as she rose around the corner. She slipped the railgun back into its sling and drew her revolver. The hammers were the only sound as they clicked to load.

Boots squelched on spongy ground, somewhere in the smoke. She stopped and took aim into the darkness. The smoke cleared, revealing a camp strewn in death. Twenty to thirty bodies in grey were scattered on the ground like so many dolls tossed aside. Holes in the front, holes in the back, weapons scattered about. At her feet lay a young woman. The hat had rolled off her head, revealing deep brown skin and dreadlocks that had taken years to grow out. Blood had gone still already in her slack mouth.

Bootsteps. Around the outside of the tents.

"You don't sound like a Covenanter." Voice was a controlled drawl. Every mispronunciation was carefully articulated over. "Are you a farmer?"

She aimed into the gaps between the two nearest tents Deckard and Claire walked around her, making a ton of noise with their boots. They froze upon seeing her, too late.

"Really, I'm sorry I didn't come sooner. I could have balanced the battle in your favor. I rode all night for three days to get here, slept in the saddle on the straighter parts of the road.'

Claire rushed forwards.

"Wait!" Deckard gasped. Sam started after them, revolver up. Claire rounded the corner and stopped short on a lake of blood. Sam stepped around her.

The man was untouched in the carnage of the massacre. His black hat was pulled low over his eyes. He wore all black from the trench coat tailored perfectly to his slim shoulders, down to the black pants tucked into black boots. In his hands were two pistols of a design she'd never seen. Black, with a single chamber. Looked like magazines inserted into their straight handgrips like a smaller version of her railgun. Their barrels glowed with magnetic energy of railguns.

The Beast of the East looked up. His eyes were pale blue. His brow, clean and smooth with a complete lack of concern for the three pieces pointed at his chest.

"State your business," Sam said.

"I came to protect this valley. I was terrified I'd been too late, but I must thank you, gunslinger. You protected them long enough," he said.

"Hell do these folk mean to you?" Sam said.

"I have a soft spot for this valley. My job here is done."

"And fifty thousand could buy them a lot," Deckard said. Sam glared at him out of the corner of her eyes. Idiot was poking at a monster.

The Beast of the East frowned. "I was hoping to just walk away."

"Not with that bounty." Deckard said and took a step forwards.

Sam realized what was about to happen. She shifted aim to his face. Just to be sure.

"Mom," Deckard said in a tiny voice.

Something cold and hard pressed into the back of Sam's head, lifting her hat up. She knew what it was.

"Claire. What are you doing?" she said.

"Miss Samantha. I love you. But I can't let you hurt my pa."

"Are you…" She saw the smile forming across the beast's face. Deckard's jaw had just about hit the mud. *Rumors were that he had a son. No fucking way. No one could imagine a monster would have a daughter, not even her.* She kept her aim on that pale forehead. If Claire shot, her dad was going down.

"I'd rather not do this," he said. "However, I do need another body for what I'm about to do."

"No," she said.

"I think the boy would be better."

"Dad. Don't," Claire said.

"I'm not going to hurt him," he said. The drawl was gone from his voice. It was a pure, smooth promise to his daughter. His brow had furrowed as he addressed his daughter around Sam's railgun.

"I don't know. Why are we doing this?" Claire said.

"Because it never stops," he said. "Until we're all dead."

Sam heard a whoosh. She tensed on the trigger. The world split open white hot. "Mom!" Deckard yelled.

■■

"Samantha." She opened her eyes. Jesse stood over her. The ground had opened up and sucked her halfway down. Mud soaked the back of her head, pressing into the gaping wound. She sat up and it sloshed off her. The mud was red all around. A pale hand stretched out to her from a gray sleeve. A wedding band sat on one finger. The long nails had been carefully manicured. She grabbed it and hauled herself up.

The world went sideways. She vomited and added some steaming green to the floor.

"Samantha, what in the inferno happened?" Jesse said. Two pairs of arms seized her shoulders. She twisted away.

"I'm going to gut them both and bleed them dry," she gasped.

"Who? What happened to Claire and Deckard? We can't lose any more." It was…she didn't know who.

"Where's my railgun?" She sloshed over the bodies and the discarded weapons. Deck's rifle lay in a puddle amongst circled boot prints. Gone. Beast had probably taken it. "The Beast of the East…"

"He's here? Was he with the Covenanters?" someone said. It was Wyatt, kneeling in the mud.

She snatched out her knife and grabbed him by the throat. Shouts rang out as his eyes went wide. Couldn't see, couldn't care. "Why didn't you tell me."

"Sam, tell you what?"

"Claire's father is the Beast of the East? You met him. How could you not know?"

"I don't know what he looked like outside the posters. Was he here…"

"He killed all of them to protect her." She shoved him away. "Then he took my son and left. I'm going to kill him and kill her. They have my boy. Where's my bike?"

"You're bleeding from the back of your head," Jesse said. "Look. If they're going into the Fangs, they'll make slow time. And you've seen the dirt in the Fangs. All that ground up sandstone makes easy trails." He held her out a weapon. She had to grasp her hands around the dark wood and glossy black metal to realize what it was. Her fingers found the scope.

"That's yours," she said.

"He's got your railgun, right? You'll need a proper marksman's rifle. That's this. It fires a forty-five, one-ten," he said.

"That's not a cartridge," she said.

"Yes, it is. The Alberrie Sniper corps uses that. I have to order the bullets once a year. The gun isn't their standard rifle, but I've modified it. I promise you it will hit your target up to a kilometer and a half," he said.

She held it to her chest. He added an ammo pouch.

"Sorry, Wyatt," she muttered to the other man.

"Not Wyatt, I'm Matt," he said.

"Well, fuck."

Act III: Summer

Chapter Thirteen

Sam's bike made a high, uneven buzz as it tore over the packed rock and dust. The humming carried through the mountains and reverberated back into her face. Dust kicked up in her wake, kicked up by her fans. The cloud rose with each branch on the trail, spreading down ravines and over the narrow breaths of open space down the mountain flanks and into the shadows of the teeth rising all around. It faded, leaving a thin track in her wake, that would be blown away by the first spring breeze

Following the monster and the children was easy. They left their own fine trail of fan-sculpted dust. She followed to the left when she could, and only crossed and erased it when the trail narrowed between high cliff and over deep ravines. The sun rarely showed through, except in the few warm hours of noon, or when she caught a break in the teeth and got a face-full of white light.

On the first two days, she had but a trail. On the third, she spotted a hash of brown dangling from a cactus. Her bike purred as she pulled up. The dust cloud billowed as it caught up to her. She closed her eyes until it faded and wiped the grains from her brow before opening them again.

It was the handkerchief she'd given Deckard way back on that river. The cactus had pierced it in a dozen places. Sam pinched the corner and plucked it free. A couple thorns came with it and dug into her gloves. It was still warm against the cooling evening air. This had to be from earlier today. She pinched each spine and wrenched it out. They had thick barbs on the tip that carried chunks of her glove with them.

The farm had sunk into its own misery. Men and women from across the valley laid out their dead. Wyatt gave Mattie a kiss on the cheek and left her to her husband and kids. He presided over the rest. There was the weeping, Sam could stand that. The moaning of the still-living wounded was what she needed to tie a rag over her ears to sleep for. Perhaps it was the concussion, or exhaustion, but the boundless terror of losing her son didn't stop her from falling right to sleep in the hay loft.

No one had stopped her and no one disturbed her.

Come sunrise, she'd started them off in terror by doing target practice with the dead covenanters strewn across the yard. The gun had been a straight shot.

Twelve shots, eleven hits. She'd thanked them copiously as she ate breakfast to the stench of dead bodies and whimpers of two who'd been too badly wounded for liquor and exhaustion to silence. They'd stocked her with everything, including a blanket from Mattie's bike that kept the dust out of her saddle, a fresh structured pack from Wyatt's days in the army, and the scarf she wore that kept the worst of the dust from her face.

She palmed the handkerchief in her hand and pondered the road ahead. The path wound around the side of a mountain, with cliff faces preventing any easy exit. She still crawled up, with her eyes to the road. The blatant track never changed, so she leaned into the throttle some more. Halfway around, the trail took a right and soared up the shoulder of another mountain, before dipping out of view.

She reached the top and breathed in a breath of fresh air. She'd broken the mountains. The mountain tops rose above her, sharpened to smooth predator pincers as though meant for puncturing the thick scales of the wind. A waterfall bubbled out from below and plummeted into a wide river that spread between several mountains.

Leaning forwards, she tore down the slope and back into the shadows.

She continued two hours after sunrise, cutting her headlights and creeping forwards.

Kindling was minimal and time to gather it nonexistent, so she ate in the cold darkness. Her dinner had been cooked under the saddle, the last leg from one of Wyatt's goats. Then, she slept in darkness.

White sunlight shocked her awake on the fourth day. After finding the trail, she set off.

Jesse had said the Fangs went three weeks across but that they grew more hospitable as they went. She saw this as dry, reddish branches emerged from cracks in the rock, and grouped in masses as tall as her. These were unhealthy plants that squatted low in tangled masses and rustled and flaked as her bike passed. They burned easily that night, and she got a brief, vicious fire.

Something moved in the distance. A pale man sat down on his rear across from her and balled his hands into his fists on his knees.

"This is your fault," she said. "You wanted him to be whatever he wanted, so when he asked to go hunting with you, you fucking melted. But daddy, I want to be like you. Fucking, please. I saw you shoot a maiden down running away. And then you melt for him."

She spat. It dropped onto her boot toe. Spitting had never been her thing. Better to just shoot someone. "You tried to be hard to be nice. All that about how we lived hard life so we've got to be nice when we can. Fuck that!"

The figure cocked its head. Like he did when he was trying to deflect her anger.

"I'm not just going to start giggling at your stupid face," she said. "I blame you. He could have been graduating school and having a nice job. That's being nice, giving him that life. Instead you did him a cruelty. What was I supposed to do? You were just the first guy I met that wasn't a priest?"

The face straightened. That had been cold, but her anger burned too hot. "I told you that last hunt was too dangerous and you still went off. You got him into that, and he got himself out alive. All him. And the worst part; I blame myself because I couldn't stop you from going. All me. It's not even my fault."

The figure stood, and walked back into the blackness of the fangs. Sam warmed her hands and lay back in her bed wrap. The stars were framed by teeth. Neither moon was out.

"Look, I'm sorry about that. You were a gentleman, and what happened, could have happened to anyone. I just want to save our boy." She closed her eyes. Only then, did she feel a calloused hand on her forehead.

"Sam, you grew up hard. That made you tougher," he said.

"A million terrible men out there, and I happened to stumble on you," she muttered.

"Other way around. A million terrible women, and you wandered up to me," he said. "And remember, that was the winter of the famine. I went after Mojan because we were starving and needed the money."

"Yeah. Well, it was still stupid," she said. "I should have gone instead." No reply as she posed herself a problem she couldn't answer. She just imagined his hand on her forehead, until she drifted off to sleep.

Deckard awoke to a boot. A pair of blue eyes glared down at him, framed by the jagged mouth of paling sky. The Beast withdrew. Deckard sat up and shivered beneath his blankets. The dirt was caked in frost. Their bikes beaded with melting dew. Pots crashed as the Beast made their usual oatmeal.

"Pa, I'll do it," she said.

"No, thank you, love. I'll get it. Make sure he gets up."

Silence. Deckard hadn't spoken in four days. There was a boundary around him, as the hostage, the stranger. If it shattered, he'd shatter out of shame for how hard he'd failed his mother. He was weak, and he shivered like a coward while tougher riders slept in bare snow.

He stared off into the wilderness. They didn't hold him with bonds. There was nowhere to run. The entire world was out there in a mess of fangs and barbed cacti. It shouted back at him with every word they spoke, daring him away into its depths where hundreds had been devoured before. It wasn't something to rebel against.

Rebellion was trying to kill the Beast in his sleep and dying. Or grabbing the handlebars as he rode back-saddle on Claire's bike and sending them careening to mutual annihilation. He was too terrified of death to do that. And now he was glad for it because he'd realized something. Something that made him excited enough to break the barrier.

Claire crouched before him, and he saw nerves reflected in her own bleak expression. She was rumpled with dust. They'd all tied scarfs around their faces but it hadn't stopped all the dust.

"Hey, pack up or pa's going to kick you," she said with zero heart.

He was the first one ready. They rode on in silence.

That night, they camped under a waterfall. Deckard hoped the handkerchief he'd bundled in his sleeve and let go had landed on the cactus. He hadn't dared check.

Claire cleaned the bike fans of dust while the Beast cooked dinner.

"Did I ever teach you hunting?" Beast said.

"No, but I learned from Wyatt," she said.

The Beast sighed as his expression broke into a frown. "Well, he's a good man."

"I'd like to go hunting with you. Is there anything to eat out here?"

"There's a bounty of food out here, hiding beyond human reach," he said. "We get further out and I'll show you." He stared straight at Deckard. "The boy can watch the bikes. Or die alone." Deckard shivered.

He stared up at the starscape, narrow as the maw of fangs gaped down at him. The cold seeped into his blankets and made him shiver. Why had he opened his mouth? The Beast would have taken his daughter and gone, and he and mom would have been safe. Instead, he pissed off a monster.

Blankets rustled.

"Up," the Beast said. "Come on little lady."

"What's going on?" Claire murmured. Deckard shivered harder. They walked past him. A lantern flicked on.

"You see that?" Beast said. Gravelly words rattled the air. Like he'd merged with the fangs and spoke through them.

"I don't see anything," a very human girl said.

"Follow my finger, look for the shadow cast by the lantern."

"Oh my. What produces a track like that? That's six toes, right?"

"Good eye. Six. Those are greywalker tracks. We're coming up on the edge of their territory. There's more prey this far into the mountains, so they stick to out here," he said. Deckard bit his lip. He hadn't heard that howling.

"Pa, we need to keep a fire going, right?"

"The wood out here doesn't burn long enough for an all-night fire. It's too dry, stores all its water in the tuber. The stuff we see above ground is expendable. We've got to keep watch, half a night each. I don't trust him enough. I know you're awake boy, I hear your irregular breathing." A pair of blue eyes appeared over Deckard. He stared into them.

"Pa, stop scaring him."

"No, because this is me and you and we have a stranger here by necessity. There's a reason I work alone."

"Okay.

Mom was coming for you, Deckard thought. Not too loudly. Mother was death at range. She'd find his handkerchief and she'd follow their trail all the way through the mountains. He promised that to himself, as Claire lay back down, and the Beast took up pacing around their camp.

Deckard tried again the next night. Claire got the furthest from the Beast when she cleaned the bikes. So, Deckard knelt beside her and picked up a spare brush. She looked over at him in shock as he brushed the fans with a shaking hand. Simple mechanic work didn't stop the trembling. He knocked the brush against the blade over and over, tapping out a rhythm to anything hiding in the dark.

"Claire." She turned suddenly, hanging on every word. "You hit mom to save her life, right?"

"I did," she said.

"Okay." They brushed both bikes clean. By then, their rawhide meat was ready.

The Beast fell asleep silently. Only then, did Deckard abandon the warmth of his blanket and crawl over to Claire's side. "Hey."

She sat up fast. He threw up his hands.

"Wait don't shoot."

She said nothing, but sat back on her haunches.

"I…" he trailed off.

"I wish you were back home with your mother," she said.

"Me too," he said. She hopped up on her knees. "How'd your mom meet him anyways?"

"My mother was a sporting woman." She shrugged. "Pa found out and paid her to give me up."

"Did…" he trailed off. There was nothing he could say to that, but he had to say something lest she take him for insulting her. "Do you miss her?"

"Not really, if she was willing to give me up for money," she said. "I used to live with Pa, out in the wilderness."

"Was he a good dad, like, he didn't lay hands on you or anything?"

"No. He loves me," she said. "Like your mother does."

"I'm sorry I opened my mouth and got this whole thing started," he said.

"I'm sorry I put a gun to your mother and you." He could see her face by the shadows under her brow and around her lips. Her expression didn't change.

"I don't feel any better."

"Neither do I."

He opened his arms tentatively. She threw hers around him and squeezed the air right from his lungs. It was all he could do to hug her back and savor the warmth between them. "We're missing the summer dance. You were pretty good in the rehearsal," he said.

"I know, gods damnit," she said. A wind blew up and the fangs howled like a locomotive steaming down the bend. The deeper mountains boomed, then the upper peaks screamed. All that drove Deckard to hug her tighter. He buried his face in her bonnet as the wind swayed him on the spot. Her fingers dug into his jacket but even their mutual comfort provided no warmth.

The next morning, as they ate cold porridge, he said, "what should I call you?"

"What?" the Beast said, surprised that his hostage had finally spoken.

"I keep thinking of you as the Beast. Do you have a name?"

"The Beast works aplenty." A laugh broke from beneath the black hat. The mountains laughed back at him.

"Well, I'm going to be here for a while," Deckard said.

"A while means nothing out here, and it won't mean anything to you." The Beast finished packing up.

"Must I make up a name for you?" he said.

"Do that at your own risk, boy." The beast slung his bedroll onto his bike. Deckard had gotten a look at the bike. Like the one he'd left behind lonely at the farm, it had been made from custom parts. Except, all the manufacturer's marks had been filed off. Only Deckard had noticed the parts didn't line up.

"You have a nice custom bike. I built my own bike from scratch. I didn't have the time to file off all the marks," he said. "How'd you get the two motors to work without them burning each other out?"

The Beast shook his head. Claire looked between them, grinning.

"Just call him pa," she said.

Beast rounded on her. "Don't take up covenant against me, not after all this time."

"Pa, we fought together against the Covenanters."

"Common enemy is still just a common enemy." He took her under the chin and leaned over to look her in the eyes. "There isn't room for sympathies out here. There's people we trust. Me and you. He's here for convenience," he said.

She stared back silently. Deckard melted into his boots.

"We must go." The Beast hopped on his bike. They joined him. Deckard left Liz's bracelet in the dirt.

Chapter Fourteen:

Sam tied the leather bracelet around her free wrist. The one she wouldn't be drawing with. Judging by the dust scattered on it, it had been dropped before the brief windstorm this morning. She was getting closer.

"Why are you still alive?" she whispered. Every day, she expected to hear the buzzing of flies and smell the death. Every day, she held against that terror longer.

She kicked the bike into gear and rolled off. The wind had cleared the trails she'd followed, but the path dipped into a ravine. The mountain ahead had split in half like a knife dropped from heaven and one side had slid down a few yards. She eyed the walls warily as she went. The wind howled on from deep, and dust flaked off the walls.

What could cause such a calamity? Ground trembling happened. Apparently, the city of Marisport had been drowned a decade ago when a new channel opened from the nearby lake and poured water in.

She caught sight of something dark and stopped short.

In the deepest shadows lay the skeleton of a dactyl. Its great wings had been reduced to slivers of bone. Brown blood matted the ground around it, meaning it was too fresh to have rotted. She knelt and scooped the carcass up.

The bones were decorated with hundreds of tiny scratches where teeth had scraped them bare. None of the bones had been broken.

A chill ran over her skin as she identified the predator. The realization that her skin was just a bag covering flesh that greywalkers could punch through at any moment, at their leisure. That she was alone and wasn't safe at any time. Looking up and down the corridor, she saw nothing moving. She drew her looted revolver, grateful she'd taken the Covenanter's Ranger with its glinting gold handgrip, excessively etched frame, and .45 cal bullet. She kept up the aim until she was on her bike and didn't release it until she was free of the tunnel.

At sunset, she left the trail and climbed a ridge. She emerged right in the upper echelon of the fangs. She stood in the open air and breathed the cold in. She spun slowly, taking it all in. The mountains had become jagged shards of darkness against the clear stars.

There, in the crown of a distant fist of rock, she spotted a flickering orange light. She drew out binoculars. The range was too great to make out shapes, but she saw something move out there. That was them. Given away by the need for a fire against the greywalkers.

She could slip across in the dark and find them, but the same virtue that let her track them now turned against her. A rider alone at night was a morsel to three greywalkers. A quick scattering of claws, a scream and a loose shot, then a gurgle as her own blood drained into her throat. She'd seen it once, twelve years ago. The next two times, she timed the shot right and dropped the beast off.

Being the target was a different story. A few stubby trees grew near her with brown branches. Sam carved them up and lit her fire at the base of the mountain, where the trail was. She found a corner and bivouacked her bike to block it

Sunrise showed no sign of Greywalkers around her. She looked about, and realized she'd missed the trail entirely and ducked into an alcove. It was a stroke of luck she hadn't walked eight steps further and plunged off the edge.

The wind blew up.

"Fuck, no." Grabbing her bike, she kicked it into a low rumble and spun about, searching for an exit. Sides sloped up in all directions. She didn't remember crawling over any of that last night.

"Come on, dear. Forget what you remember. What looks like the best exit?" he said, a warm breath on her ear.

She spun slowly. The soft slope of bare rock, scoured clean by the wind, called out to her. Testing her bike, she found it shockingly easy to climb.

The trail unfurled beneath her. She skittered down and was blasted all over by driving dust. In the distance, low clouds rolled in. The clouds split and reformed as they engulfed each tooth of the Fangs. Rain would be coming. And with it, tougher racking. She had to find the track first.

At first that was easy, as the ravine continued for a mile of windswept rock. Then it opened and three trails presented themselves to her.

One was a trail as common folk would recognize it. A path of bare rock running between two fangs. On one side rose the mountain, and on the other a gorge fell another hundred yards to a stream, then rose a thousand to the summit of the next fang. The other two could only be recognized by those who'd ridden the hard lands. One rolled over flat ground covered in angry red brambles and continued into a wide gap between fangs. The other climbed upwards at a steep angle and continued around another mountain.

A couple dead batteries and burnt campfires meant the covenanters had come through here. All it did was cast Deckard's trail askew. She checked all three and found openings for each. Buried amongst the branches, she saw a glint of metal.

It was an angel with six arms reaching out to embrace her, carved from a single block of marble. The eyes were beads of pure silver. Definitely covenanter. Or, Deck could have grabbed it and left it as a trail. It was all she could do to step back and look at each path. Three chances. Get it right or lose her son forever. As she looked between them, her fingers wiggled like she could just go for her railgun and shoot her way through.

"You were the thinker. Deck got your business mind," she said.

"And my luck. Remember when I tried to buy a general store?"

"Fire, I had to haul you out with Deck under my arm," she said. She remembered the town burning that dry summer. Screams from children trapped in their lofts, and howls of desperate parents who couldn't get to them before the blaze engulfed them both. Horses shrieked as the stable burned.

"You saved us," he said.

"Yeah. Now, help me here," she said.

He paced around her once. His feet kicked up a few ashes from the dead campfires. "Well, there's no clear sign, is there?"

"Nothing," she said.

"You're overthinking. If you were leaving somewhere in a hurry, which path would you take?" he said.

"It doesn't matter. He's clearly going somewhere. And he needs our boy for something nefarious," she said. He paused and stared at her. "What?"

"Took me a moment to remember what nefarious meant," he said. "Well, I think an educated guess is better than none," he said. He resumed pacing. Her boots ground dust as she pivoted continuously to follow him.

"I agree."

"So. If you needed to get somewhere, and you were an outlaw which trail would you take?"

She looked between the three. The easy one went winding across the mountains. The bramble-filled one had been cut apart in the distant past by vast wagon wheels. The third just went straight up and over.

"The third one," she said.

"Yeah. Definitely the shortest route between two points."

She had to turn her bike sideways to climb up the incline. By the top she was sweating. She looked out over miles of hard ground. In an eave where the rock rose, she saw signs of a bike. Encouraged, she powered straight down. There was a gap in the fangs as the trail crossed a gnarled shelf of bedrock, one that had been forced up from below by tectonics and now sat, an unbreachable barrier for mountains trying to rise below. That made easy riding.

At sunset, she kept going until the next mountain rose. Here, she saw the light far in the distance.

This time, she found her own branches and lit a fire. With warmth billowing up, she fell asleep quickly, hand on the trigger of her borrowed rifle.

Deckard clung to Claire as she maneuvered up the pass. Her hands shook as she clung to the steering bars, making every movement an effort not to overcorrect and plunge them over the side.

Deckard felt Claire take a deep breath when they lowered back onto solid ground. He patted her under the arm, then leaned forwards and whispered, "good riding."

She leaned back and rested her head on his shoulder. Hair got under his scarf and tickled him.

As the trail widened, the Beast fell back to ride alongside them, riding dangerously close to the drop-off. He raised a hand suddenly, and they halted.

"Pa, what's going on?" Claire said. The Beast got down on their side and walked around until his toes were over the edge. Deckard and Claire clambered down and approached, albeit a step back lest the edge suck them over and into the patchwork ground of oblivion.

Far below, broken across the banks of a stream, was an upturned wagon. All the doors had been blown open on the impact and crates of…were those brass cartridges? Yeah, they were.

"Them covenanters could never drive," the Beast said with a dry laugh. "That's going to be shelter for some explorer a decade from now." His voice bounced across the valley and blew back in Deckard's face.

"Hell of a fall." He snatched Deckard by the shoulder and slung him over the edge.

Deckard screamed. He couldn't stop his feet from kicking even though there was nothing. His right arm ached as the Beast held him up. "Please!" he said. He looked back and saw only pale blue death.

"I see you with my daughter. You are alive out of necessity. If you keep your mind on her then I will no longer consider it worthwhile," he said.

"I…we fought together," he gasped, searching for something the monster would understand.

"Pa. Bring him back." Claire had drawn her rifle and aimed it.

Deckard shook in the beast's grasp as he pivoted to face his daughter. A pebble, dislodged by the movement, fell past Deckard's boots and into forever.

"You won't shoot me."

Claire thought it over. She canted the gun high and fired. Thunder roared and roared again as it echoed. The beast's hands shook. Deckard's shoulder slipped, and he dug his fingers in.

"Next one's in your head."

The Beast swung Deckard back over and dropped him into the dirt. He lay there, too weak to stand. The ground was the only safety in its dusty solidity. "You're choosing this boy over me, your father."

"I'm choosing neither of you. I cracked his good ma's head to protect you. You're the one doing all this," Claire said. Her voice gave Deckard the strength to rise. He grabbed the pedals of the Beast's bike and hauled himself up.

"What the fuck do you see in this wretch?"

"We fought alongside each other. And I love him, he's sweet and wonderful and a gentleman."

"When I was your age, I thought every one-toothed sporting woman was after my heart," the Beast said. He looked at Deckard, who'd gathered himself into a crouch. "What are you doing, boy?"

"If you shoot her, I'll tackle you and push us both over the edge," Deckard said.

"I ain't shooting my own kin. Fuck you think I am?"

"Your hands are on those railgun pistols," Deckard said.

The Beast looked down. The double-take nearly sent him off the edge anyways. He buttoned his jacket shut over his famed weapons, then turned and spat onto the wagon wreck an eternity below. He strode to his bike. "Mount up."

Deckard sat by Claire's side at dinner that night. The only comfort was feeling her pressed against him, moving and bunching up their jackets as she ate.

"Where's your daddy, boy?" the Beast said.

"Dead," Deckard said. "Yours?"

"Might be still alive, if real old. I ran away when I was fourteen," Beast said.

"My father was a good man and died because someone better got him."

"How life works out here. Your mother teaching you to shoot?" He drew out his railgun pistols and laid them on his oilskin outer blanket. Mother's railgun remained strapped to his bike.

"Unwillingly. She wanted me to finish school and get a job. I'm starting to think she was right."

"Well, when I was your age, I wanted to go out and shoot. Now, if I had the chance, I'd just sit down and run a bank," he said. He stripped off his gloves and sacrificed a few drops of water to scrub his hands. A brush and black polish appeared from a saddle bag and he began dismantling his famous weapons.

"Well, you seem awfully better at shooting than I am. When did you get started?"

A look passed between Claire and her father.

"I was a filibuster. I ran away from home and joined at the first recruiting table. We went off and raped and murdered just about every settler in our target area. Then we were ambushed, led into a pass by the promise of a settlement. I'd call our captain an idiot, but I fell for it too. Sixty-seven of us went in. Only I came out, after playing dead for two days," he said.

"Good for everyone else," Deckard said. "Except Claire." She giggled. The Beast smirked ever so briefly.

"Our side lost the war. And my face was on wanted posters everywhere. So, I got together a few of my fellow survivors and we continued the life," he said.

"I saved a little girl. Her father went crazy and massacred their entire family except her. I saved her and carried her back to an orphanage. She's sweet and adorable," Deckard said.

"Does that make you better than me?" he said.

"Yeah," Deckard said. "You kill because you were paid for it, and then for fun. You never tried to be anything else. I went out of my way to protect this little girl."

"And if I killed you and her?"

"Doesn't change that you're a monster," Deckard said. "I met a man who talked like you, once. My mother blew his head off." He realized Claire was no longer beside him. Which was understandable, because that was still her father. He wished he had any strength without her.

"Never said I wasn't. I suppose the only reason I regret being unable to settle down is because age is catching up to me at last," he said. "Time always wins." For the first time, he looked directly at Deckard. His eyes were small and blue. The face around them had been handsome once. A sharp, hawk's nose and a jagged jaw made for the kind of rugged appreciation all the girls back at school loved. They wanted themselves a frontier man. A long white scar across his left cheek proved he wasn't, in fact, invincible. His hair was neatly cut despite weeks on the trail, and even beneath the brim of his hat, a few gray flecks fell through.

Deckard slipped far back from the fire as he could, to sleep. The sky had grown black and damp with fog.

"Hey," he said. The other two were still talking at the fire, Claire huddled against a rock opposite her dad. They looked up. "Does it rain out here?"

"We've got rainy seasons. What you need to worry about is if the wind kicks up hard when the clouds roll in. That means there's a storm big enough to cause a flash flood. These mountains become river rapids," he said.

"You live out here?" Deckard said.

"I've spent a few years out here. Not recently, or I would have visited more." He patted Claire's shoulder. Another reminder that no matter what, Claire was his daughter. Deckard was alone. "I need to make up for four birthdays."

"Time for that, dad," Claire said. She withdrew a step. Her father didn't follow. He looked from her to Deckard. Something lethal flashed in his eyes. He undid his belt and laid his holsters and spare magazines at Claire's side.

"I'll be back. Keep these safe."

"Pa, I've got first watch," Claire said.

"I know. I'll be back." He drew a long, curved knife from his belt.

"The greywalkers are out there!"

"I know." He dropped his jacket and vanished into the dark. Gravel crunched off into the distance.

Deckard slid closer to the fire as the visible world seemed to retract by fragments of jagged shadow. He kept going right until he was at Claire's side. She slumped across him. "I'm scared," he said.

"Me too."

"Does he do that a lot?"

"No. He used to tell me stories around the fire until we fell asleep together. One night, it was so cold we couldn't fall asleep or we might freeze. So he made me walk in circles around the fire all night until the snow stopped. And he never ran out of stories." She lay down so her face was devastatingly close to him. He rolled to face her. Her skin glowed in the flickering firelight. Her lips were open slightly as she stared at him in awe. Her eyes were framed by black curls, as they were wide, the fire glinting in them.

"That, I wish mom did that. Instead she keeps having to save me. Thanks for saving me, by the way." Too cold to free an arm, he scraped dirt to nudge her with his forehead.

"Anything, my dear."

Something screamed in the dark. Inhuman, shrill. Claire sat up hard. "What is he doing? Pa!" She stood and stepped forwards, then stopped at the edge of the circle of the light.

The beast's pistols lay just out of reach. The handgrips glinted in the firelight. They were checkered rubber like he'd never seen before. Glinting metal at the end marked the magazines. He could grab them and kill the Beast. And then he'd have to kill Claire because she'd want to avenge her father.

He lay back and waited until she sat back down.

"He's gotten angrier since I last saw him," she said.

"Really?"

"I don't know what happened." She lay down next to him.

They were whispering when gravel crunched again. The Beast came upon them so fast they barely had time to roll away. He stared down at them, dark form outlined in the flame as his eyes flowed. Then, he sat down on the other side. "It ran from me at first blood.

"What? Did you attack a greywalker?" Claire said.

The beast laid down without answering. "I'm going to sleep. Don't die."

Chapter Fifteen:

Sam had lost the firelight that day. She found it that night and kept going through the night with revolver in hand. She stopped when her light beams dropped off the face of the earth. A quick walk forwards sent rocks skittering down a ravine. She stopped short and turned back.

Dawn revealed a break in the fangs. A river had carved a vast v-shaped valley through layers of sandstone, dark and bright. Hundreds of millions of years of rock accumulation had been cut open. Sam drew her binoculars and surveyed up and down its length.

Far ahead, a fang had been undermined and toppled over. Hundreds of feet of rock lay strewn in the valley. The river dammed and swelled until it bubbled through the gaps in the rock. Something jumped in and out with a splash.

She swung back, along the trees and scattered cacti. Directly in ahead of her and over a kilometer away, she saw something glint.

Sam found the nearest rock and tucked herself and her bike behind it. She found the spot again and put the binoculars to her eyes.

A bike leaned on its rest. Claire walked up and threw a bedroll on. Deckard followed, straining under two bags. Her son didn't look hurt from here. He'd gained a gauntness around his cheeks as the trail wore onto him, but she saw no obvious injuries. Deck turned to the left. She didn't see who he spoke to. A shadow traced itself on the ground. It turned, and a vast hat brim was outlined in the new sun.

Sam slid down the rock. Jesse's sniper rifle been too long to keep in a saddle scabbard, so she had to untie it from her bike, then pull the knit cover off the scope. By the time she'd scampered back up the rock, Claire was atop her bike. Dust billowed out as she warmed up the fans.

Sam sighted at the junction between fan and saddle, where the motor was spinning. "Range, one-thousand four hundred and fifty meters. Zero wind," she muttered as she adjusted the zoom wheel on the scope and centered the windage dead on. Then, she remembered she was using a regular rifle and aimed a centimeter higher to account for bullet drop, so her sights were settling at the base of the saddle bags. Deckard stepped into view. Sam breathed out. She didn't feel the trigger, only the weapon hammering her shoulder as it roared.

She hit the lever beneath the trigger and launched a smoking brass cartridge over her shoulder and clattering down the slope. She yanked a fresh cartridge from her belt and jammed it into the breach. Then, she hit the lever and sealed the breach shut. Finally, she popped the hammer back.

The bike rocked but Claire held on. A black hole sat in the belling fan mount. Too low. She aimed a bit higher and breathed out.

Flames burst from the hole in the engine mount. The bike swung to the right as it vomited its fans and burning motor oil out the bottom. Claire threw herself from the bike just before it hit the rock. Deckard caught her midair and lowered her. Sam smiled. Good boy.

She dropped back out of sight. Hit the lever, shove a fresh cartridge in the top. Close the lever. Pull the hammer back

She slid off the rock, kicking up a cloud of dust that she hoped no one would notice. Ducking low, she headed left to where two rocks made a natural shooting platform.

Deckard tried to lower Claire to the ground. He ended up staggering awkwardly, until her feet hit the ground and they threw themselves into a heap behind the rock. Several sharp somethings jabbed into his back. "Are you okay?" he said.

"Yeah, thank you." She rolled over and kissed him.

"Get up!" the Beast howled. He sprinted at them. Another shot roared. Beast's vast collar kicked up. He ducked low and slid into cover beside Deckard.

Deckard was hauled up and slammed face-first into the ground. A shard of rock jabbed his jaw and he felt wetness immediately. He kicked out and struggled to roll over. Beast planted a knee in his back and tied his hands behind his back.

"What are you doing?" Claire shrieked.

Twisting his head, Deckard saw her from the dust-stained stockings up, kneeling over him.

"That's his mother who you let live shooting at us. Do you trust him? Where do you think he'll run to?" Beast snapped. She fell silent "Stand guard over him." He tied Deckard's feet together and left him in the dust.

"Get me off these rocks, please," Deckard said. Claire obliged, hauling him over onto his belly and dragging him out. He saw the Beast crouched behind a rock, mother's railgun in hand. That was her weapon. He had no right to it.

Sam sighted at the puffs of dust. She settled back on her elbows and waited. The sun crept higher in the sky, and the shadows rotated with them. A wide-brimmed hat emerged from an outcropping of rocks, and she aimed there.

As she moved, movement flickered between brown branches. She fired into the center of it. Drop the lever. Jam a fresh cartridge in, seal the breach, cock the hammer. Her shoulder ached. That forty-five one-twenty had a massive kick. She brought the scope up in time to see the glint of light from another scope. Then the rock split all around her. Shards rattled off her scarf and hat. A piece of hot shrapnel got into her collar. She ducked away as another shot cracked past.

So that was what it was like, she thought as she slumped against the shattered rock. No muzzle flare, no gunsmoke. Just a crack and destruction. She rolled to her knees and slid down the rock.

The greatest problem was where her next perch would be. Stepping back, she saw the expanse of the ravine wall, until a break and shattered boulders between two fangs, as if some titanic force had blown the side of the ravine open. She mentally marked out where her bike was parked and sprinted towards that opening. It was giving up height advantage for some nice cover.

She darted low and scrabbled over the rocks. The cover she found was a sloped boulder that gave her a meter of clearance to crouch behind and aim her rifle over. She pulled out the binoculars and swept the ridge. Claire's bike lay in a smoking heap.

Movement. She aimed there. A dark ankle-boot kicked out for an instant. A black thought crossed her mind. She shook her head. That motion nearly cost her a shot as something emerged from the ruined cluster of bushes. She barely had time to catch the picture of a black hat silhouetted against dun ground before she slipped the trigger. The rifle roared and buried itself into her shoulder.

A hat rolled across the ground. Dust blew in the air. She reloaded, shifted a few yards to the left into a shadowed perch, and aimed. A green dress emerged, then retreated.

"Pa!" Claire screamed. Deckard's heart soared as the Beast went down. He twisted and dragged himself forwards. Please, he thought.

A black-clad arm emerged from the tangle of broken rocks. It grabbed a handful of gravel and hauled itself forwards. The Beast crawled out. His hat was gone. His head bled mightily from the right side, but he was very much alive.

"Pa, stay put," Claire said and leapt up.

"Stop!" he howled. She retreated.

"Lady got me. God damn, that's the closest someone's ever gotten." A smile broke across the Beast's face. His jagged mouth spread wide, showing off white teeth. "Good for her."

He hauled himself up to sitting. Took out his flask and fountained a drink through his dust-caked lips.

"Pa," Claire said.

"Stand guard, I'm fine." He followed the liquor with water. "You see my hat?"

"No," she said. "Pa, can we run?"

"She'll chase us down. That's why she took out the bike first; to make one of us walk." He scampered towards them. Then stepped over Deckard and kept going a few meters the other way. "We have to go on foot and she can just ride until she finds a comfortable position and open fire. I'll kill her now."

Deckard shifted around. His wrists ached under the thick ropes the Beast had used. As he turned, he smudged blood across the ground. "Claire. I'm bleeding," he said.

She rolled him over and pulled a handkerchief from her bag. Shaking hands blotted up the blood, then tied it around his chin.

"Water, please."

She drank half her canteen herself, then poured the rest into his mouth.

"Let me go. I'll run to mom. She'll leave with me, and we'll all go home," he said. She nodded and fished into her dress for the knife.

"Don't you dare. I need him," the Beast howled. She stopped, blade hovering tantalizingly close.

"Come on. I don't know if we'll meet again, but our parents are going to kill each other," Deckard said.

"Damnit love, if you let him go, I'll shoot him down," the Beast howled. He fired two shots off, then moved a bit further away.

"You take that shot, my mom will kill you," Deckard said.

"I'm sure she will," the Beast replied. Claire hovered over him. If she dropped the knife, it would stick Deckard through the belly. It trembled in her hands.

She lowered it back into her dress.

Sam was tempted to cross the valley on bike there. She'd seen a path that could give her a smooth ride. The water looked shallow enough to ford on bike. A shot rang out as she moved, obliterating a poor cactus just above her head. She leapt back away from the shower of shrapnel.

The railgun stayed her. When he caught her in the open, he had twenty shots. One would catch her. So, she sat back and took aim.

Based on the wreckage of the cactus and how it had blown apart, he'd moved to her left. She used the black hat, still laying in a divot where she'd blown it, as a landmark to track him. She caught a few shadows among the rock, but she didn't take the shot. There wasn't enough certainty. That could be Deck. Without the all-encompassing shadow of that blood-stained hat, she couldn't tell anymore.

Sam switched back to the hat. It was crumpled to its right, the ten-gallon head bucket caved in. A ruddiness filtered around the edge. She'd wounded the Beast. She'd been so close to killing him right there. With the railgun, he'd be dead.

When she returned to her mark, she couldn't track him against the broken ground.

"Fucking hell." She ducked out of the line of fire and into shade. The sun was high enough the temperature drop was relaxing. She took a drink of water, ate a few pieces of salted pork, and breathed for a second. Then, she circled left, around the closest fang. She crawled in amidst a tangle of brown branches, ignoring the flurry of tiny minnow lizards she disturbed by upturning their nest, and took aim over the ravine.

For long minutes there was nothing. The lizards decided she wasn't there to eat them and squirmed around her to slide back into their nest. A dactyl let out a shrieking call she'd never heard before.

The ravine cried out to her. A quick dash, and then she'd be on his side. Being a hostage, Deckard was probably tied down near the ruined bike. She could be right there.

Except, she had no advantages in kit at any range. He had all the railguns. Long range offered her the least disadvantages.

She scoured the terrain, making movements in fragments of inches. A bramble bush at nine-hundred meters had been blatantly trampled. Rustiness on sandstone looked like blood drops at a thousand meters.

He was opening the range. Forcing her to move in towards the ravine just to get a shot. There! A shadow of black between two rocks at thirteen hundred m3534w. Sam had to lean dangerously far into the open to sight at it. The rocks had been eroded into a natural V shape, and the patch of black was nestled right in the base. As she watched, it moved. Sam flicked her fingers over the zoom wheel and rolled back.

Something moved. She couldn't tell specifics, but to the right of the V, borders shifted slightly. She zoomed back in, and over five breaths shifted down and to the right. She aimed high to adjust for bullet drop.

"Sixteen-hundred twenty meters, no wind," she said. And fired.

Rock exploded, clouding her view with brown dust. A grey cloud puffed out into the open air, unveiling her position.

She didn't bother with hiding and scrabbled behind solid rock. The first shot dug the lizards out of their nest. The second blew a few of them to bits.

"Missed," she spat. Then reloaded and slipped out.

A shot immediately tore the open air around her. She withdrew but felt something burning next to her cheek. She ripped off her scarf. As it flew it split into two pieces separated by smoldering ends. Infuriated, she stamped the cinders out and bundled the two halves into her jacket.

She had to close the range.

Sam slid down the slope to the dried riverbed below. She weaved between the tufts of heavy bush, boots clapping on the dried mud. The rock dropped away and she kept moving.

Deckard saw a black speck just under the ridgeline. It dipped and wove but moved at a steady clip toward the next fang. Mom. Please.

He looked further up the ravine and saw the Beast staring him right in the eyes. He turned towards the ridge. From his position, he must be invisible behind the next fang. But he had to know. Oh no, Deckard thought. He scrabbed up on his hands and knees. "Over here!" he yelled.

The Beast only grinned as he swung mother's railgun up.

Deckard threw himself up with such force he caught his shoulder on a rock. "Mother. Get down! He's aiming at you!"

Mom disappeared behind the next fang. The Beast stepped out of cover and knelt, aiming at the spot she'd emerge. He had a gap in the rock between fang and fallen boulders, a few meters to register and shoot.

"Mother!" Deckard said and lunged out. He landed on a patch of rock that had baked in the sun all morning. It burned his skin.

A speck flashed through the gap

Sam's railgun cracked. The speck toppled forwards, and tumbled out of view, hitting every rock on the way down. Deckard threw himself forward with a scream. His forehead slammed into the rock and he rolled to the ground. He squeezed his eyes shut and curled up in a ball. He slammed his head into that rock over and over, until blood trickled down his forehead.

"Deck," Claire said. A hand gripped his shoulder. He twisted and kicked into the heavy weight of her knees. She took it wordlessly, gravel rattling as she fell back.

"Just kill me," he said. "Please. I've nothing left. I left my home and got my mother killed. If you love me just put me down," he said.

A revolver clicked. The blast never came. Deckard opened his eyes. The Beast had grabbed his daughter's revolver out of her hands. He leaned to his side. Blood trickled down his cheek and into his collar. His eyes were wild and unfocused as the adrenaline faded from his body. In the sunlight, Deckard saw how thin he was. A gust of wind could blow him over and end everything right here.

"Love, we need him. Stay down here, I'm remaining on guard until sunset. Just in case."

"Dad, your face." Claire scrabbled to the ruins of her bike. She came back with bandages. "Sit down.

He did and held the railgun across his chest as she cleaned him up.

Chapter Sixteen

Sam sprinted around the Fang. She'd already sighted her next spot of cover behind a mess of boulders precariously atop the lip of the ravine. That meant crossing ten yards of treacherous open ground, but if the Beast was still aiming at her last location, she had plenty time to cross. He should be if he was any experienced sniper.

A copse of trees, sheltered in the lee of the fang, was her last cover. These had deep blue needles, but their branches were withered by drought, gnarled by decades of standing fast in the wind. Sam went around the trees lest she disturb any branches.

A reflection glinted. A tiny speck in the distant mountains. Something flashed brown in front of her face

A hammer blow snuffed the lights from her eyes. The ground hit her over and over, throwing gravel into her open mouth. She wasn't moving, the entire world spun in darkness. Every rock rang another bell on the way down. Until with a final crash that shook her joints from her bones, she went still.

She lay there but she didn't pass out. The sun baked down on her and the dirt roasted her from below until her jacket and boots were ovens. Jagged gravel dug into her cheek, her eyelids, and something's sharp claws tore into the open side of her head. She thought it was greywalker, but it wasn't accompanied by the rest of her being devoured.

Sam could tell the sun had dipped behind the fangs, as the heat on her head faded. The ground remained a furnace. It must have glowed red hot every evening, how had she never noticed that as she rode? Her throat was dry and she felt the dust grains stuck in her teeth and down her throat. Her canteen sat on her hip, but she couldn't move to reach it.

Sam stopped thinking and darkness reigned.

When she opened her eyes, vision only returned to her right side. She craned her head up. Shadows had engulfed her in their march across the valley. The sky was a distant grey poking between the fangs. She tried to move in bits. Her fingers wiggled, her toes. She tried her left arm and found agony. So, she reached back with her right and fumbled the damn round canteen from her belt. She unscrewed it with her teeth and drank, dust and all. Once that terrible film washed away the cold water tasted delightful. She felt it slide through her all the way down.

Drinking left her too weak to move. The sun dipped lower and the ground around her turned a pale grey, with dark spots of blood.

Sam scrounged for a handhold. None offered itself, so she tensed, and with a groan hauled herself up into sitting position. With her left eye not cooperating, she had to waste more energy turning all the way about to see where she'd fallen.

A dried streambed stretched around her, populated by brown brambles and yellow grass. Painfully, she craned her neck back, and caught her bike glinting in the dying light a long walk away. The trees were far overhead, her path marked by little tracks of blood and the occasional wide stain. Where had that come from? Sam felt up her left side. Quickly, she hit blood and jagged bits of wood. She got higher, until she felt over the torn remnants of her cheek.

She had a mirror. It was cracked when she balanced it on the rocks, but the picture was clear in any light. Her left eye had disappeared beneath a massive splinter of wood, blood trickling around the white and red of the socket.

"I'm going to kill you," she spat. "I swear, you and your daughter are going into the same hole."

Sam built a fire with broken branches. Somewhere in the grass, she turned up the Peabody rifle with fresh dents all along its venerable frame and tucked it under her arm. She drew her knife and placed it in the flames, then waited as it turned red. That would ruin the true of the blade.

No alcohol. She'd seen a man die once because his fingers slipped, the splinter dug deeper, and he bled straight into his brain. She needed all senses focused.

The knife was hot in her hands. It burned on the skin of her eye. She grabbed the splinter and held it tight, so it remained in place as she slid the knife in. Her eye tightened as she howled in pain. With a hiss of flesh she wrenched it free, and screamed as some ropy things popped out with it. She froze, staring at a ruined sphere made from her own body and dangling by pieces of her own body. She shivered and it shivered with her. Her eye was gone. Inspecting the damage, she knew no surgeon could save it.

Her vision flared white as the knife seared that connection at its source. A howl tore through her. The Fangs shook around her as they took up the cry, the scream that shook the world and her. Then the knife slipped and added a hot nick down her eye socket, and she clamped up for a second, before pain stabbed in.

The knife clanged as it fell against the rocks. Sam fell back and stared up at the sky with her one eye. She didn't notice when she stopped screaming. Just that the echoing in the mountains had stopped.

Now, the alcohol went on a rag and dabbed into her eye.

She sat back up, cursing every which way under the sun and every person she'd ever met in the last year (except Wyatt and the orphanage staff.) She spat on the ground and came up with blood.

Now she went after the little fragments peppering her face and collar. They had to go before infection set in. That would kill her. Not the disease, but her body weakening until it collapsed in the saddle would get her. She'd die huddled by the side of her bike, too weak to ride, or fetch water.

Those were easier. Pinch around the wound to drag it up, then wrench the splinter free with bare fingers. A couple of the larger ones required slipping the tip of the thin blade in to jar them loose. The one lodged in her collarbone, she dug a bit into the bone beside it, twisted until it jarred loose, then wrenched it free. That required more searing, more screaming.

The mirror showed half of her. The other half had been torn open and swollen up.

She fell asleep right there, rifle in hand. Shaking on a suddenly cold patch of stone amidst the rubble of a seasonal oasis.

Dawn didn't wake her. Something deeper dragged her up in the middle of the night. Her eye opened and she shot up. Agony had torn the confidence from her reflexes and left them bare with survival instinct.

And she came face to face with a slender skull lined with four eyes down the center. In the dying embers, the eyes glowed red, unblinking pools devoid of pupils. The mouth peeled open.

Peabody's rifle snapped up so close it jammed the beast's nose. It withdrew.

She held her fire on the kill shot. Greywalkers always came in threes, and she had only one shot. Sam kicked the dying fire, scattering embers and touching off a few more sparks. A single flame flickered as air reached an untouched branch smothered beneath the ashes. She grabbed it up, ignoring the burning on her knuckles, and swung it up. The flame burst to life.

And the lithe forms of all three greywalkers leapt away. They flowed, serpentine, from their front two feet to their back two as they raced off. Three howls rang out, like dozens of screaming victims. They echoed over and over until a city of misery wailed around her.

Sam snatched her revolver and laid it on the ground. Then her knife. Greywalkers never left their prey. Out in the wilderness, they couldn't afford to let meat get away. They would keep watch in shifts, driving them until they let their guard down, or simply collapsed from exhaustion. Greywalkers would stalk humans for days, snapping up their own food from the crevices, fixating on their bigger victim. She'd hunted the beast. Now the real beasts hunted her.

Red eyes flickered in the distance. They tracked left, then right again, appearing in and out as the beasts looked up from her to track. Sam laid the rifle on her knee and waited.

The Greywalkers realized she wouldn't waste her shots on ghosts and fell still. Twelve red eyes stared out at her, three banks of four.

Sam grabbed dry grass off the ground and piled it in front of her. The branch wouldn't last forever. Where were the moons? Both were high overhead, almost atop each other.

Fuck, she wasn't sure how long until sunrise.

■■

The Beast knelt and let his daughter sear his head shut. She held him around the head with a gentle arm, and pressed the superheated knife in. Blood hissed. A guttural cry rumbled from the beast's clenched teeth. Sam lowered the knife, and pressed her forehead to his ruined hairline.

"How's it feel, pa?" she said.

"I'm fine. Now my face matches my reputation." He laughed. Claire slapped a palm to her forehead and grinned.

They separated. She sat down at the fire. He sank back on his haunches, tying the scarf back around his head. He pivoted to stare across the fire and leaned hard on his right palm. "That was the closest I've ever come to death. One centimeter closer to the mark and it would have split my skull and boiled my brains. Your mother almost got me."

Deckard stared back. His hands were bound in front, so he could take care of himself, but he couldn't survive in the wilderness. His back ached from carrying saddlebags across the Fangs.

"I've been waiting for that moment for a few years now. When someone finally bested me. She came the closest. So close. Unfortunately, if your mother's the best, I might need to wait a while longer." The Beast tipped his flask back and drank deeply.

"What does that mean? Are you trying to get yourself killed?" Claire said. "What would drive you to do that?" She lunged across and snatched up her dad's shoulder.

"You're young and have a life ahead of you. You don't understand," he said.

"You're my father. I'd like to have you around," she said.

"He's had everything taken away from his twisted soul," Deckard said. The Beast nodded. "I'd like to offer you a chance. Give me one of your sidearms. We'll draw and see who's ready to die."

The Beast didn't budge, as Claire gaped at him.

"A tempting offer. I respect you, boy. But I need you alive, so I'll refuse your invitation to suicide," he said. He sat down stably. Those railgun pistols glinted in the firelight, flat and blocky without all the chambers of a revolver. One was worn across the beast's belly in the gunslinger style. The other sat on his left hip, halfway under his body as he leaned on the rock.

"Well, fuck you, then," Deckard said, and stood.

Dozens of dying children screamed in the night. He froze to the ground as the greywalkers wailed on and on. The Beast's laughter rolled in with their hunting cries. "You can't even walk off. You have to get me to do it. Go on, then, let them have you."

Deckard sat back down and huddled to the fire. The Beast took a drink. Claire stared back and forth between them. What did she want? He didn't care. He laid back.

Except he did care. Claire was the closest thing to friendly out here and every thought clung to her like he was crawling along in her dust trail. He couldn't stop himself. Every time he tried, he remembered how warm he'd felt as they'd kissed in the hay loft.

"I recognized that ravine. We've maybe two hundred kilometers to go, so it should be a week of travel left, at most," the Beast said. No one replied until the greywalkers had ceased their cry. Somewhere out there on the backside of a ravine, tangled amongst the dry grass, they were tearing apart mother's corpse into bones and teeth marks. Her bike would lie wherever she parked it, forever.

"Is that the edge of the fangs?" Claire said.

"Nay. As we go, the fangs are broken up by the great north rivers. Think of it as an inlet, but it's near the edge," he said. "There was a town there for twenty years, a farmer's republic like the valley I left you in. It was the covenanter's previous victim."

"Were you working with the covenanters?" Deckard shouted out. Claire stared at her father.

"I was working for the guy who founded and paid for them. I was running my own errand north when he sent them out. He sent me out to reinforce them. Not my plan. Never, for you, or any of the only people who showed me friendship," the Beast said.

"They wiped out an entire caravan of families," Deckard said.

"Why are you taking us back to him when you betrayed him?" Claire said.

The Beast shook his head at Deckard.

"You can say you don't care. I reckon you've got a mountain of corpses," he said.

"Yeah, you kill enough you stop noticing. Has your mother told you that?" he said. That didn't answer the question.

"She doesn't commit murder."

"I'm sure not with you around," the Beast said. "And, love, he doesn't care about things like bands of filibusters. I just saved him from paying a lot of salary. He'll be fine," she said.

"I'm not," she said, and scooted back a step. She hiked her knees up to her chest and buried herself into her dress. The Beast reached over and tugged her bonnet down over her eyes. "Hey." She grabbed it back up and only succeeded in tangling her curls. She flailed about as the Beast chuckled. He burst into coughing right as she finished.

And the coughing didn't stop, he hacked away until Claire slapped his back.

"Thanks." He lit his pipe.

Claire slipped back in and snuggled against him.

"You're shivering." He pulled off his duster and draped it around her shoulders. He leaned over and took the time to do up every button and lace the collar around her. "You take second watch tonight. Get some sleep."

She nodded. "This is real comfy. No wonder you always go around dressed in black."

"Yeah, I got that from a fine tailor in exchange for a job. No labels, everything silk and fleece lining. I've been meaning to get you a dress from there, they do ladies and gentlemen," he said, and patted her shoulders. She giggled and snuggled against him.

Deckard slumped on his back and stared into the stars. He saw mom staring back at him. *Shouldn't have come out here. Just finish school,* she snapped at him.

I'm so sorry, mother, I'm so sorry.

Chapter Seventeen:

Dawn laughed at Sam as she lay curled in the dust. Long after the greywalkers withdrew, she rose to her feet. The fangs swayed and she caught herself on a stumble. The valley wasn't safe. Patches of eternal shadow lurked in the corners. She couldn't see her hunters but she knew they were there. One was always awake, watching her.

A look back shocked her at how much blood she'd lost. In daylight, the hill she'd rolled down was positively streaked with rust. The dust around it was carved up by three-clawed footprints, elongated as the greywalkers loped past.

All that because she shot Tow then, instead of waiting until they got into town, she thought. She spat into the dirt.

He'd said that Greywalkers didn't like water. A monster like him might know a thing or two about them. Except there was no water around.

There was a set time until the sun went down. Sam holstered her revolver and clutched the Peabody in both hands as her lifeline. She didn't even look in the mirror when she picked it up.

She found her bike nestled under the rock where she'd taken her first shot from. A long brass cartridge stuck open-end up out of the dirt beneath it as an exclamation point to her failure. She snatched it up.

The bike ran fine as she edged into the ravine, floated across the rocks just below the surface (refilling her canteens on the way), and clambered up the other side. It stopped halfway. The fan whined and churned dust. She kept pushing until the bike screamed and shivered under her.

Sam backed down. She crossed the valley, then turned around and gunned the throttle. The valley roared up, then tilted back as she climbed the side. She swung right, then left. Her bike slowed, engine growing in volume until it howled and chewed the air. The entire seat grew hot under her.

"Fuck." She cut the throttle and fell back to the riverbed. Her bike coughed and dropped down. She killed the engines and kicked out the stand into the dried, compacted mud to give them a chance to cool down. And her a chance to survey.

While on the side she'd come from, the ravine sloped heavily but raggedly, with lots of uneven ground for her fans to get a grip. On the other side, the sandstone had broken away outright to reveal a striped face of different ages of sandstone canted at a heavy angle. It stretched on in either direction as far as she could see.

She thought about hauling the bike up. She had some finely woven rope, and there were a few rocks she could loop it around.

Too risky. She wasn't strong enough to haul sixty kilos of bike up thirty meters.

She turned left—the direction the Beast had shot her from—and gunned the throttle. The riverbed was ragged with boulders and vegetation, but the mud had dried out and it made easy purchase for her high-performance fans. She had to keep the throttle down as her vision couldn't keep up.

By nightfall, the granite face had sloped a bit, but remained a solid twenty meters overhead. She pulled up next to a copse of spiky green trees and dismounted to make camp.

A howl rose up. The ravine acted like a tunnel and blew the greywalker's cry towards her. A second came from that way. Then a third, almost on top of her and above.

Sam grabbed her newspaper and lit it up without thinking. She ripped two branches off the ground and ignited hem right there without clearing the site. The flames flickered up, revealing a dark shape creeping across the stream, slowly to avoid splashing.

Sam grabbed her rifle, and with a splash the greywalker leapt out the other side and scampered for cover. She didn't try a shot. She only had one. The red eyes peaked out between towering shadows of a crease in the ravine. They stared at each other in their eternal standoff. A life for a life. Greywalkers could form bonds and feel loss. Killing one would set the other two on you.

Soon she heard a massive, mangled lump of branches crackling. The greywalkers circled. She couldn't see them, but she heard the occasional click of talons on exposed rock. She didn't sleep that night.

The sun burned holes in her vision when she climbed on her bike the next day. She had to tip her hat low and proceed at steady pace.

The ravine widened into a veritable floodplain, barely damp, and the sandstone fell further. If she were rested, then she'd have tried hauling her bike up now.

A fang sprouted from the center of the ravine. It was fat and unyielding. The river trickled around it. Flood stains and dead moss rose ten meters up its length. Sam tipped the steering bar and swerved around the long way, avoiding the stream.

A bleached metal hull lay upended in the river. It was a bare structure, an axle for wheels and a solid frame. A few rotted wooden furnishings lay inside. Sam slowed to a stop. This had once been a wagon, an old one with a towing axle for a tractor or some other vehicle to drag it along. She puttered around it.

Wagons lay in a bonefield all through the flood plain. Two had gotten stuck in the river flow itself and subsided up to their roofs. The rest were stripped by nature. Sam pulled up in the middle of them and leapt off. She landed in a patch of grass, and something crunched under her boot.

Sam knew what it was before she had pulled the dismembered half-ribcage out. She fished around with her fingers and closed around the eye sockets of a skull. A morbid curiosity overwhelmed her, and she soon had the upper half of a petite figure. A rusted-out revolver lay amidst her findings, six bullets still lodged in the chambers.

Sam left the young man, or woman, to rest and strode around the wagons. Fingers reached out from another overturned wagon. She saw crates, and shattered plates. A silver spoon lay shining just below the surface of the river. A crayfish circled the light.

Sam flicked her wrist and snatched the cray fish up by knife tip. She finished it as she looked among the wreckage. Lots of wagons, but no tractors.

She found the tractors piled up where the ravine was at its lowest before climbing up again. Three tractors formed a rusted base of sorts, and someone had leaned wagons up against them, reaching two-thirds of the way up to safety. Over the decades, mud had caked around their wheels and dried.

Sam sprinted forwards and stopped. Around the tractors the bones lay in great quantities. They reached out in arms and legs for each other as they held on against the decades of weather threatening to scatter them forever. They came in all sizes down to the slender bones of children, wrapped in the larger bones of parents. One was strapped into the driver's seat of the tractor, a rifle and ammo bandolier strapped across the blackened remains of his shirt. Under that tractor she overturned the remnants of a wooden ladder.

That settled her hypothesis; they'd all been caught here. If the summer rains were as bad as Jesse said, it would have ended in minutes. Maybe they'd found the ravine as impassible as she did with their heavy wagons, and travelled along the harmless river for a safer passage. The weather would have caught them, and the flash floods drowned them all in minutes.

Hours. They'd known what was coming and built their escape. The planet had been too fast for them.

There was no use searching for supplies in a ruin this old, but Sam tried anyways. The weapons were all rusted shut and liable to explode if their barrels were still open. The clothes were remnants. She found a belt buckle and picked it up. Faintly, holding it up to the afternoon light, she saw an embossed 'J'.

Sam ran through the wagons until she found another J on the side of a wagon.

"Johbert," she said to herself.

Night was closing but fuck camping here. She scaled their ladder with rope over her shoulder and picked her way up the burning face. She found a great rock and looped it around.

She strained on the rope. Her bike lifted off the ground and crept up. She rested it on the tractors and sat down to breathe. She was sweaty under her jacket. Her fingers were bloody. She pulled out the halves of the bandanna and tied them around her hands, then resumed pulling.

The bike rested again atop the last wagon. The entire pile shifted. Sam rocked on her feet.

"No, fuck you," she spat and wrenched the bike up. She kept going until it lodged above the ridge.

Then came the hard part. She tied the rope off and scampered up it, slipping every few steps but not daring to slow down. Up top, she wrenched the bike over the top, and with a gasp, collapsed. It clattered down at her feet. She gasped for air. The twilight reached out to her from all sides.

She grabbed the sticks out of her pocket and built a quick fire. With her back to the edge, the greywalkers could only come from one direction. There were no trees, but by the time the sun set she had a massive pile of brambles and grass.

A set of red eyes glowed in the night, a dozen meters above her and in the distance.

Chapter Eighteen:

Sam napped for an hour in the morning. She'd leave an hour at sunset to cut down wood and eat. That cut down her travel time. This wasn't about hunting the beast down anymore. She was tracking him to wherever his destination was. Then she'd kill him and Claire and take her boy home.

She backtracked up the river until she found the Beast's old position. He'd stripped the destroyed bike of anything useful and left it on its side right on the trail, surrounded by prints from Deckard's big boots, Claire's smaller heeled boots, and his own fairly large print. Just a few meters beyond, a dried splash of blood behind a rock, and a shred of black fabric flickering and impaled on a cactus.

"I can bleed you," Sam muttered.

The wind felt strange driving into her empty socket. Like it was trying to pry into her brain. She tied half the scarf around it and tucked it under her hat.

She made good progress. The footprints were easily visible along the way, as was the pile of tobacco where someone had tapped out his pipe. She camped for the night by a pair of trees, alongside a sheer cliff a hundred yards high at least.

This time she built a sizeable pile of wood, and stacked logs far from it, then lit it up just as the sky turned from grey to black.

She cooked her dinner properly and waited. The loudest sound, above the crackling logs and bubbling beans, was her heart hammering in her ears.

Something hard tumbled to her right. She spun and saw a set of red eyes, a log in its mouth. It stared at her, fangs jutting over the log, looking like a smug child, delighted with the cookie they'd stolen from the jar.

She drew the revolver and fired two shots after it. It hissed and the log clattered into darkness. Half her pile was gone. The rest were terrifyingly little to last a night. Sam could only haul them closer to her. She heard a single footstep on the other side.

And fired without looking. The second greywalker averted course and raced off into the dark. Sam spat after it. Then broke open her revolver cylinder at the hinge and replaced the three wasted cartridges. Two sets of red eyes stared at her out of the darkness. In the flickering flames, she saw the outline of one of her lost logs, leaning against a rock on the edge of darkness.

"Fuck you," she muttered. "I left you a whole nest of lizards back there. Go eat those."

Once, she'd gone hunting greywalkers. Her group had left animal bait and they hadn't bit. Then, they'd dragged out the body of a drowning victim and left the body in the trap. The greywalker came. The lizards belonged here. Humans, goats, and chickens did not. Greywalkers always went after humans and their preferred domestic livestock. They'd driven sheep farms out of the frontier entirely, along with any free ranging animal that could be picked off en masse. She wondered if some instinct in that reptilian brain knew what belonged and what didn't.

Or, worse, that the greywalkers had had a thought about it.

Sam had a theory. She stood, backed up all the way to the edge, and took a quick peep down. Then leapt back. Her boot caught a rock and she fell. Her elbows hit the ground hard, but her aim kept true at the two closing sets of red eyes.

There, frozen in the single image she'd taken of the cliff face, was the third greywalker's red eyes, pacing far below.

When she refocused, the two red eyes were gone. They were out there. She didn't see them or hear them, but they were there.

Greywalkers couldn't be hunted in the open night. They had to be tracked back to their burrows by day and burnt out. Sam huddled behind her fire, adding logs whenever it got low. And waited.

She made it to sunrise. Her limbs were heavy and when she stood, she stumbled and nearly did their work over the cliff.

The last log was gone. The ground had been scoured clean of tracks by their tails, so she couldn't track them if she wanted to.

Breakfast was her last bit of beans, eaten cold as she rode. Lunch was a single salted biscuit. To keep her on her bike. When the sun was highest, she stopped right on the trail and threw herself down, heedless of the dust painting her back yellow. Her arms were the comfiest pillow she'd ever experienced.

The screams of dozens dragged her up. She stood in the combined bedroom of a mining family's little hovel. Five beds, five stains of blood. Five sets of eyes wide in terror. She walked the wall. Two little boys. A girl who looked like she'd died without waking. Two parents with tears still wet on their cheeks.

And the single clawmark scraped onto the dirt floor. Where the greywalkers had left.

She awoke with a start and swung the Peabody up off her chest. The lone greywalker leapt sideways and raced off the trail. Sam rolled and took aim, but by the time she'd gotten a sight picture, the predator was a tail disappearing behind a stand of cacti. It left a single footprint in the dust. Three toes.

They wouldn't let her sleep.

She'd been there. The town of Navarya had burnt three greywalkers in their nest. Except, there had been another nest. So they'd come in the night and taken their revenge. And now, they wouldn't let her sleep. Oh yeah, they could think. And they'd been here long before humans had arrived.

Spotting a bush, she got an idea.

Sam set it ablaze and stabbed at the lizards that skittered free. She got four.

They made a filling dinner after she roasted them on the fire with her captive audience. She tossed the bones at their feet.

"Choke on them, reptile scum," she said.

A crunch disappointed her.

The trail straightened the next day into a facsimile of a road. When she found a longer stretch, she throttled down the engine and dozed in the saddle. She awoke to the jolt as the steering fans hit rough rock and bounced her away.

Dinner was half the remaining salted biscuits. A soft slick chewing told her the greywalkers had found their own game. One to stalk, two to maintain supplies. God forbid they learned collective government, they were already working like a good army.

She caught a nice, long stretch of riverbank and napped a good fifteen minutes along its length. When she awoke, she saw crawfish struggling against the current, forced near the surface by the bend. She stopped and leapt down.

Her knife had split the carapace and given her easy access. It was a matter of boiling everything, then scooping out the innards with her fork. A decent dinner. With an audience.

Sam was suddenly face down in the empty shell as endless fangs lunged across the fire at her. She snatched coals from the fire and hurled them every direction, heedless of the burns going down her arm and ash lighting on her face.

The greywalkers withdrew and the cinders died out. She grabbed a fresh branch and the fire burst bright for a few moments. Then, she threw the shell at them. The revolver remained in her lap, her rifle across her waist, attached by its sling around her.

They swarmed. She snatched more coals and swung them about. Her campsite resembled a volcano as she threw fire forth. The monsters withdrew. One lay down just out of view, tempting her for a shot.

He sat down on the other side of the fire. "I always wanted a khola crawfish. How was it?" he said.

"Sweeter than I expected," Sam said.

"Yeah. The water up here is probably pure snow melt. No salt to get in through their shells," he said. He looked around him. "Sam, I once was standing naked in the snow, with a guy pointing a revolver at me."

"I know," she said. "Are you telling me I can't make it, or I can?"

He lit a cigarette in the fire and puffed once. "I think you already lost when you took that branch to the face. You're down and have a lot more than a revolver pointed at you."

"Thanks for the support," she said. Cold rushed into her from the inside out. "Hell happened to you?"

"I picked on someone better than me and died for it, and almost got our son killed," he said. He blew a smoke ring of perfect shape at her. She let it land on her forehead.

"Well, that was you walking into danger. I didn't fucking choose this. Filibusters, and an outlaw chose to come here," she said. Maybe she should have waited another day and crept up to the beast at night. Once again, she stared at the shadow of the Beast, as his daughter clambered onto her bike. What could she have done differently?

"Sam!" he howled.

She fell back and fired her revolver without thinking. Red eyes, flashing dust, all blinded by the muzzle flare of the three-eighty.

The trigger kept clicking long after they'd withdrawn. Sam cracked it open and shook out the empty cartridges. They clinked off the dirt and rolled away. She had ten shots left of .38 pistol ammo, and twelve of the massively longer 45-110 rounds.

"Thanks," she muttered. "Don't hold any bullets on you?"

"No, I don't." He held up empty hands. "You've lost the trail of our son, haven't you?"

"No. According to Jesse's information, there's a river somewhere." All the information faded away beneath the blanket of sleep. "I can't find all this shit, okay? I've got to get our son back, and that's all that matters."

"Can you? He already beat you at your best. Now you're far away and surrounded by monsters." He spread his arms. Red eyes flickered at his fingertips. They were out there. Waiting.

"I don't care. That's my son," she said. "I'm picking up the damage you did with your stupidity."

He stood and walked off into the night. She saw his dark form against lighter ground. Until he climbed the river bank and disappeared over the side.

Sunrise. Sam followed the trail. Until it split into half a dozen slivers of plateau and disappeared into rock.

Sam ventured down each of them in search of signs of life. She had nothing. There were no footprints left to follow. The only bike tracks were her own heading back towards the valley. Among them walked a few three-toed tracks.

New plan. Take the fight to this fucking hellscape. Valery had gathered the morning after the attack for a vote. Unanimously, they'd agreed to fight. So, they hired everyone around. Sam, Valerie, and a dozen Marshals followed the tracks back into the hills. The first night, they'd lost one man to the greywalkers and killed zero in return. And learned there were two pods out there working in tandem.

Sam returned to her old campsite by the ravine that night. She piled wood high on either flank, then scattered brown brambles around the ground beyond them. Then, she lit them up. The only path was right down the middle into her guns. Then, as the sun set, she laid on her back and amused herself tossing her remaining biscuits up one by one and catching them in her mouth.

Dry brambles crackled on the ground.

"Hey," she said and propped herself on her elbows.

"Hey," he said, and sat down.

"Tell me. When we got married, did you think it would go down this way?"

"No, love. I was eighteen and I thought we were invincible. If this was a world where we could find each other, how could we ever lose?" He raised a fist and studied his wedding ring. They hadn't the money for gold. So, he'd ordered matching sets of twisted silver. Years later, he'd added the emerald to hers, after a particular profitable summer.

"What about when I had Deck?"

"This place eats the weak and nothing's more helpless than a babe suckling at its mother. After he turned five and survived that fever, when he was safe and strong, I figured we'd all be fine," he said. "And I figured he could follow in our life one day."

"Even when he learned his letters at six?" she said.

"I was a bit rigid. Riding got my family for three generations. It seemed like the only way. What did your family do?"

"The orphanage wouldn't tell me. They said it wasn't important, save that they'd rescued me from a much worse state," she said. "I swear, a couple different choices and I'd be leading a gang of rescued orphans, torching men and women of the cloth." She made sure her rifle was still balanced on her chest. Shooting reverse prone was a certified position at the shooting competitions. When she looked up, he was gone.

"Don't worry, I'm getting him back," she said. Then, closed her eyes.

They were on her by the time she'd opened. She launched the first ember right at their feet.

The ground ignited. Brambles crackled all around. A yelp split the air. Not the howling, but a singular screech of pain from a wounded beast. She snatched up her rifle, but that one was gone. She had to swing her whole body to see the other two, and by then they were racing away, trailing embers.

She grinned over the flames and lay back down. "Choke on that."

The second night in Valery, the posse had burned the entire forest down. A drought had driven the greywalkers to the town initially. Now the dry heat let the fire spread. And those reptilian brains realized there was nothing left but to fight.

And the town had won. Sam closed her eyes and fell right to sleep.

Chapter Nineteen:

Sam awoke at sunrise. A full night of sleep hadn't been enough. The bare dusty rock was too comfy. She had to think of Deckard alone and tied up to force herself to her feet. Her limbs were heavy. Climbing onto her bike was like lifting iron. She slumped in her saddle and closed her eyes. Her hands itched with fresh scabs. Her eye ached. A dozen spots along her neck ached, and her back was locked up.

Yet, she found a little fire deep inside. She'd outsmarted the beasts. And dug the Fang's dead out from the dust. They could do this. She and her bike and Jesse's borrowed rifle. She opened her eyes. Dust flaked off the bike as she keyed the engine. It roared to life, the high-performance engine finding new life.

She found the Setbow river the next morning. The fang directly behind her was a two-stepped mountain with a broad top. Definitely a molar. She got up there and surveyed the landscape with her rifle's scope. In the distance, a dark patch of green spread between the fangs, disappearing behind each mountain and yet emerging undaunted from beyond the other side. From there she traced the route with ease. A smile crossed her face.

As she clambered down, she saw fresh three-clawed footprints in the dust.

Crossing open ground from point A to B was a challenge. A ravine yawned halfway over, forcing her to turn aside and find a different route. Except, a fang rose and forced her to break contact. She stopped halfway around and came back to the edge.

The gap was barely twenty feet. The drop, dozens. A skeleton of some larger reptile lay smashed at the bottom, picked clean and white.

"You've taken leave of your senses," Sam muttered as she backed away from the lip. "Survive all this just to commit suicide on the rocks." She picked a cactus about a hundred paces back and turned around there. Then stood up in her stirrups to get final ranging.

"Seven meters. Wind is twelve kilometers an hour dead right." She stared at the dark gap.

Then yanked the throttle all the way down. The bike roared as its vast engine finally stretched its legs. High performance fans screamed through dust and rock as they surged her forwards. Dust blew out all behind her. Immediately she ducked low and let the wind paste her right to her steering bar.

The ledge came roaring up. Immediately there was no room for second guesses, as there wouldn't be enough time to stop. So, she grabbed her rifle to be sure and pressed her chin right to the handlebar. She hit the lip of the fang and bounced around as the bike raced up the hill. Only for her weight to vanish as she left the ground.

The ravine split far below. Hundreds of layers of different hued sandstone, compressed by millions of years only to be split open by sudden geological anger. The air was clear as she left the dust behind.

At the last instant before landing, she switched the fans to full reverse.

Then she slammed into the ground and bounced up. A fang rushed up to smash her.

With a shout, Sam spun the bike sideways and leaned against it. Her engine cowling and steering bars scraped on the ground, throwing up dust and sparks as they hit bare rock. She came to a halt with legs straddling her bike, staring back over the edge she'd just left.

When her heart finished pounding, she switched her bike back on and hovered off down the trail.

■■■

The fangs ended abruptly. It was like emerging from a curtain of bare rock and seeing a forest of lush blues and greens. Deckard heard the river but couldn't see it through the trees.

He stopped and looked back. The fangs loomed in the darkening sky like a wall of doom, and he followed them all the way around. Even beyond the trees they poked up.

"Like I said, out here the fangs are broken up by the major rivers. A couple decades ago, the city of Jarwei tried to settle up here. It went bad. Loggers got eaten by greywalkers, another war started, and they couldn't fund the settlers," the Beast said. Deckard absorbed it all but didn't answer.

The air grew hotter in direct sunlight. Deckard undid his jacket and let it hang open. The fine white shirt he'd gotten from Matt had been soiled around the collar by weeks of dust. He'd certainly smell bad if he could still smell it. Perhaps the river was safe for swimming.

"Is this our goal?" Claire said, removing her outer jacket and slinging it onto the bike. They'd taken to hauling all their bags on the Beast's unflappable ride and walking alongside.

"Nay, we've got a ferry ride ahead of us."

"Can we swim?"

"There's running water and soap where we're ending up, promise," the Beast said and patted her back. With a surprised look, he pinched her shoulder. "You've picked up some muscle."

"Well, working in the fields tends to build one's back and legs," she said. "You look skinnier than I remember? Have you been eating alright?"

"Been a long winter," he said and burst into that deep, sickly cough, and that was the end of that conversation.

Deckard saw some familiar tracks as they strode through the trees. That grazer they'd tracked. He forgot the name. Maybe if he ran here and got a rifle somehow.

Mother's bare skull lay way back in the Fangs, staring forever ahead. Scraped with tiny teeth marks from the greywalkers that had chewed up her skin and flesh and muscle beneath. In school, they'd dissected dead krowkers, tiny six-legged amphibians that flitted about the river piers. That was mom now. He shivered. How could he survive where she'd failed? The trees loomed in, and the fangs rose beyond on all sides.

"Stop fidgeting," the Beast said and clapped him on the shoulder. Deckard settled back to a walk without words.

"Who goes there!" a dry voice cried. The Beast held up a hand.

"It is I, the Beast, returning from my ride to report to our master," he said. The man that emerged looked barely older than Deckard. His beard was scraggly and half grown, his jacket hanging open to reveal a white undershirt. He carried a single shot rifle with a bit of rust across the barrel. The white-handled revolver at his hip looked brand new by comparison. Not even dust in the grip.

He stared at them dimly, jaw hanging open.

"May we pass?" the Beast said.

"I was told to look for a tall man with a black hat. You do not have a black hat," he said. He stumbled over every word.

"Here." The Beast plucked the remains of his famous cover and waved it.

"You're not wearing it. The instructions said you'd be wearing it. Therefore, you cannot be the man I was told to look for."

Deckard had to bite his tongue to keep from laughing. At the Beast, who'd suddenly gone red with frustration.

"Son. I have his signature pistols. I ride the bike. I know where Captain Robinson and her dear mother are," he said.

"That does not matter. I have instructions. A sentry on watch does not relinquish his guard," the man said.

"So, go get someone else."

"I cannot leave my post. We will wait until my relief arrives at sundown," he said.

"You're serious," the Beast said and took a step forward.

The man stepped back and snapped his rifle to his shoulder in one fluid motion. "Listen mister. I-I don't know what you're trying to pull here, but you are not the man I was told to look for. So you're going to stay right here until we can get someone higher up to look at you."

Deckard burst into laughter. He coughed, then let his laughter hit the most high-pitched obnoxious note. Twice, he'd been caned for laughing like this in school. All three of them stared at him. All he could do was point at the Beast, to clarify whose misery he was laughing at. Even when he fell down on his rear he kept laughing.

Claire sat down opposite and stared at him.

Deckard kept laughing long as he could, knowing he was keeping the poor sentinel alive. Maybe he could get the Beast to kill him in frustration, instead.

Until some heavy boots crunched through the undergrowth.

"What is the situation?" a woman said. She was tall, with a mousy face that made her look in her mid-twenties at most.

"Captain Robinson. These three were claiming to be the Beast of the East, but they don't match the description," the sentry said.

"Let me see that." While this was going on, Deckard just glared at Claire. You got what you want, he tried to tell her with that glare. Choke on it.

Captain Robinson slapped the sentry over and over, doubling him over. "Damn Lamont you idiot fuck. Does that look like the Beast? Yes, it fucking does. You've seen him before. Who gave you this job? You're supposed to fucking think and you can't even do that." She kicked him right in the ass, making him howl. Claire covered her ears and cringed. Deckard just glared deeper.

"Sorry, miss."

"Go back to your fucking post. You're worse than having noone out here," she said. The man stumbled off, clutching his rifle like a lifeline.

There were frantic apologies. This new woman wore a smart suit of men's clothes. She wore grey breeches tucked into knee-high boots, and a white button-down blouse. A red scarf was wrapped around her shoulders. Deckard stopped laughing on a dime. Claire glared at him.

"Well, welcome back Beast." She bowed low, scarf fluttering around her. "I never got your name."

"You won't," the Beast said.

"What happened to the filibusters? We'd hoped to hear about our new conquest by now."

"They're not coming. The farmers proved tougher," he said.

She shook her head. "We sent an army. You're telling me they were wiped out by a group of dirt farmers with their grandfather's rifles.

"And I warned you not to underestimate anyone thriving that far from civilization. They're excellent shots with veteran experience and knowledge of the terrain, while your filibusters are city folk used to gunning down lone homesteads. And they got some help from a gunslinger with this railgun," he said.

Captain Robinson's eyes went wide at mother's weapon.

"I killed her and took it, but it was over by that point. You should have sent a bigger filibustering party," Beast said. He walked past her. "Is Bogdan still here with his boat?"

"He'll never leave," she said. She put a hand over her mouth and shook her head. Her eyes lit on Deckard "Fuck is this welp here for?"

Deckard guessed her maybe eight or ten years older than him. Then he saw the river and lost track. Deep black water flowed clean. A few fish leapt from it and splashed back in. Deckard's stomach rumbled.

Bogdan's boat was a sizeable launch with benches enough for all of them. Bogdan himself was a scrawny man of the same peaked eyes and black hair as the Beast. He cast out the sail and steered with a rope attached to it. Deckard leaned out and felt the cool breeze blow across his cheeks. It smelled clean and fresh, free of the dry dust and pollen he'd gotten used to this year.

"You look a bit lost," someone said. Deckard nearly jumped, then realized Bogdan was speaking to him. He nodded, then settled back into his seat.

"Well, there's two of us." Bogdan stood up straight, balancing impossibly on the rocking boat. He canted his neck back the way they'd come and sniffed the air. "Look at those dark clouds. Storms coming tonight. Winds and floodwaters to blow us all away." When he sat down, he patted Deckard's shoulder.

Something fell out of his hand and into Deckard's lap. Deck scooped it in his hands and clutched it tight.

They hit the other bank and Bogdan leapt out. As he hauled the boat into ground, every muscle in his back stood out through his shirt.

The banks rose with lush blue grass. The village sat on the other side, hidden from view by the river. Two streets unified a silent collection of houses. Dark windows stared out from under sod roofs like a skull's empty eyes. The wind whistled as it swung doors open and shut. A tiny parish sat in stone, bell hanging on a tripod over the roof.

They strode past the cemetery. All the graves had been smashed and left in the dust.

"You don't live here?" Deckard said to Captain Robinson.

"No. This place is filled with ghosts. Our camp's around the gold mine," she said.

"You created the ghosts," Deckard said, and spat on her shining new boots.

She snapped and a revolver came up to Deckard's forehead. He withdrew a step.

"Yeah, easy to make jabs when you don't have a gun in your face, isn't it?" she said, grinning.

"Put that gun down and cut me loose, let's find out," Deckard said.

"Why would I do that?"

"None of you are doing anything. I need him alive," the Beast said. Robinson shoved her revolver away. She hurried to the front of the line. Deckard spat after her. Now, with all eyes off of him, he opened his hands.

Sitting in his hand was a tiny razor. It wasn't metal—it looked more like bone. He shoved it into his jacket pocket. Thanks.

They continued through a copse of trees. The camp was a line of freshly built cabins, guarded by a proper palisade that formed a semi-circle. Between them, a host of metal pipes rose from the ground. A handful of men and women lounged about.

"Make way," Robinson cried. They saw who was coming and scattered. Robinson strutted down the street and stopped them at the mine entrance itself, a gaping hole in the ground. "She's moved her quarters down here now that the rainy season's started," Robinson said.

The sky flashed bright. Deckard saw a scar running down the Beast's throat. He caught his breath.

Thunder boomed. Robinson spung about. Deckard followed her gaze. The clouds rose like a true mountain of their own, black and towering overhead. Beneath them, sheets of rain fell so thick the fangs were awash in water.

"Cover up!" Robinson bellowed. Hatches came out and tarps were thrown over the exposed bikes. The mine entrance was sealed by two oiled shutters of wood.

"Beast. This will have to wait," she said. "Do you want to be put up in the hotel?"

"I can't wait. Take the children to the hotel and put them in separate rooms. Keep him under guard," Beast said and pointed at Deckard.

The door swung back open. The woman who rose out of it wore a dress of white, tied about the waist by a sash of red. Her hair was done up in excessive blonde curls, under a feathered hat Deckard knew could only have been ordered from a city's most expensive catalog. Nothing about her belonged out here. That much had he learned. That made him terrified and he shivered as she stared at him. Someone who could dress like that and be strong enough to exist out here. That terrified him.

"Hello, mother," Captain Robinson said.

"My dear Marienne. Who are you to send a guest away? I'm always free," she said. She strode up. "Beast. Good to see you back. Have you received word from my filibustering party?"

"They're all dead. I warned you several times over," the Beast said.

Emma scowled. "You should have warned louder." Deckard was shocked at her superficial anger.

"Who are your guests?" she said.

He took Claire by the shoulder and spun her around. She grinned faintly. "This is my daughter, Claire. And this." He seized Deckard by the hair. Deckard scrabbled at his hands. "This is my sacrifice. I come to use the machine."

What? The shock froze Deckard. What the hell was he sacrificing? "What are you doing?" he said.

Emma chuckled. Her makeup cracked along the worry lines on her face. "You didn't tell him? Should I now?"

"What are you doing?" Deckard said and fought free of the Beast's grasp. He spun about. There were a dozen soldiers standing around them, smirking at him.

"Pa, what did you do?" Claire said and reached for Deckard. He leapt away from her.

"I'll tell him," Emma said. "Boy. In the basement of this here graphite mine, we found a machine that had been buried by our ancestors. I don't know why they'd bury such a powerful device, but we dug it up. It heals people from the brink of death. Only, it can't produce new flesh. It can only take from a healthy source to an injured one. And it can't be a willing sacrifice, though I'm not sure why that is. Perhaps our ancestors were fans of sadism," she said with an ugly chuckle. "Anyways. The priests of the Second Covenant, and the industrialists they support have paid tens of thousands each to heal themselves. And there are always sacrifices."

Deckard gaped.

"The Beast is invincible in a gunfight, but he's still flesh and bones that can grow warped and diseased. So, you're going to be stripped to your bones to restore him," she said. She chuckled smoothly.

"Pa, what the hell is wrong with you?" Claire punched her father. He stumbled half a step back and held up an arm to block her next swing at his throat. He caught her by the wrist as she wound up again and twisted it behind her back.

"Love. This is something I have to do to keep myself alive. I know if you were in my place you'd do it, too."

"No, I fucking wouldn't," she said and kicked at him. "Give me the railgun. I'll put them all down." The Beast spun her around so she had her back to him. Captain Robinson burst into laughter. Emma and the rest looked away. Deckard couldn't. He could only watch the monster who'd taken him all this way just to offer him as a sacrifice.

"You haven't looked death in the face like I have. And you don't have a kid waiting for you," the Beast said.

"You're sick with something and you haven't come and seen me for five years, don't tell me that," Claire said and elbowed him. He took it silently.

Deckard just looked from them to Emma, who was frowning at the spectacle. There was nothing left for him here, just these monsters.

"Beast. I'll stow your charges in the hotel and put them under guard. We just used the machine. It needs a week to recover."

"That will do." the Beast said. Claire had given up and slumped against his side, sobbing. He stroked her back. "Don't worry, love." She shoved him away, and only fell to ground.

The soldiers came for Deckard. He punched the first and was proud that the man staggered back and fell to the ground. The second buried her rifle butt into his gut and he doubled over. Breath wouldn't come, his lungs just wouldn't expand. They cuffed him behind his back. They even waited until he could wheeze down air before hauling him up.

Chapter Twenty:

The sky tore open and water poured right through the roof of the world. It hammered Sam into the saddle. She tipped her hat forward, sacrificing the back of her neck for some clearance over her eyes. Ahead, the fangs receded into jagged shadows rising and falling with the terrain. The ground around her sloshed brown as dusty earth struggled to take in any water and the hard rock below offered no relief. A tree on her right surged with the current, then stopped. Beneath the rapidly receding ground, she saw a vast network of roots going straight to the rock.

Airborne, Sam had no respite. She trundled on at a slow pace. Until the road took a dip off her current ridge and vanished. The river had risen up past its banks and flooded into the surrounding valleys. A horde of little lizards scurried past her to high ground, splashing furiously.

Sam turned back. She found a gap in the nearest fang and stepped through the sheet of water. A tiny patch of soft earth met her. She poked the walls with the peabody's barrel, finger on the trigger. After making sure those were the walls and not shadows of a deeper tunnel, she slipped inside.

Her bike wouldn't fit, so she was soaked to the bone as she spread her oilskin blanket over it and hauled her saddle bags in. She had a bit of salted pork and felt it drop like a rock into her empty stomach. There was nothing else to do but check over her saddle bags for damage, clean her weapons, and then watch the rain pool in the little divots around her boots. Every time the wind picked up, the solid rock around her rattled and water slicked off the fang.

She got tired of cringing whenever that happened. So, she watched her bike's tarp rattle.

Something dark blocked it. Sam snapped her revolver up.

A fresh howl rose into the din. It touched her ears and then whipped away into the wind.

"You want to come in?" Sam said. The greywalker remained there, waiting. Something flashed past the narrow opening and thumped close enough to splash water. The second walker galloped out of view. Even in the rain it flowed serpentine, like it was swimming.

Sam only noticed the sun setting when the rain went grey, then black. She began shivering. Quite a bit of water had gone down the back of her jacket and soaked her shirt beneath. Now it clung to her and just soaked cold. Not even the warm late spring air could keep it away. And her jacket kept all of it inside, draining her body's heat away.

After a thought, Sam stripped everything off from the waist up. Then, she buttoned her jacket over her bare body. She shivered still, but at least the soaking had reduced to a general dampness. She leaned against the wall and waited for sunrise.

"I found the river, you dummy," she said. "I did learn some navigation from you."

"Good, because you got us lost on our honeymoon trek," he said and laughed.

She joined him. Her bare skin brushed against the looser jacket. That fleece lining was soft. This had been a good idea. "Well. When this rain stops. If it stops. What do you know about monsoons in the Fangs?"

"I know Johbert's Fangs are part of the twin river deltas. The entire area gets monsoons in late summer that last for days. In the off season, the farmers grow an entire year of crops on half a dozen storms of rain."

"Does it snow like that in the winter?" She said.

"It does," he said. "I'm not sure how the Covenanters got through here in the winter. That many murderous people; either they needed some serious snow equipment, or they had to dig their way through the pass and haul their own firewood," he said.

"Maybe god was on their side," she said. She slumped back. He slipped in and tucked his knees to his chest to fit beside her. "I guess the Beast is a devil, then," she said.

"Yeah, and you're the misguided pilgrim," he said. All the warmth vanished.

"Let's stick to lighthearted banter. I know you wouldn't say that."

He shrugged. "Being helpless on the end of a gun with your son, and dying for it, changes you."

"Yeah, it kinda changed me too." She raised her free arm. He snuck under it. He'd grown his straight hair long and it brushed against her bare neck. She grinned as he went in for the kiss. He nipped her lips, then dipped low, into the collar of her jacket. Warm breath rustled it down her chest.

And she snapped up as the watery footsteps splashed close. He was gone.

And didn't return by sunrise. At first hint of grey, Sam burst forth.

Howls rose up as Sam sloshed through the rain. She ripped the blanket off and took a quarter second to stuff it—and her molding shirt—into the saddle bag before leaping on the bike. The engine sputtered. Motors whined up slowly. A road bike would have had no problem. Her racing bike splashed water from the low-set fans. Two greywalkers streaked out. In the dim light she tracked them by their splashing closing in on either side.

She drew her knife in her free hand and swept her head back and forth, splitting focus between the two. Then grinned as her bike rose from the water. Steam billowed around it. The greywalker leapt from the left. Splashing rolled in from the right.

She swung her revolver and shot it blindly, staggering back, then swung just as the second leapt onto her.

Her bike surged forwards, jarring the greywalker's jaws away from her throat. A couple stabs and an elbow sent it tumbling back.

She flew a hundred yards and swerved to a halt.

The canyon had become a tributary. Fangs and high hills poked out. Tops of trees swayed just below the surface. A cactus floated past.

Searching, she found a narrow line of rock, nearly awash. She tore off and headed across.

They came after her. All three loped through the water. She heard them directly behind, on the same narrow path but didn't look back. With only one eye she couldn't afford to.

The next island was a long patch of flat rock, with a fang at either corner. She gunned the throttle to halfway, and only then slowed down and swung with her aim.

The greywalkers broke to either flank, moving along the dark line where shallow water fell off into submerged ravines. She turned about and put her body to the chassis, then pushed her hat back to keep water off her back. At the end of the oval, a treacherously narrow trail led to another island. She hit the path and crossed the white foam. A lone tree guarded her way, roots bare and soaking up water through reddish veins. It bent double as she roared past.

They came together as she closed. She looked back. Two were right behind. The third had dropped back considerably. That must be the one she'd shot. Like a bike taking a hit through the fan, it was limping.

Ahead, a long maze of broken islands, a few fangs protruding. Beyond that, a wall of forest. It was the end of the Fangs. The solid boundary where the planet's madness finally subsided and friendly forests stretched out. Sam had reached the river

Sam raced forwards. As she did, she switched to high steering, and whipped out the Peabody. Ten shots. She kept it slung across the chassis and wrapped the strap around her hands.

One of the greywalkers came from the right and she hit the throttle, turning aside. She swung right and crossed a land bridge. Now she ran parallel to the river. Ahead, a fork in the trail. One led to a dead end. The other, back towards the trees she needed. She turned towards the fork. The bike hit deep water and stalled for a precious second. Her boots dropped into water.

The fan caught the shore and boosted her back out. She looked back for an instant. One greywalker was ten paces back. The second loped off and moved to intercept her at the fork. She took another look. The third was far back but followed the first directly on her steaming trail.

The fork loomed up. Sam switched to thigh steering. She took her rifle in hand and swung towards the trees.

Then turned away. She caught the water and swung in her saddle. Her bottom caught air and the stirrups crushed her thighs. She screamed and threw herself the other way. The bike rightened and kept going.

Jubilant howls rose behind her. She spun around and raised the rifle.

The greywalker leapt. She caressed the trigger and held it. The greywalker splashed back down. She tapped the trigger.

The Peabody roared and jolted in her grasp. Four eyes widened in surprise, then splashed snout-first into the water.

Sam hit the brakes and spun as she jammed in a fresh round. She heard shrieks, then a splash and bubbling as her bike toppled.

She ripped the stirrup straps and kicked free. The current drove her back into it, so she caught the ground in her knees and let it roll her up and out. Her back slammed into the bike, and she jammed the rifle into her shoulder.

A dark shape came out of the rain and launched itself into the air. She fired. It slammed into her and bounced off. The last she saw of it was it's thrashing in the bloody foam as the current carried it away.

Sam sucked in a cold breath. Then, reloaded. The third greywalker stood at the fork, eyeing her. It turned and limped off into the rain.

She took another breath, and another. Water coursed over her thighs and bubbled around her waist. It drained into her pants and filled her boots. It carried her body's warmth away until she shivered and rattled her body against her bike.

She stood and looked about. The first greywalker lay in the trail a few meters ahead, water bubbling through the hole dead-center in its head. She put another hole through its chest, where its heart and lungs were for good measure. She righted her bike and drained the engine. It sagged as she hefted the corpse over the saddle bags.

"Done," she said, and eased the throttle into drive.

In the trees, she found a two-level shack on stilts. The bottom floor was a storage center, and she bivouacked her bike to dry off under its tarps. The upper floor was a three-room home, long covered in dust. The greywalker looked real nice with a stick shoved up its ass, slowly rotating over the hearth. The muscle was thick and hard, but there was a nice layer of fat underneath. She ate well and slept even better.

Act IV: Autumn

Chapter Twenty-one:

Deckard woke with the sun. He showered first thing and drank from the sink. They'd taken his clothes and left him with two silk dressing gowns of pale purple. He dressed and waited. Breakfast was served on a silver tray. He ate, then waited for lunch, then waited for dinner. Sometimes he stared out the window and watched the trees sway in the rain

The hotel had been built for mining executives. The bed was vast and comfy, the floorboards covered in rugs, and the bathroom a full set. There was a shower, with actual running water. On the first day he'd toured his room and estimated that the value was more than any single building he'd lived in since running away.

At least he had comfort. The dressing gown was fine silk. After weeks in the same clothes, it wrapped around him like clouds of heaven. It must have been made for some executive to relax in after touring the mine. And now a doomed schoolboy was enjoying it. Wasn't that something! He thought.

On the sixth day, the clouds broke and the sun shone through. He saw that water flooded everywhere and the fangs punctured the sky like teeth. A couple dozen strings of black smoke rose from chimneys in the mining camp. By contrast, the town was empty and abandoned.

He saw Emma sitting on a swing under an awning, a spot of vibrant red amidst the green and blue and grey. She read a thick book. Her gloved fingertips turned the pages delicately. For all the world she was one of the fine ladies back in the city. Several of whom he'd gone to school with and read books with just to flirt with them.

Sam wondered what a lady like her was doing out here. She didn't just survive. She looked like she fit in as a bright spot amidst the wilderness.

Captain Robinson strode up and began pacing. She took out a revolver and twirled it in her fingers. Emma pointed at her with the book.

The answer came with a clenched fist.

The gap in the clouds shut and rain drenched everything again. He flopped on the bed. The knife balanced on his belly. It was a tiny blade, but a brush across the pillowcase on day two had created a wide tear. There was a guard outside his door. He could cut his throat with a quick slash. He'd bled a couple chickens under Matt's guidance. Completely different organism, but exposed veins merited a similar motion. Then he'd have weapons, and time to run. He'd seen bikes moored outside.

Someone kicked the door.

"You own this place, come in," he said. They kicked the door again. "I said, you own this fucking place so come in here!" he said over the rain hammering the roof.

The silver doorknob turned. Claire entered. She wore a dressing gown like his, but of deep blue. It was too long and she'd tied it up with a knot at her waist. All that did was make it flow around her as she walked, showing off natural curves no calico would reveal. Deckard tried to pay attention to her face. He stared at her blankly. What was this? A final apology? Some last romance attempt?

She placed a revolver at his side. One of the covenanter's own brass plated weapons. He broke it open. Six loaded cylinders. Real bullets. He closed it and laid it out on his fingertips. The muzzle, he left aimed into her belly. Then looked up. Claire stared at him blankly. Her hair was tied back in a sky-blue ribbon. She looked about to cry.

"What's this for?" he said.

"I'm getting you out," she said.

"Why?"

"I'm craven and should have cut you loose a long time ago. He's my pa and I trusted him. And everything is my fault because I could have just cut you loose or done something, and I didn't because of my craven heart. You didn't deserve any of this and I'm so sorry."

Deckard stared at her mutely, because there was nothing he could say to that. After everything, there was nothing left to say. He scooted over and patted the space he'd warmed up.

Barely breathing, she curled up against the headboard with her legs tucked up. Her shoulder was a fine pillow to rest his head against. Hair tickled his cheek. When she was wearing a calico and her usual petticoats, he couldn't see much of her beneath the folds of dress. Now, he felt a strong shoulder bone beneath, and saw a burn scar fading under her collar.

"You need better taste in boys."

"You taste delicious, thank you. Especially in hay lofts after having cinnamon buns for dessert." A finger slipped against his bare neck. It drew little circles in the hollow of his neck, ruffling his collar over and over. Which made everything harder because his throat got all tight and heavy and he couldn't breathe. "Where are you going when you get out of here?"

"There's an orphanage and a little girl. Her pa went crazy and killed the whole family. I saved her and she loves me like nothing else. She's the most beautiful girl I know. Sorry, you're second."

"I don't mind losing to a little cutie," Claire said with a giggle.

"Well, this orphanage needs a coat of paint and a new radiator. They could use me, at least for this year," he said.

"Could they use me?" she said.

It was dumb. Deckard couldn't decide if he was just dumb, or he had that hot flash his teachers had warned of. When boys and girls did stupid things for each other. He didn't care. "I'll take you, Claire. Is that what you want to do?"

"I don't know. I can farm, I can hunt a bit. I can ride. I don't want to be a farm hand my whole life, there's just too much to do out here. Is it true that in the civilized world women are expected to sew and stay at the home their whole lives?"

"There's a bit of freedom. My school was one of the first to admit girls as well as boys. I'm not sure what their opportunities were once they graduated, but they studied everything we could. Even fencing," Deckard said.

She twisted to look him in the eyes. "I want you to come with me. Wherever I go."

"Sure."

She rolled a bit and settled her legs atop his. His forehead bumped her temple. "These dressing gowns are so comfy. I'm not wearing anything under." Her ears grew hot against his forehead.

"Me neither," he said. They exploded into laughter. She kicked her legs over him. And he couldn't stop laughing even as his ribs hurt. He clutched her in his arms and kissed her over and over. Her eyes were like emeralds.

"Do you know how to…" she trailed off and gathered up his gown in her fingers.

"Yes! Wait, you do?"

"I work on a farm." Her brow furrowed as she stared at him like he was an idiot. Then she kissed him again.

"So, do you want to?" He found his hands sliding down the length of her gown, over the gentle curve of her belly.

"Yes." He caught her gown around her thighs and started rolling it up.

They didn't roll them back down after. They couldn't let go after. Deckard clutched her tight as he could, his gown pinned under his arms.

Her fingernails dug into his bare back as she nuzzled the inside of his neck. Everything had turned golden and beautiful.

∎∎∎

It was midnight when they awoke. With a finger to her lips, Claire slipped out. Deckard paced about the room and tried to remember mom's instructions. Never stop checking your gear. Always keep moving in a fight. Aim just below your target to account for recoil. He cracked the revolver and checked the brass cartridges over and over.

The door creaked and he nearly spilled them out. Claire returned with both arms full. "I got our everything. The door guard's passed out drunk at the front gate. Pa's asleep in his room." She threw everything on the bed. Then shrugged at him.

"Yeah," he said. They turned around and dressed. "We keep the dressing gowns, right?" he said as he pulled his underwear and slacks up under the gown. Only then did he pull it off.

"Oh yeah. We're wearing those wedding night," she said. He stopped, undershirt halfway over him. "I'm sorry, that was a joke."

He pulled his shirt on. Then buttoned up his heavier flannel. Even in the middle of summer, the nights were cold. Probably the altitude. "I was thinking about it, before everything went down," he said.

"So was I. I was hoping we'd figure something out at Summerfest," she said. "I'm ready."

He spun around. She was all buttoned up in her green dress. Her hood was back around her neck and bonnet over her head. "We make a nice couple of war, like mom and dad," he said. He slapped his revolver into his holster and cherished the weight. She shoved her own revolver into hers. "Ready?"

"Yes."

He threw her arms around her and kissed her on the lips. Once, briefly. "I love you."

"Love you, too."

They slipped out the door, grateful for the luxuriously thick carpet to muffle their steps. As they reached the stairwell, snoring rumbled up. Two soldiers were slumped in the doorway, empty bottles around. They'd doffed most of their gear.

Deckard grabbed the bandolier of pistol cartridges and made sure they matched his weapon on the way down. He saw Claire holding a lever-action rifle.

The lobby was empty and hollow in its grandeur. Deckard could barely breathe as he padded out the front door. He pushed the door open and winced as it squeaked. Then, he stepped outside. His boots sank into the mud. Rain drizzled on his head, tapping on the brim of his hat.

Claire waved him around the side. There, under an awning were four bikes. She took the first. He leapt onto the second and found the key in the ignition.

"Wait," he said. Then stood in the stirrups and looked around. In the distance of the right, the mining town was a cluster of lights. The camp was a much nearer, larger spread of lights. The river. "Where's the river?"

"Straight ahead. The boat was towards the town, so we find the river and head toward the town until we hit the boathouse," Claire said.

"Right." He hit the ignition switch. The bike had smoother rumble to its motors than his own, though the fans had a weaker tempo. A low power cruising bike, meant for staying on the limits of roads and garages. He put it in neutral and hovered a solid half-meter off the ground.

"Stop!" The command whipped through the air.

Captain Robinson stood in the hotel's front door, wearing only a white shift that fluttered around her shoulders. She raised a rifle.

Deckard aimed low. She vanished as he fired. Claire kicked her bike into full and raced off. Deckard jammed the throttle and tore off after her. He threw himself low on the handlebars as Robinson fired into the night after them.

"Are you okay?" he yelled at Claire. She gave a thumbs up. The muddy ground raced away beneath them. Their headlights projected their vision a few dozen yards ahead. Deckard squinted into it. As quick as they left, the mud vanished into an all-consuming darkness. He threw his steering bars to the right and slashed through the rain. The fan threw up a spray as he hit the shore and carried right along the waterline. Claire thrummed behind him.

Looking ahead, the lights did not grow larger, but spread into individual buildings as they approached. Until two lights broke away from the edge and curved out towards them like greywalkers going for the kill.

"Claire!" he pointed at them. His voice vanished into the wind but his arm got the message across.

"We can't shoot them."

"No, just keep riding, they have to catch up to us!" he said. He pointed ahead. The lights drew abreast with them. Deckard teetered as he stared out across. There, far in the distance, a light glowed in a window. "Claire, he's on the other side of the river."

"Wait. He shouldn't be, his dock was on this side," Claire said. Deckard cut the throttle and she drew alongside him. Panic was wide in her face, and that made his arms go weak.

"Maybe he moved it due to the flooding," Deckard said. Then the world spun. His bike dipped with the riverbank and caught the water. He was up and helpless. Then a cold fist slammed him in the side. Air blew out of his lungs. He sucked it back in and cold water poured in.

The ground hit him. He wrenched one leg from the stirrups and tried the other. It didn't budge. He jammed his foot against the bike's sinking frame and pulled until his knee ached.

Until he realized the bike was upright. Grabbing it, he pulled himself out. And burst out of the surface. He gasped for air and only made himself cough.

"Claire!"

Someone sloshed behind him. "I'm here," she said and grabbed him from behind. There was no time to spin around, as the two bikes roared in. Deckard went for his revolver. He wrenched it free and took aim.

"What the hell are you two…" the man trailed off. He'd been expecting a couple of his own people. Not the hostage. His hand dropped to a holster on his saddle pommel. Another silver-pommeled revolver came out.

Deckard fired. He grabbed his belly and howled terribly as he fell out of his saddle.

The second man gunned his throttle. Deckard swung about but Claire was already firing over and over. The bike cut between them and kept going until it vanished into the water with its rider.

As he watched it, he saw a light on the swollen river itself. Bogden's boat trundled across, the current pulling it downstream. "Hey!" he yelled.

"Deck, behind us." Claire grabbed his hand and pulled him back. Lights swooped in from the town and the camp alike. Claire tugged him away down the shoreline after the boat. Water sloshed out of his boots with every step. She stopped and looked at him.

"We'll have to swim for it."

"I can't fucking swim," he said.

"I can't either. So." She reached out with a foot and stopped a log. "I guess we float."

The black water was bottomless. Yet Deckard had just decided how he would live. So, he splashed out with her. They caught each other's arms around the dead tree and locked together. They waded out until the current plucked them up and shoved them out into open water. His toes felt nothing but depths. The light of Bogdan's boat grew, until he saw the man standing up in the bow as they passed. The sail fluttered, but the boat couldn't turn in time to catch them.

Another log slammed into them, spinning them around. Then another. He felt a thump, and Claire's grip slipped. "No." He caught her, face just above the water. The current spun suddenly, catching them in its immense fist. Another log caught him under the ribs. He let go of everything but the girl.

Cold blackness swallowed him. Shadows poured out, hitting him over and over. He caught sight of Claire, pale skin barely visible, eyes wide in terror. They pressed their foreheads together, finding comfort in each other's touch. Then a mass of trees tore them apart.

Deckard tried to grab something, but the bark slipped through his fingers. Claire appeared behind him, upside-down, and then vanished from view.

And then his shoulder slammed into the solid bank. He stuck fast, mouth just above the water to gasp for breath. Lightning crackled across the clouds high above.

Someone seized his shoulders and hauled him ashore. "I give you credit. Going in there takes a special desperation. Most sacrifices just live their last night in comfort," Captain Robinson said. She dropped him hard. A drumbeat rolled through his skull and his vision flickered. She stood. "Did you get the girl?"

"We've got her," a man yelled. Deckard breathed hard.

"Bogdan, take your boat back across the river. This doesn't fucking concern you!" Robinson said. She stepped over Deckard. Beneath her outer coat, she only wore a shift and boots. "Sergeant, what about the wounded?"

More voices. "Derian's gone, river took him. Gast's alive but he took a gut shot. He's still screaming."

"Then get him to the fucking doctor and pray he lives, go!" she said. Deckard propped himself up on his elbows and looked around. There were dozens of soldiers about in dressing gowns and clothes alike.

He stood. Someone clubbed him across the shoulders and he fell back on his hands and knees. He went for his revolver and found it missing. Claire leapt up and sprinted to his side. She threw her arms around him.

"Let him go," she said. A massive man with a handlebar moustache seized her shoulders. Deckard caught her, and they were both dragged along the mud.

"You know what he's here for, right?" Captain Robinson said. "Ah, who cares. The Beast is coming." The man let them go, and they fell into a shivering heap.

Deckard sat up. His body was spent, he couldn't even raise his arms against the cold. Claire was pale and soaked. All the lights around glowed off her paleness and the water all around them. He shook his head. "Claire, I'm sorry."

"No, I'm real sorry. This is my fault," she said and grabbed his wrist.

A familiar fan roared. The Beast rode right up to them and hopped off his bike.

"The girl had a romantic spot after all," Robinson said, almost with amusement. "I figured I'd let you separate her. For some dignity."

Beast approached without word. Claire buried her face in Deckard's shoulder. "You can't take him without me."

"There's a million boys, and only one of your old man," the Beast said. Even as he spoke, half a dozen soldiers closed around them. Deckard looked about. All of them had their hands right on their revolver hilts. One held a double-barreled shotgun across his chest.

"And you're a terrible person. I should have stayed on the farm with people who build things. All you've ever done is kill," Claire said.

Beast dropped on his hands and knees. Deckard smelt something foul on his rasping breath. And saw under the bandage and fresh black hat, a look of utter desperation. "I created you. And I sacrificed everything for you. You are the one good thing I've put into this world and I'm not losing it over some boy."

"It's not about Deckard. It's about you. Wyatt raised me," Claire said.

Deckard hugged her close. His breathing got faster and faster until he wasn't actually getting air, he just couldn't stop gasping as he stared into the bottomless death of the Beast's eyes.

Then something flashed in them. A bolt of emotion. Deckard didn't understand it until his brow softened and death became a deeper expression of despair. Like mom, when Deckard had first met her under the dome. He reared up. Captain Robinson saw it too, because she screamed and dove into the water.

Gunfire roared out in all sides, but no muzzle flare accompanied. The Beast was a blur with empty holsters and whirling coattails. He spun about, and covenanters fell like the scythe had harvested them from the open field. A couple shots fired from men already falling in bloody spray to the ground.

The beast came to a halt where he started and switched to the soldiers on the bikes, who were only now firing. Their shots cut the air around him, fired in pure panic from the hip as they screamed. He plucked them from the saddle, railguns firing in alternate. A bike spun slowly on spot with an arm caught in the steering bar.

The remainder behind him finally had their revolvers up and return fire roared back from rifle and pistol, illuminating the night in the yellow flicker of igniting powder. Their hands shook too much and they hit nothing but air. The beast seemed to stutter. Footwork of a dancer.

They fell so fast Deckard couldn't track the shots. Bodies exploded and flesh and bone sprayed into the air. One boy ran away, screaming. The Beast stilled for an instant to aim, then thought better and resumed his rampage. His hands dropped to his sides and the magazines were replaced in an instant.

Robinson rose from the water with a splash that sprayed Deckard. Her pale skin shone in the gunfire, and the rifle in her hands simmered as she brought it to bear. Deckard saw the twin belling barrels and realized it was a shotgun. She couldn't miss.

"Pa!" Claire screamed. The beast didn't hear as he engaged the new reinforcements roaring out from across the land.

Robinson sucked her jaw in. Her shotgun roared hard enough to kick her entire body back into an S.

The beast contorted in a mirror to Robinson's as the blow struck him. Dark blood burst up from his shoulder. He fell. Robinson threw the smoking weapon aside and drew her revolver.

"PA!" Claire leapt from Deckard's arms and raced at her. Robinson clubbed her right across the head, sending her reeling. She would have fallen into the water and drowned had Deckard not caught her.

Silence fell. "God damn," Robinson said. "He's not human, what the fuck was that?" She dropped her revolver and sloshed over. She looked utterly dreamy as she twirled the pistoles in either hand and stuffed them into her holsters. Then she grabbed mother's railgun and cradled it close to her chest. "Lost for decades. Holy shit."

Bikes roared up. More soldiers leapt out.

"Check the bodies over for survivors and get them straight to the hospital," Robinson said, gesturing with the butt of the railgun. "You three, guard the Beast. We'll hang him from the execution tree at dawn, I want him alive until them. You four. Bind the two sacrifices. We're going to need them soon."

Deckard tried to stand. Something hard and metal slammed him facedown into the water. A boot clamped onto his neck. He gasped for breath as his hands were bound behind his back. Then he was hauled out and slung over the back of a bike. He looked up, and saw Claire dropped onto another. She stared up at him, eyes rimmed red and crying.

He opened his mouth. There was nothing to say. They were dead. He slumped back down and shivered as his soaked clothes sucked the warmth from his body. The engine rumbled and he was driven away.

Chapter Twenty-Two:

Sam awoke dry and hungry. The air was humid but lacked biting heat. In daylight, she saw the house she was in was well-furnished with finely made furniture and solid walls that had kept the damp out. The greywalker was deep brown and smelt like steak on its spit over the dark cinders.

She dressed it and packaged it first. Only then did she dress herself. Her outer shirt was in ruins, so she discarded it and went with her jacket, undershirt, trousers, spare cotton socks, and boots. She counted out her last six revolver cartridges and eight .45-110 bullets and stowed them on her belt. She tipped her hat at the empty house and stepped outside.

She stood on a wide band of deep blue forest, with brown floodwaters on one side and black river on the other. From here she saw a few more houses, one of which had smoke coming from the chimney.

The trees were too thick to ride through, so she set her bike to neutral and walked alongside it with a hand in the stirrups. The river emerged, having grown to engulf the last few rows of trees. Across the river, she saw plenty of smoke trails set against the grey sky to her north. So, she headed that way.

She stopped and gaped. Bodies were strewn across the far riverbank. Grey forms lay amidst torn up mud, amongst fallen bikes and lost weapons. She popped out her binoculars. None of them were Deckard. Wait! She saw his brown hat in the river, nudging the shore with every ripple from passing flood debris. Her heart quickened.

A branch snapped behind her. She spun and aimed her rifle at the small, shirtless man. His body was wrapped in ropy muscle gotten from a lifetime of hard labor and covered in tattoos. He raised his hands slowly.

"Please. I only steer the boat. You want to talk to the town forewoman," he said.

"Did you see a boy? Bit taller than me, curly black hair. Pale skin. Wore a brown leather peacoat," she said.

He nodded eagerly. "He came with a girl with black curly hair, and an injured man. His hands were tied, so I slipped him a knife. I hoped it would help," he said. "Are you hunting for them?"

"The boy's my son," she said.

His expression fell. "The injured man was the Beast of the East. He works with the forewoman."

"And I injured him," she said and hefted the Peabody rifle.

Suddenly he looked like he was about to cry. "My name is Bogdan. Do you know the Second Covenant?"

"I've killed a ton of them and if my son is here, I'll kill some more," she said, and looked back across the river. No movement. It was a test. She looked back. No movement from the boatman.

"Listen to me. I am from the city of Acavia. Fifty kilometers down the river. Three years ago, the Covenant took over the city. This town refused to join. So, the Covenant sent filibusters here and killed everyone. They're buried in a fork of the mine that went dry. They send prisoners like me to work the mine," he said. "I can sail and navigate the river. My family has fished for five generations. I have a valuable skill, so I don't go into the mines." He smiled softly.

Sam slung the rifle over her shoulder. She stepped closer and put a hand on his gnarled shoulder. "What would they want with my son? There's a reason the Beast took him all the way through the Fangs alive."

"The Covenanters discovered a machine here a year ago. If you put a healthy person in one end, and a dying person in the other, it will strip the flesh and bones from the healthy and give it to the injured. High ranking Covenanters come here and pay the forewoman to be healed," he said.

Then the beast was dying. Hope raised her for a second, until horror took over. Deckard was a ticking clock until he was shoved into a piece of lost technology and…

"What happened on the other bank?"

"Your son tried to escape, with another. When the monsoons come, I store my boat on this side where the trees will protect it, I think they didn't know that. The Covenanters stopped them. Then the Beast turned his guns on them. There were too many."

"Get me and my bike over," she said.

They had to brace together and lift the bike onto the boat, then tie it down. By the end, both were panting and sweating in the sunrise. Sam sat down in the back and left her hand on her revolver. She watched him launch the boat and rig it to sail himself. "I was worried I'd have to swim," she said.

"Can you swim?" He said with astonishment.

"Forever," she said.

"Your son and his companion tried to swim the river. They were lucky the current washed them back to their side instead of drowning them," he said. "Where did you learn?"

"I grew up in a convent on a river. They wanted me to be a fucking woman of the cloth. I learned to swim from local fisherman so I could find other careers," she said. The man smiled. "What's your name?"

"Bogdan."

"Where's your family?"

"I don't know."

The boat grounded on the far bank. Sam unbuttoned the bike and hauled it off. All that work just for a few hundred yards, she thought as she unbuttoned her jacket and panted.

"Do you need anything?" Bogdan said.

"Stay on this bank and hide. I might need to leave in a hurry. How many soldiers are here?"

"There are usually about a hundred, a full company," he said, which made her curse. "They are split between the mining camp over that way and the town. And, obviously, some of them are dead."

"Where's this machine?"

"Still in the mine. I think they're afraid to move it and damage it."

"Well, thank you," she said. She mounted her bike.

"Good luck," he said.

She throttled up the bank and stopped just below the lip. Only her head reached above the muddy crest to get her bearings. There was about a twenty-minute ride from town to camp. Once she made her assault, she had a time limit to clear out before reinforcements showed up. That limited sniping.

Then, she saw a single tree in the gap. Three soldiers clustered around it, as they looped a noose around a fourth. Sam snatched up her binoculars and stared in shock at the bloodied form of the Beast. She braked and leapt down, then whipped out the Peabody. She set the sites to eight hundred yards and crouched.

The first soldier walked out the hanging rope. At eight-hundred meters, Sam plucked his brains from his skull. By the time the others had seen her, she'd put a shot through the center of the woman's back. The last man took off running to the right, for the knoll that was the only cover around. The bullet met him at the hillside and slapped him into the ground. His legs kicked up muddy divots until Sam made it over and put a mercy kill into his forehead.

The Beast was slumped on the ground under the tree. Bandages, stained red, were wrapped around his left shoulder. He'd been stripped to the waist, revealing a gaunt body. He straightened at the site of her.

"Kids. They're the death of us," he said.

"That's because you're doing it wrong," she said.

He cocked his head to her busted eye "You sure?"

"All in the job," she said. "Now, tell me what the fuck happened."

"My daughter tried to get your son out. I had a soft spot and tried to protect her. You really did do me in. That bullet you winged me with, claimed the hearing in my left ear. I didn't hear that Captain Robinson raising her shotgun on that side until she hit me," he said. "I'm guessing I hit the tree next to you?"

"Yeah," she said.

"You made your shot. I got lucky where I missed. You bested me." He sighed and slumped against his hanging tree.

"Will you get your head together? Our kids are about to get fucking murdered by lunatics and you're worrying over who's better. I'm going in for my son. Are you getting Claire?" she said. She leaned back and spat. It landed between his splayed legs.

"I want her back," he said and stood.

She aimed the gun at him. "I have two questions first. One. Why did you want to put my son in that machine?"

"I'm dying. Smoker's lung. Coughed for years out in the wilderness. Finally went in to see a doctor. Too late for treatment or surgery. I've got a year to live, less at this point," he said.

She almost shot him right then. For trying to kill her son. "Does she know?"

"No. I didn't come back because I didn't want her to see me waste away," he said, and shook his head. "Don't shoot me yet, please, I want to go get her." The menace died in his voice. His words were scratchy and horribly pathetic.

"Second question. What's your real name? I'm not calling you the Beast because you're not worth the title," she said.

He stood on his own. Swayed on the spot and stabilized. "Clan name Sima, personal name, Yi. Call me Sima, please."

Sam grabbed revolvers off each of the dead. They were all standardized. Double action, .38 caliber with a brass handgrip. Judging by the proof markings and big C emblazoned on the barrel, these had been made by the covenanters. A solid, sleek weapon of high-quality construction. She draped the holsters over her bike. "You get these when we go in. How's the arm?"

"Useless." They had put it in a sling. Sam checked over his wounds with what was left of her own medical supplies, then searched the bikes for rifles.

There was one lever-action, but it was chambered in .38 like the revolvers. Good for up to 200 meters, useless beyond.

On the last bike, she found something new. A rifle chambered in…45-110. She collected all thirty rounds and restored her empty cartridge bandolier

The same bike also had a revolver in a pommel holster. It was a monster. Long as her forearm, so massive she needed both hands to aim it properly. She recognized it; a Grand Dragon, an antique from when weapons technology was at its lowest. It required percussion caps to fire.

"Don't take that, it's obsolete," Sima muttered in exasperation. "Seriously, it's a muzzle-loader."

Indeed it was. Yet, that was a massive bullet. The Grand Dragon had the power of Deckard's .45-70 rifle. It had been designed to smash a bike at a hundred meters. She strapped the whole holster to her saddle, to a groan from Sima.

"You lead," she said. They mounted up. She switched to thigh controls and rested the Peabody in her lap, aimed directly at his back. "What are we facing?"

"There's about twenty of them left at the camp, fifty more in the town. There's always one sentry on guard, and the rest are probably in their cabins getting drunk," Sima said.

"What about our kids? Are they still alive?" she said.

"They will be. There's no need for sacrifices right now. Or she'd have tried to buy Deckard off me. So they'll be held by the machine, ready for the next old man or injured noble who comes here and pays for a new life," Sima said.

They bivouacked in a rocky outcropping overlooking the camp, an island of solid ground amidst the mud. Sam dropped on her left side and lay so she could peak over the top with Jesse's binoculars. "They're about eight-hundred meters from here," she said.

"Nay, a kilometer and a half," Sima said. He plucked a telescope with a gold eyepiece from his pocket, then held it in his teeth and pulled it open.

"What?" she said and took another look. The area looked far too flat. She tried to close an eye. And remembered, there was a reason one shot with both eyes open. "Well shit, with one eye I've lost my depth perception," she said.

Sima nodded sadly. "The range is about fifteen-hundred meters from here to the mine itself. That's the big hut in back, with the metal vents coming out of the ground around it. The rest of the buildings are supply storage and guard barracks. There's one sentry atop the barracks. And there he is, with a big rifle."

"What did they mine?"

"Graphite. They still do."

"Did the townsfolk consider paying in graphite when the filibusters came?" she said. She spotted two women walking the center of town. One was dressed as a soldier with a sky-blue shawl that fluttered in the post-storm breeze. The railgun was slung across her back. It was stuck into a tiny rifle holster that barely covered half the barrel.

"I don't know. I wasn't there for that," he said. "My guess is they tried everything down to pleading for their kids, to no avail," he said. "Mining building, upper rightmost window."

She saw Claire pressed to the window. It looked like her hands were tied behind her, judging by how she was pressed by her shoulder to it. "They've got our babies."

"Not for long." Sima's voice rolled from the pits of his throat like the commands of hell. "The redhead woman is Captain of the guards, Marienne Robinson. She's a blooded veteran and dangerous, given she's the one who wounded me." He sighed. "Now she's got the most dangerous weapon of all."

"Thanks," Sam said. Something flickered in the window. A woman in a red gown. "Who's the lady of high society?"

"That's Emma Robinson, her mother. She was supervising the mine when they dug the machine up. And she was its first case. She was wasting from pancreatic failure when she went in and came back healthy enough to make it to a hundred," Sima said.

"Does it resurrect the dead?"

"It's engineering, not a miracle from god," he said. He sank back below the rim. She joined him, leaning on her left shoulder. They stared at each other in mutual concern. There was a lot to go wrong. And too much pressure to waste time.

"I reckon when the shooting starts, they'll all come running out," Sam said.

"I concur. I suppose I'll go in and start killing. You cover me."

"No. You go in. I'll take the sentry and you'll be ready when they come running out," she said.

His stone mouth twisted upwards ever slightly into a smile. White teeth showed.

"I need one thing first," Sam said. She crawled back over the top and started pointing. "I need you to give me ranges."

“What?”

“Normally, I can range-find with my naked eye. I’ve gotten very good at that. With one eye, I can’t tell how far the enemy is so I can’t adjust the sights appropriately. So, I’m going to pick a few points and you tell me how far they are from the mine, you understand?” she said.

“Yeah, shoot.”

“That upturned boat.”

“Eight hundred fifty meters.”

“The stand of trees on our right.”

“One-thousand meters roughly.”

“That boulder on the far side.”

He stuck his head up a bit further. “Thirteen hundred meters.”

“And the rusting wagon on the way towards town.”

“Nineteen hundred yards.” They crawled back below the lip. Sima’s good fingers tapped away at the nearest revolver hilt. “Just another hit job. One more bloodshed for the land.”

“No. This our fucking kids,” she said.

“Does it matter to this world?” he said.

“Yeah,” she said. “One more thing, though.” She rolled and tapped the Peabody’s barrel on his good shoulder. “Anything happens to my son by your hand and Claire goes in the same hole. You can kill me, but she’ll still be gone.”

Sima’s eyes narrowed. She already had the trigger pulled to its limits of tolerance. He’d have to roll to get any revolver to bare. “I understand.” He stood and stomped back to his bike. She was lining up her shot when he rode past.

Sima stopped a bit out of town and leapt off his bike, landing on one knee. He stood and strode forwards. He was a long, impossibly lean figure with a wide-brimmed hat. The wind picked up, billowing his black coat around his gaunt body as he went. A revolver caught the light under his jacket and glinted at her.

"I see you boy," she said. He passed the first house and entered the town proper. Two covenanters stepped out of a building, laughing as they walked. They froze.

Cries rang out, murmurs from far away. The sentry leveled his massive rifle.

She didn't feel the trigger. The Peabody roared and belted her in the shoulder. A second later, the sentry stiffened, and slid right off the roof. Sima strode forwards as she reloaded.

The first three out of the barracks died by his hand. Sam took the opportunity to pluck the head off a woman leaning out a second story window with a shotgun loose in her grasp. When she looked back, Sima was firing through the door as he ran past.

A man and a woman stumbled out of the bike shed, fumbling with short-barreled carbines. Sam hit the man in the shoulder. He grabbed it and fell, screaming. The woman turned right around and ran at Sima. Sima pegged her with his empty gun. As she reeled, he drew and fired two shots into her chest.

Sam spotted a few soldiers creeping out the back of the barracks. She swung her rifle about and dropped the first. The rest took off running, not into town, but into the bike garage. Her next shot splintered the door as they swung it open. By the time she reloaded, were inside.

"Shit," she muttered. Sima was firing into the windows of the mine house, astride the end of the street. He grabbed a revolver off a wounded man and ducked behind one of the air vents. Someone flickered in the window. Sam fired two shots through and was rewarded on the second as a single arm flopped over. She grabbed her binoculars and peered through the upper window.

Claire was gone. Movement. Something red.

Sam ducked as the first railgun shot split the air over her head. She scrabbled back as repeated shots excavated the hill apart around her. Time to change spots. She leapt on her bike and rolled out.

She left the safety of the hill and threw herself low across her chassis. A single shot missed by meters, and Robinson gave up. Sam angled toward the trees, then reconsidered as her eye tingled. She went for the boulder.

Immediately she realized her mistake, as she twisted her neck all the way to see the three bikes racing from the garage towards her. One man must have had leg controls, as he took aim at full throttle. Sam took aim and waited till his trigger finger jerked. She swung her hips and swerved left so the shot hit air. Then she settled in and returned a shot at his chest, that hit his shoulder instead. He kept firing, and she needed a second to finish him off.

There was no time to reload and adjust sights as the other two tore at her. So she slung the rifle over her shoulder and roared right at them as she drew up the massive revolver. A railgun shot whipped past both of them. One of the boys flinched and started firing.

Sam aimed center-mass and fired. A flame burst from the revolver's muzzle and the weapon wrenched her wrists in their sockets. Something exploded on the front of the bike, and its steering fans died. It slammed nose-first into the ground and somersaulted into the air. The rider flailed like a ragdoll until he hit the ground and bent double backwards.

The second soldier came on, jaw set and revolver lining up a steady shot. Sam swung the gun up.

She jerked her hips and braked hard. His shot clipped her sleeve. Hers blew a hole in his chest big enough to aim through, and he whipped past, slumped forwards on his bike. She heard the crash amongst the trees.

She swapped back to the Peabody and adjusted the sights to nine-hundred meters. Another shot raced past. Now between two of the buildings, she saw the redhead leaning out the window. Sam swept behind the outcropping of rock and raised the rifle to her shoulder.

She looked out at her long shadow and realized what could happen.

As she emerged, she hit the gas, hard. The shot left a ringing in her ears as it coursed past.

Sam saw Robinson in the window. A tiny speck. A shadow on a flat wall. She didn't need to think. The angle, the range, and her sights met perfectly.

■■

The three people standing in the room clustered around the windows, pouring fire through the sills. A shot split one's skull. Lying on the ground, Deckard bunched his knees up and pushed himself forward. His hands ground on the bare boards. He gritted his teeth as he caterpillar crawled across the floor to Claire's side. Then he squirmed up next to her.

"Claire, here," he said, and pressed the knife into her belly. She nodded and rolled over to take it.

"Godamnit, she's weaving in and out," Captain Robinson said. She fired another shot with mom's railguns.

She? Deckard thought with a start. Claire rubbed against him as she worked the knife back and forth. He pulled closer to cover her.

A man screamed out in a high-pitched warble that Deckard didn't know men could make. It was a cry of desperate agony, as someone out there died. Then another flurry of gunfire claimed a few more. That had to be the Beast, somehow. Which meant Deckard was dead no matter what.

Just live then, my dear, this is for you, he thought. She winced suddenly and stiffened. He took a handful of her dress in her hands. Just keep working.

"I see her. Aim for the other side of that boulder," Robinson said and swung so far that she leaned out the window with the railgun. The remaining soldier aimed with his rifle. Deckard fixated on Robinson.

The railgun roared and she grinned in triumph.

Then she was spun halfway around in a spray of blood. She fell to the floor.

"I'm hit, fuck."

The remaining soldier leapt back. "Ma'am!" he said between thick sideburns. He pulled out a medical kit.

"No, fuck that." She hauled herself up. "Get them down to the machine. I'll sacrifice one to heal myself, then I'll kill these fuckers.

Deckard kicked at the soldier, who stomped his ankle into a painful pulp before hauling him up by the back. "You're a couple animals, you know that?" he said. Another soldier appeared in the door and grabbed Claire.

"Boy. You get to be something more than just a rider wandering the earth, isn't that great?" the man said. He made sure Deckard bumped every step on the way down into the basement.

The basement was an open tunnel of rock. One way ended in an elevator and stacks of air pumps. The other.

It was a black cube with two human-sized hatches in front. A control panel winked red. Deckard thrashed hard as he could. His feet just dragged on the ground.

"Please," he said.

"My girl what happened?" Emma said. She stood beside the machine. Her hair had come down from its curls. It framed the wide-eyed worry on her face.

"I should have just killed the Beast. He's here, with a sniper friend. He'll be here shortly and I need to heal first," she said.

"Of course," she said and tapped the control panel. Both hatches slid open. Red lights glowed within only one. "Oh god dear, does it hurt? You look awful."

"Mother, I was shot by a large rifle," Robinson said dryly. Then to her soldier: "Throw the boy in, then both of you stand guard. The

Beast has to come through that door. Shoot as soon as it opens, I don't care what you see," she said.

"Yes ma'am!" they chorused.

Deckard screamed. He threw his shoulder against the man, fought with the bonds until his wrists burned and bled down his sleeves. The device radiated warmth, making him sweat.

Claire rose up and stabbed the second soldier through the throat. She turned, as the man collapsed on the ground and gurgled.

"Look out!" Emma cried. The soldier spun just in time to catch Claire's wrists. Deckard staggard back and his boot hit the lip of the hatch. He threw himself forwards and slammed headfirst into the back of the soldier's neck. Through stars menacing his vision, he felt the man stagger forwards. The man grunted in pain and staggered back into him.

"Hell," Robinson said and drew a railgun pistol with her remaining arm. She took aim at Claire's leg.

Deckard spun on her and charged. He planted his shoulder into her chest just as her finger squeezed the trigger. She crumpled, and a roar filled the air.

Pain split him open from the legs up. Deckard collapsed in a heap, but the agony wouldn't stop. Pressed to the ground, he saw his legs. The right one slumped from halfway to his shin, down to the ground. White protruded. His bone, he realized. Everything turned cold and painful.

"Deck!" Claire screamed from somewhere far away. The soldier had her pinned under his knee, bleeding as he tied her hands back behind her.

"Get him in, he's dying," Emma said. She helped Captain Robinson up by the shoulder. The soldier grabbed Claire. "No, the boy, before he bleeds out."

The soldier loomed over Deckard. He didn't have the strength left to fight.

The soldier's head jerked suddenly. The light fled his eyes, and he folded up on himself.

Captain Robinson raised the railgun and reeled back as she was hit in her other shoulder. She gasped something and dropped the weapon. The beast strode into view. He was hunched badly to his wounded left side, but his jacket remained impeccable. He dropped his revolver and grabbed one of the railguns off the ground. He grinned as he weighed the familiar weapon.

"Your daughter is right here unharmed, and here's your hostage. Take it and leave us, please," Emma said and knelt before him. "I have money. Please don't hurt us."

Captain Robinson groaned behind her

The Beast paused. "Would you do anything to protect your daughter?"

"Yes, please take anything!"

"Cap, would you do anything for your mother?"

"What do you think? Do you understand family?" Robinson gasped, trying to rise on her legs alone.

"Then you are of no use to me." He shot Robinson first. Emma screamed and screamed until his boot crushed her windpipe. He fired a couple more shots into her.

"Claire?" the Beast said.

"Dad, I'm fine. Deckard's hurt!"

The Beast knelt before Deckard and looked him over with those empty eyes. He grabbed Deckard around the waist.

"Don't put me in there, you monster," Deckard said. He felt a knife at his wrists, and the bonds dropped away.

"My name is Sima Yi," he said.

■■

Sam dismounted and shouldered through the door. A single soldier, chest bloody and eyes glassy, fumbled for his revolver. He barely had a moustache. She blew him off his feet with that cannon and he crashed into a crate.

She found them strewn outside the mine. Deckard lay in a puddle of blood and her heart raced. Until she saw Claire tying a splint around his leg as Sima guided her with profanity every other word. She raced to her son's side.

His eyes opened slowly. They were sunken into his skull and rimmed with red and grime. "Mom?"

"Hey Deck. Mommy's here." She cradled his head in her lap. Seventeen years, and nothing changed now, did it?

"You died." He raised up on his elbows. She forced him back down.

"Don't move until you have to," she said. "We're going to get out of here now. Sima, where's the nearest friendly doctor?"

Sima's stare told her everything. They'd have to go all the way back across the fangs..

"That's about two weeks," she said. "No, I give it ten days. The hell happened to him?"

"He took a railgun round to the leg. It cut through a bone and a vein. We stopped the bleeding, but infection or just bad treatment is going to get him," he said.

She got Deck over her shoulder and hauled him out. While she laid him onto the saddle and figured out how to secure him, Sima and Claire sprinted out. Sima returned hauling a single massive cylinder of explosives.

"What are you doing?" she said.

"I'm blowing that thing up," he said and vanished into the mine.

Deckard slipped off the saddle. She caught him and lifted him back. "Sorry mom."

"No problem." She hopped up behind him and kissed his cheek. "Ew."

In the distance a dozen specks emerged from town. Then two larger blobs of wagons. "Deck, we've got to go."

Sima emerged. "Fuse is set. Get down to the river. We'll lead them away."

"Dad, you're not in good shape," Claire said.

"I have a trigger finger and an eye," he said, and shoved Sam's railgun into her hands. "I need you to make it out alive."

Sam gunned the throttle without a word. She took a left and looped around the tree cropping. From there, the land dipped and she broke eye contact with the approaching force as she gunned it for the landing.

Bogdan had the boat ready. Sam dropped her wallet in the boat.

Halfway across the river, she saw a pillar of black smoke punch its way above the bank. Half a second later, the blast rolled through in a single titanic boom that rustled the trees and shoved the boat through the floodwaters.

Chapter Twenty-Three:

Rain hung like a sheet for Sam to charge through. It restricted the fangs to dark shapes looking into the distant sky. Somewhere overhead, the mist and silhouettes merged into deep gray of the calm between storms. The fine details emerged at fifty meters. At full throttle, the frozen Sam barely reacted in time. She couldn't slow down, as Deckard heaved against her with every breath. There was only the split-second touch on the throttle.

Sam raced past the bloated corpse of the drowned greywalker. She came close enough to make the upturned legs wiggle, and she caught a single waft of festering sceptic waste. It lingered for long after, even as she leaned out of her jacket and tasted the breeze. In her lap, Deckard slewed about and vomited over the side.

"It's okay Deck," she howled over the roaring engine. Deck twisted back and said something, but his words were whipped from his lips. She rubbed his side. He sank back into her arms.

Under the gap between his ear and shoulder, a former ravine presented itself as a long channel of harmlessly blue water. She swung away and cut to the high point of the ridge. Just in time for a narrow fang to suddenly widen into an obese molar. Sam checked to the sides and skewed back towards the ravine. As she closed in, the molar spread to fill the land. She pulled up hard.

And spotted a steep, sloped gap between rock and depth. A knife's edge to shave minutes off their trip. "Deck, lean to your right!"

Deckard slumped over. Only the straps she'd jury-rigged kept him in the saddle. Sam leaned. The racing gyroscope swung with the weight and the bike tilted to hug the ridge. Her coat flapped as it brushed the rock and came away frayed as they emerged. A long stretch of flat land rewarded them, growing muddy as it dipped between two plateaus.

"Good work son," she said and rubbed his shoulder.

"Mom, I don't like your kindly tone. It worries me," Deckard said. His voice rasped out. It shivered like he was trying not to cry, and that scared her more than everything. Nine months and not a tear.

"Shut your mouth," she said and pinched him. "Sleep if you can."

The rain kept him awake and her alert. Mixed blessings. Better than negative, she thought as she kept them straight down the center of the ridge.

Mud became swamp and they threw up a trail of mist. Sam closed her eyes. Eye, fuck. Last time she'd come through here, she'd descended from a long shelf. There'd been a steep drop and a narrow trail, like a shelf.

She felt it first. The rain shook. The very damp air shivered as something massive moved. It became a roar. The water picked up its flow until she had to increase her hovering height to stay above the current.

"Mom!" Deckard shrieked. A white wall loomed. An eternity cascaded from dozens of meters overhead to smash itself onto the ground she approached. Nature had pulled one last trick. A transformation really, to show the life that had been here since creation that it would always be welcome, and that the two humans were not welcome in its domain. She aimed towards the left corner. She pushed Deckard's head down, and he bobbed back up. "Mom!"

"Stay down, please," she said. She switched to thigh controls and hugged him with both arms. The seam of rock she'd descended on was there, and the waterfall shifted around it. She hit it and slipped under the waterfall. Darkness fell and she could only hug the trail in the headlights as she zig-zagged up and up. Until only water was overhead, going over the side in thundering doom.

She hit the throttle. A wet fist slammed into them, soaking everything at once. Then they burst through and crested onto the banks of the new river.

"Hey, trust mom, okay?" she said and hugged him tight. "How's the leg?" She swerved around a bend in the rock, and they went from a gulch to rising in the air. A higher stage of the waterfall burst beneath and fell into the abyss.

"You're scaring me," he said.

"How's the leg?" she repeated.

"Hurts."

"Good. Means infection hasn't gone gangrenous yet," she said. Yet. Infections always spread and devoured until the afflicted limb began to die, or modern medicine stopped them. "You're tough, you'll be fine."

"Seriously, stop being nice mom," he said.

The sky ignited. For an instant she saw clouds, the mountains stabbing them, the trees blooming all around, and the trident of lightning straddling them. Sam's hair stood right on end as the mist steamed around them. Then came the roar like artillery straight from heaven.

Immediately the curtain of mist crashed down in a torrent of rain. It hammered them down a few centimeters.

She threw up her arms. "Fuck!" Whatever god was up there laughed at her as they threw lighting down to light the way, and thunder to shatter their thoughts. Sam twisted to point her one eye straight ahead. Every flash, she blinked and framed it to memory. Which was why they lived when the trail bent into a steep plunge and she swung just in time to scrape water off the eternity. Now they descended. The water billowed up after them, accelerating their fan thrust. Sam pulled up on the brake.

Nightfall. She tried in the dark, but the headlamps had a range in centimeters. They found a ledge of dry land. Deckard slumped on the ground, spread-dactyl.

Sam produced the last leg of greywalker. "Eat," she said and carved off a muscle for him.

He mumbled something.

"Seriously. Your body needs everything right now." She placed it on his chest. "Go on, that's greywalker."

"No, it's not," he said without rising.

"Yes, it is." She tapped him with the knobby thigh bone.

"You can't kill them, they're the second most dangerous thing on the planet," he said. Wait. Then what was the first? The thought stunned her for a minute, until she decided there were too many possibilities to worry over it. The affront on her kill was more urgent.

"I hid underwater and held my breath until the monster got too close. Then I blew its head off. Eat it. It's the flesh of the apex predator," she said.

Deckard hopped up on his elbows and bit down. "That's good." He wolfed it down. "It's thick, but damn tasty."

"They're greywalkers. They eat only the best," she said. She tore into the leg and ripped off a fine, fatty piece of meat. Fat to give them energy for those stupid all-night sprinting sessions.

"What did dad see in you?"

"Two eyes and two tits," she said. He burst into laughter, until he choked.

They left at the first greying of the ground. Deckard tried to walk out. He seized the rock and hauled himself up on his left leg. That held, so he tried the right. The ground swung suddenly as pain rocked his world. Something shifted hard in his lower leg, where there should have been tendons keeping his bones intact.

"Deck!" Mother caught him and cradled him to the ground. "It's alright, we'll fix your leg."

His blood ran cold. His throat froze shut as she hefted him up and hauled him to the bike. He pinched something on the way down and a wince escaped his lips.

"Sorry," mother said. She adjusted him.

The bike roared to life. He was used to the heavy thrumming of Claire's workhorse farm rider. Sam's was as much greywalker as his dinner last night. Speed and a high-pitched fan. It was comforting as it roared along. Soon, the pain in his leg faded into a dull tingling.

Looking ahead was a terror of racing monoliths and shifting ground. All of it thrown up across the alien landscape. He closed his eyes. Soon as he did, the bike vanished and he fell away and away.

He forced his eyes open. His body caught up with his stomach. "This hurts," he said. Sam said nothing. She adjusted slightly to steer them under an arch. Rain vanished for a blessed instant. He breathed once in the dryness, and it returned.

"Mom," he said. "Mom!"

"Yes?" she said.

He slumped back. She caught him. Thigh controls. Genius advancement in steering. A high-sensitivity gyro in the bike's seat let her steer with easy movements in her legs. High maintenance and high performance. He grinned at the thought of such a fine technology under him.

They came to the ravine. Deckard knew without thinking. The river roared through in a torrent of white water. Wedge into a rock was the remains of Claire's bike. Rust spread out from under the plastic dust covers across the ruined fan blades and bare axels. A strip of green was wrapped around the steering bar. It swung back and forth in the mist wafting off the flooded gorge. Somewhere, dozens of meters beneath the surface, he'd ridden across a few weeks ago.

There was no way across. Deckard slumped back. Sam turned them left and ran them parallel. He lost track. He shut his eyes.

Sleep didn't take. Fangs flashed in and out. Every time he came up, he forced himself back down.

A jolt lurched him awake. "Mom!"

"We're fine," she said. "There has to be a way across." They were riding upstream.

"What if it's the other way?" he said.

"That's the way I came. Nothing down there but Johbert's caravan and all their bones under the water," she said.

"Wait, seriously?"

"Yeah, I found him. Looks like they got stuck in the ravine and drowned when it flooded."

He closed his eyes and imagined doom rushing towards him as he waited helpless in the dry ravine. Nothing changed. His leg was throbbing…He opened his eyes

There was no ravine. They ran over a ridgeline or something, over bare wet rock. "How's your leg?"

"Stopped hurting," he said with delight.

"Can you feel this?" she shifted. The bike swayed.

"What? Your shaky steering?" he said, then looked down. His bandages were green and red, and the splint had jarred loose. With his flesh swollen and twisted at that angle he should have felt something down there, but the pain stopped just below his knee.

"You've lost feeling. The infection's turning the gangrene," Sam said, and terror slipped through.

There was no getting off the bike. He tried to fall asleep in the saddle, but somehow ended up on a blanket he couldn't feel, head elevated by a rock.

At sunrise the cold rain continued, but he burned. Mom put her palm to his forehead and shook her head. "Don't worry," she lied. He could fucking tell. As the day went on, everything vanished behind the endless fever burning up.

He was on the ground, still burning. Claire and all his school friends circled him through the night, keeping him awake. Claire boxed with the boys and lost to every one in turn, as the girls cheered their boyfriends on. He yelled at them and reached for his revolver to even the fight for her. It wasn't in its holster. And everyone was laughing at him for being a weak limb in a weak relationship.

When Sam unwrapped her son the next morning, his eyes were glassy. They stared past her and through the tarp, into space.

"Deckard?" she said and shook him. His cheek brushed her hand and it burned.

He mumbled something.

"Deck, we're almost there," she said. She hauled him up. Her legs shook and he plunged into a puddle. The water was warm. Brambles had grown towards it, thirsty. She dragged him to the bike and hauled him into the stirrups.

Her strength didn't return. Something had broken loose in the bike and rattled under her. She put her head down low as she passed brambles and cacti. The brambles had turned red and gone heavy with pink buds of flowers. The cacti clung to bare rock above the floods.

The day darkened as the rain picked up again. Rivulets of water slipped down the back of Deckard's coat and ran into her jacket. She opened it and let water flow free.

She passed the clearing lined with abandoned wagons and corpses stripped to bone and sinew. Grey shadows loomed long in the evening, reaching for her as she raced straight down the center of the caravan's massacre. She heard Johbert's followers whispering from the ravine, begging their new comrades to stop her and add her son to their number. They reached past the raging waterfall towards her.

The sensor post still stood tall with its destroyed sensor. The windmill spun like a rotary saw in the wind. She coaxed every bit of speed out of the bike and outran the last figures of shadow. The plane opened around her and she roared over growing green stalks.

The bike shuddered; she tilted forwards and accelerated towards the dark ground. A wall of water opened up and snatched her in its cold embrace. Sam screamed and bubbles rose up. She ripped out the stirrups and hauled herself out of her seat. There was darkness all around and still water. Something flashed and she looked up just in time to see lightning crackle above the barrier of the surface.

Where was Deckard? She kicked a bit with her boots and spun herself around. Her bike's headlights were behind her and slowly drifting. She swam after it and felt along its hot frame until she found something soft. She cut his stirrups and grabbed him. He was a heavy weight. She got beneath him, found solid ground and planted her shoulder into his back. The last she saw of her bike, the lights flickered somewhere in the depths and died.

Gasping for breath, she hauled them out and collapsed on her back in mud. Deckard lay face-up in her arms. She cried for air but her lungs didn't refill. There was nothing left in her but water and shivering.

She patted Deckard. His eyes fluttered open and stared at the clouds overhead. "Come on son." She put him on her shoulder, tucked a hand under his rear, and trudged onwards.

The ground became mud that sucked in her boots. Then it gave way to row upon plowed row, and she smashed seedlings open with every step. Deckard's bad leg dragged up a furrow. When she was nine, the women of cloth had taken the entire convent out beyond the town and taught them to plow. One day they'd be married off and would need to work the farm, or they'd be wearing the black wrap and work the church gardens.

She'd loved the hoe and plowed lines, until she'd grown bored and started drawing her name, tearing up rows of freshly planted seeds. A scream had startled her and a sister ran over, face red and switch already brandished.

There were no boots ahead. Just the fresh life she snuffed out with every step. And Deckard slowly dragging her down

She hiked him up a little higher on her shoulders and strode on. Now his leg wasn't steering her, but her back ached as her vertebrae compressed beneath him. A field gave way to another. Then a hill rose out and the furrows returned to mud. She patted Deckard, wherever she was reaching.

A wall rose from her right. She passed the skeleton of a wagon, stripped bare by human hands. Then she was past the camp, and walking beneath the hill that still carried the gatling gun's frame. Then more wagons. More dead reaching out to her.

Then her legs folded and she knelt in the mud. Deckard slid down a bit and she caught him. She raised herself up on her haunches.

She saw a bridge, then a river, then the great house, covered in fresh yellow boards. White smoke curled up from the chimney.

Sam found the cannon lodged against her frozen belly. She ripped it out and raised it high. She yanked the hammer back with her thumb, then pulled the trigger. The weapon roared. Recoil buried it muzzle-first in the mud.

A light came on in the house. "It's okay Deck," she said. "We did it." A lone figure in dressing gown strode out, lantern in hand and rifle on his shoulder. Wyatt stared her straight in the eyes across the farm.

Chapter Twenty-Four:

When Sam opened her eyes, she lay in a bed softer than snow, wrapped in sheets of thick cotton. A brick fireplace across from her housed a roaring inferno. Its glow across the dark walls nearly dragged her back to sleep.

She sat up, hard and fast. She was completely naked. There was a window, with slivers of light stabbing through the drawn shutters. The air within was warm and dry as can be. Her bare skin tingled at the feeling of such comfort. Also, that it was clean of grime, and felt utterly bare.

On either side of her were ornate night tables, glowing with veins of the trees they'd been carved from. On one, she saw a fresh set of clothes neatly folded. She yanked it off the table, and a note fluttered out.

Samantha

This was Mattie's walking skirt, from the cities. She never wore it. If you can't rise, please ring the bell and a hand will come.

-Wyatt

She donned it tenderly, smoothing down every wrinkle and making sure the creases fit just right. It was a waist to floor skirt with a single set of buttons, but a row of slits on either leg. Some fiddling made her realize she could unbutton the skirt front from the left leg and fold it to her right, changing a fashionable skirt to pants. Since it was a skirt, first she had to put on the shift and the sweater it came with, before pulling it on and setting it to pants.

These all came with pale grey stockings. When had she last worn stockings? Well, these were for someone taller and went all the way up her thighs. They were warm and comfy. The boots were a size too big and required extra lacing to get right. Once she'd put it all on, she saw her massive revolver in its holster. They'd reloaded it and replaced the spent percussion caps. She strapped it on her hip, where it weighed far too much.

The door swung open with a creak. The children paused on the hallway floor, chalk sticks and slates clutched in their little hands. The littlest one leapt up and sped off. His cry rang through the house.

"Grandpa, Sammy's awake."

He came bounding back and threw his arms around Sam's knees.

"Hi Marian," Sam said, patting his head. "What are you doing?"

"They carried you in and you looked like you were dead," he said.

"No."

Wyatt appeared and tipped his hat. "Ma'am."

"How is Deckard?" she said.

Wyatt steered her away from the kids and into the empty dining room.

"In Mathias' room, with the doctor presiding. He's alive."

"His leg?"

"We had to amputate below the knee. The infection was too far gone and his fever only broke after we took it off," Wyatt said with a deep bow. "You don't look much better."

"How long was I out?"

"Three days, roughly. Rain's over, for now," he said. "You want to see him?"

"Now," she said. The pants swished around her legs as she followed him. In better times she'd probably laugh at that.

Deckard was so pale. His cheeks had stretched tight over his bones. If his chest didn't rise and fall beneath the blankets, she'd think he was dead.

Doc stood and stepped away.

"Fever's on its way out. Another day or so and he'll be healthy," he said. For whatever passed as healthy now. The door shut behind her.

Sam huddled over him. She made herself a corner on his bed and wrung her hands in her lap as she waited. There was nothing left for her to do but wait. And that terrified her more than anything.

Deckard's eyes fluttered open.

"Mom?"

"Back to sleep."

"Where's Claire?" She nearly slapped him.

"Get your priorities straight boy."

"Mom, didn't you say my dream was to have a beautiful girl throw herself at me?" he said.

She slapped him over the forehead. "Fine. I don't know where she is. You're at Wyatt's place."

"How'd we get there?"

"I hauled you through a monsoon," she said and shook her head. "You're heavy."

"Sorry." He sat up on his elbows, and she pushed him back down.

"Sleep."

"Mother. Something's wrong. I'm wiggling all my toes and I can't move the sheets." He sat up again and looked down. "I remember getting shot in the leg."

"They had to cut it off. I'm sorry, I couldn't get you back fast enough."

He nodded. Face blank. Took a single breath that rattled his weakened frame. "Mom, please don't leave."

"I'm not going anywhere," she said, and swapped the stool for the armchair in the corner. "Promise."

The grandkids barged in an hour later, with two steaming bowls and a loaf of bread. Hers was a full stew of veggies and beef chunks. Deckard's was thick broth. He was just strong enough to eat on his own, and his exertion had the benefit of putting him to sleep. She had to shoo the kids out because they kept leaping on the bed to hug him.

The doctor returned, and she found a washroom and cleaned up properly, because she didn't intend to go back out on the trail for a long time. When she emerged, she went to the dining room. Wyatt sat alone, smoking his pipe.

"Kids. All the work we do just to get them to adulthood," she said.

"It doesn't stop at adulthood. Matt's building a new house across the valley for his family. About damn time," Wyatt said.

"Well. At least they're cute," she said. She threw both her elbows on the table. "Can I get a puff?"

He passed it over. She took a long whiff. It was good tobacco.

"Dress looks good on you. Might be a bit long, she was so tall, and her mother and I could never figure out where it came from," Wyatt said.

"Thank you," she said. "How are things around here?"

"We just finished burying the dead. The mourning won't stop, ever. This is why I quit the army at ten years instead of going for twenty. It never stops," he said.

"Well. I've got bad news. The city on the other side of the fangs. The covenanters are in charge there. There's a bunch less of them now, but they're in charge."

Wyatt shook his head. "The violent few run the many."

"Yeah," she said. "Doesn't mean we can't try."

"Definitely. A rider showed up a week ago. There's few families coming up together. They want to settle here. They have a couple relatives already living here, so we're letting them in. It'll be a good festival when they arrive, bigger than what's right to be polite, but we all need it," he said. "How'd that Grand Dragon serve you?"

She knew he'd reloaded it. "Stopped a bike at a hundred meters. Just as the legend goes."

"We were issued those in the cavalry way back when. They were old even back then. We didn't have paper cartridges, so every now and then someone would sprinkle too much powder outside the chamber, and detonate all six at once," he said.

Sam burst into laughter.

"Where'd you find it?"

"Killed someone. Ask their soul," she said. She tensed and asked. "I need to know something. Did you know Sima Yi was Claire's father?"

He winced. "I did. I served alongside him. Our city hired him to do some scouting and sent my squad along to provide cavalry support. He was a monster. Then, he showed up here six years ago with the young maiden. Said she didn't belong in the life he lived. Asked me to raise her honestly. How could I resist? I didn't ask questions because I didn't want to know. I took her. He stayed for dinner, and then left. We got cards and a sum of money from him once a season. The money's in a bank, waiting for her."

"Well. She turned out better than he did, so maybe all's not lost," she said.

"Are they alive?"

"I don't know," she said.

He nodded.

She got the master bedroom for the night. It was hard to get back to sleep. The bed was too soft, the fire too warm. Greywalkers stalked outside, waiting.

Deckard recovered swiftly. He was eating whole foods by the next night. By the third, he decided to stand up.

"If you fall, you buy me drink for a month," she said, and offered her arm.

"That's like one a week," Deckard said and grabbed her. He managed to get himself upright by hauling mercilessly up her side. His remaining leg tentatively reached over the side of the bed until it found the floor, taking the comforter with it. "Step back, mom."

She did, and he staggered upright. It was like holding a leaf in the wind. Or a cat clinging to you. Definitely a cat hanging on for dear life. He remained upright. When the stepped away, he dragged all of the bedding off the bed.

"Shit, sorry," he said.

"No worry, hang on." Sam held him with one hand as she switched around to his amputated side. "Better?"

"Yeah," he said, and hopped forwards on his leg. She kept pace. "I love you, mom."

"You sure?" She threw her head back. "Hey, kids, get in here!"

Deckard glared at her as their small audience piled in. "Oh my god he's standing!"

"He's so skinny."

"I think he's cold. Look, he's shivering."

"Now, we do a lap," she said. Huffing and puffing, they walked around the room once. Deckard sat down and got swarmed. "Relax after you make the bed," she said.

"Fine," Deckard said, but the oldest two kids, the twins, were already hauling sheets over.

"Grandpa taught us military corners," they said.

A gunshot rattled the house. Sam had the Grand Dragon out in an instant. "Deck, stay here. Don't let the kids out." She slipped out the door. Two farmhands ran past, rifles in hand. Wyatt burst into the dining room with his New Model Carbine loaded. They all took aim at a solitary figure standing across the bridge, a dress billowing around her.

Sam burst out before anyone could stop her. The ground was surprisingly solid for a week of rain as she strode across the lawn and over the dark channel. She didn't need a lantern. Claire waited, hands clasped to her belly and head hung low.

"Is he alright?" she said.

"I swear, the both of you," Sam said. "Deckard's alive." She stowed the revolver. "Hell happened?"

"They didn't chase us. When the machine exploded, they just turned around and ran back to town. We managed to sneak out and find Bogdan," she said. "This is yours." The railgun slid off her shoulder. She offered it almost apologetically.

Sam took the railgun. Soon as it was safe and heavy on her shoulder, Claire lunged in and hugged her. Sam took her and held her close, while staring over her shoulder. "Better than whacking me again."

Claire tightened her grip. "Sorry." Sam patted her back softly, until she let go.

When Claire stepped back her eyes were wet. "Thank you, miss." She started and stopped. "Pa's waiting for you out by the old camp."

Sam made sure Claire was received safely, then saddled up on the first bike she found. Her railgun and all its spare magazines were empty, so she left it behind and took only the massive dragon with her.

The Covenanter's camp had been long-emptied and the bodies buried, but the palisade remained. The figure was stark and black at the entrance. She smelled tobacco as she strode up.

"Does she know you're dying?" Sam said.

"She does. I hope she'll be safe."

"Deckard's probably going to propose soon as he can. First thing he said when he woke up was to ask about her. Damn teenagers," she said.

"I know. It's always been curious but I've never replicated the feeling," Sima said. He shook his head.

Sam almost felt bad for him. "Where are you going?"

"About that." He handed over the ruins of his black hat. "That's got my blood all over it. It will be good for the bounty office's DNA tests. And there's these." He undid his belt and handed it over, railguns and all. "My bounty should be fifty thousand. That's my dowry."

Sam tucked them under her sweater. "Thank you. What do you want?"

He smiled at her. "I want one dance at the wedding. And some peace and quiet before I get sorted into whatever hell's the real one." It wasn't justice. Fuck was justice though? They were here, they'd resolved the present issues, and going into the past would only bring up more. She remembered the necklace with all its little pendants sitting in her saddle bag. She'd done enough justice with that.

"Of course," she said. "Are you going to ask Wyatt for entry?" She lowered her hand to the revolver.

"No. I ran with Jesse far longer. I'm going to knock on his door," he said.

"I'll let you," she said, and stepped aside.

She escorted him halfway across the valley to Jesse's cabin amidst the forest, then returned.

The kids and a farm girl were listening at the door. They scattered at her approach. She shrugged, and barged in.

Deckard lay across the bed with his head in Claire's lap. It was all very adorable. Except, in the candlelight she saw Claire was streaked in grime. They stared at her fearfully.

"You, go take a bath before you make him sick," she said and crooked a figure at Claire. "And you. Get dressed."

Claire skittered out.

"Mom," Deckard said, and sat up. "Did you have to do that?"

"Yeah. She's making you and the bed dirty with whatever she picked up on the trail. She'll smell better too."

Only then, did she pull the ring off her finger. "Your father gave this to me. Took him three years in secret to save up for it. It's two silver bands interlocking around the emerald." She held it before him.

He cupped it in both hands and held it close to his chest. When he turned it over in his fingers, the freshly polished gold shined in the firelight. Five little sapphires were embedded along the middle. The center one had cracked a while back. The others shone bright as the day he'd presented them to her. Deckard's breath clouded along them.

"Mom. Can you be in the room when I propose?"

"Of course," she said. She tossed his clothes at him. "Now get dressed. One does not propose in a dressing gown. Do you need help?"

"No."

She turned away and cringed at the variety of scrapes and grunts for nearly fifteen minutes. When Deckard said he was ready, she turned back. He wore brown breeches and a fine blue button-down shirt, tucked into a slender leather belt. His remaining leg had a single white sock. There were definitely a lot of fine details to fix, but she didn't know how.

"Help me up," he said. She offered a shoulder and let him scrabble up. Someone knocked at the door, right on time.

"Enter," she said.

Claire came in in white stocking feet. She wore a dress of faded red with a white apron. Her hair was back in a simple ponytail. A silk neckerchief was tied around her head. She smiled. "You look lovely, Deckard," she said.

"High praise coming from you. Are they treating you right?"

"Yeah. It's like I never left, and it's really creepy," she said and fanned herself with a hand.

He released Sam and dropped to his knee. He would have fallen had she not stepped out a leg for him to lean on. "Claire. The lesson goes that a couple needs to find out everything about each other before marrying. And, well, after the last few months I've learned I'd trust you with anything and I love you more than anyone. That's not everything but that's been enough. Will you marry me?" He held out the ring.

Claire sank to her knees, eyelids fluttering like she'd fainted. She held out a hand. She shook so hard Deckard needed a minute and a nervous giggle to slip it onto her finger.

She threw her arms around his neck and kissed him. Sam made sure she firmly held him before taking her foot away. She strode out of the room and slipped the inside latch before shutting the door.

The entire farmhouse was crowded around the dining hall. They all stared at her.

"She said yes," Sam said. A gentle sigh of relief around the room. Matt grabbed a grimy bottle from a shelf.

"Damnit, Matt, don't pull that out," a young woman said. Sam recognized her as Matt's wife but didn't remember her name.

"Moonshine?" Matt said. Sam, Wyatt, and a couple of the farmhands drank. The farmhands were being helped off the floor when the bedroom door swung open. They limped out together, Deckard leaning heavily on Claire's shoulder. Smiles brighter than the lights in the room.

Applause broke out, even from the farmhand still on the floor. Matt tried to offer moonshine but stopped when Sam tapped the grand dragon's butt.

Epilogue:

The wedding was held on the autumn solstice, under a full moon. They erected a shrine from the dismantled structures of disabled Covenanter wagons. The chairs were brought from every farmer's house. A group of locals brought their instruments and played.

Deckard had been practicing with his peg leg for a week. He still leaned on Sam hard as she walked him down the aisle. After him, a man with a deformed right ear walked Claire down. She was utterly glittering in a dress that had been passed down for three generations of Wyatt's family. Her train was woven with silver thread. Her legs, clad in silver bangles and white stockings.

Sam stood off to the side and grinned harder than she could bare as the two of them said their vows. She kept her blind side to the audience. They didn't matter and she could hear them breathing anyways. Only the pair on the podium mattered. They clasped hands and exchanged rings. Deckard's was brass with a single fine emerald in the center.

"You may now kiss the bride," the priest said. Deckard lifted the veil. Claire leaned in and kissed him so hard he stumbled back. Sam went for him. But he caught himself and her.

As they separated, applause rang through the shrine and the valley. It bounced off the fangs and the sane mountains and reverberated back as they kissed again. Deckard stepped forwards and dipped Claire down to kiss her.

Sam whooped as everyone cheered.

No one questioned the man in the brown suit clapping on the other side. And no one asked when he took the second dance with the bride. He spun her about the floor, her gown spinning about as a pinwheel of light in the candles. The man took a plate full of browned barbecue ribs and vanished into the night.

Deckard and Claire returned to the city. Their dowry got them an apartment with running water in a nicer part of the city. It paid for all their furniture and dishes and paid the bills for the first month. He worked as a mechanic while she battered a gunsmith into accepting her as an apprentice. At night, together, they studied for the university exams by candlelight.

One day in the first days of fall, Sam clambered down from her ladder and admired her handiwork. The orphanage was freshly white and drying in the bright sun.

"How's it look?" she said to her partner.

"We're done now, right?" Elizabeth said. Her eyes stared straight through the orphanage. Something had been taken from her that night.

"No, I missed a spot," Sam said. She dabbed Liz's nose white. She clapped her hands over her face and giggled.

"Hey."

"Got it. Let's go." Sam scooped up the bucket before she could retaliate. "I wonder what's being served for lunch," she said to the little girl scampering after her. They couldn't match pace so Elizabeth ran forwards, then slowed for Sam to catch up over and over. As they came through the front door, Elizabeth smiled and grabbed Sam's free hand.

"Ready for lunch?" Sam said.

"Yeah," she said. "When are Deckard and his wife coming?"

"Next spring, I told you. Which is why we need to get this place fixed up before then." She passed the radiators. Those, she'd paid to be fixed. Deckard had demanded to look at them when he visited, but that was next spring.

Sam slapped the paint can down on the kitchen table with a thud that rattled the empty dishes.

Georgina spun around and smiled. "All done?"

"Oh yeah," she said. "What's for lunch?"

"Corn bread and chopped vegetables. The kids are all studying out back. Julie thought it was good for them to enjoy the last days of warmth," she said.

"Any more barge captains?" Sam said.

"No. All the barges today were departing." There'd been four separate captains. Two had come by day with lies. Two had slipped in with the night. Three had been carried out by the marshal and her deputies. The fourth had died on the spot from the grand dragon's butt cracking his skull.

"Good," she said. She swiped a piece of corn bread. "Hey, Liz. You can go hang out. You need to keep learning your letters."

"I want to stay with you," she said.

"And Samantha loved it so much when you read that poem yesterday," Georgina said. Liz raced across the orphanage and out the back door.

"Thanks," Sam said. "I got her to laugh, just so you know."

"Good," Georgina said. She nodded at the girl, who opened the oven. The smell of cornbread and burning wood mixed together into a delightful smell. Sam closed her eye and inhaled it.

There were a lot of outposts of humanity clinging to the windswept rocks. She could protect this one.

The End

About the Author:

Ken Wolfson has been writings since he was ten. He currently lifeguards for a living, with a side of swim instructing and supervising. He prefers lattes to coffee when he's writing, likes both cats and dogs, and playing Rugby.